Annie's TRUTH

Touch of Grace

BOOK ONE

Annie's Truth

Touch of Grace

BOOK ONE

BETH SHRIVER

REALMS

Most CHARISMA HOUSE BOOK GROUP products are available at special quantity discounts for bulk purchase for sales promotions, premiums, fund-raising, and educational needs. For details, write Charisma House Book Group, 600 Rinehart Road, Lake Mary, Florida 32746, or telephone (407) 333-0600.

ANNIE'S TRUTH by Beth Shriver
Published by Realms
Charisma Media/Charisma House Book Group
600 Rinehart Road
Lake Mary, Florida 32746
www.charismahouse.com

Scripture quotations are from the King James Version of the Bible and from Holy Bible, New International Version. Copyright © 1973, 1978, 1984, International Bible Society. Used by permission.

Although this story is depicted from the town of Staunton and the surrounding area, the characters created are fictitious. The traditions are similar to the Amish ways, but because all groups are different with dialogue, rules, and culture, they may vary from what your conception may be.

Cover design by Bill Johnson

Visit the author's website at www.BethShriverWriter.com.

Library of Congress Cataloging-in-Publication Data:
Shriver, Beth.
  Annie's truth / Beth Shriver. -- 1st ed.
     p. cm. -- (Touch of grace ; bk. 1)
  ISBN 978-1-61638-607-8 (trade paper) -- ISBN 978-1-61638-864-5 (ebook) 1. Amish--Fiction. 2. Adoption--Fiction. I. Title.
  PS3619.H7746A84 2012
  813'.6--dc23
                                        2012002334

First edition

12 13 14 15 16 — 9 8 7 6 5 4 3 2 1
Printed in the United States of America

To Shelley Shepherd Gray, my sister in Christ and my inspiration to write those first words

Never doubt in the darkness what God has shown you in the light.

—Amish Proverb

Prologue

THE BRIGHT MOON illuminated the velvet sky. Shafts of corn swayed in the soft, warm breeze as if alive, dancing a waltz in the huge ten-acre field. The cries from a pack of coyotes erupted through the nearby hills surrounding the Shenandoah Valley.

Amos Beiler made his way through the rows of ripe corn as the pups howled an off-kilter tune along with the group. Amos followed a different cry—that of a human babe, the sobs weak and intermittent, nearly drowned out by the louder yelp of the coyotes.

He used his shotgun to slash his way through the six-foot stalks in a maze of never-ending rows until a small whimper close by made him stop. He turned to his right and looked down a stretch of dirt that led to his farmhouse a good mile away. He'd come to protect his livestock from the coyotes, but finding their prey was his new goal.

Another sputter from the next line over caught his attention. He moved quickly, not wanting to lose sight of the area where the sound came from. Cornstalks shadowed the dirt path that led him closer to the child. Now in bouts of darkness, he listened with an attentive ear to any tiny sound. A frog croaked. The wind rustled through the corn leaves. Another curt howl sounded. All made him pause, listen, and discern.

Another wail from the babe made him step quickly, running through the dark aisle of soil. Finally he caught a glimpse of movement; something white flashed from the ground. As he neared, he saw a colorless blanket. He unwrapped it to find a newborn inside. As he lifted the small bundle to his chest, a sense of urgency stirred up in him. The need for protection set him into action.

The coyotes' song ended. They were on the hunt now, looking for the prize he'd found. They were downwind of him, sure to have his scent and that of the child.

Carrying the gun with one hand and the babe close to his shoulder, he cradled its head in his palm and hurried toward the house. He looked behind him only once and saw motion out of the corner of his eye. The wind played tricks on him that he dared not allow to fool him. The faster he walked, the farther away the house seemed.

When Amos finally reached a window on the side of the house, he lifted the gun and banged one time, hard. He dropped to his knee and scanned the field. One, two, four pairs of yellow eyes fell upon him. He set the crying babe on the ground behind him. Then he steadied his gun.

∼ Chapter One ∼

THE DINNER BELL rang just as one of the milk cows slapped Annie's kapp with its tail. Now she was late for the evening meal. She pulled the black kapp off her head. When Maggie swatted Annie, the pins were knocked loose. She wiped off the dirt and cow manure then hastily twisted up her hair into a bun and pulled the kapp over her mess of hair.

"Need some help?" John Yoder's dark eyes smiled at her.

She jumped at the sight of him looking down at her with a grin. "Nee, I can finish up."

Her mamm would scold her for her tardiness and her unruly hair, so she quickly grabbed two containers of milk, clutching them to her chest. When she turned around, John was removing the cups from the Guernsey's udders.

"Danke. The boys must have missed a couple." The cover of one of the containers lifted, causing milk to spill out onto her black dress. Annie wiped her hand on her white apron. Frustration bubbled up and burst out in an irritated groan.

"Now what?" John opened the barn door and shut it behind them.

Annie pointed to the milk stain and slowed her walk so he could catch up. Her mamm wouldn't be as upset with her if she saw Annie with John.

"I spilled on myself, my hair's a mess, and I'm late." She juggled the containers to keep them in place as she walked.

John's smile never left, just tipped to the side while she listed her worries. "You're never late."

"You will be too if you keep talking to me." The milk sloshed around in the containers as she adjusted them again. "Taking the long way home?"

"Jah, thought I'd come by to say hallo." He took one from her then reached for the other.

She turned slightly so he couldn't reach the second bottle. "I've got this one."

"Suit yourself." He shrugged as his grin widened.

They walked together toward their houses, which were down the path from one another, divided by a dozen trees. John was three the day Annie was born and had been a part of her life more than her own brothers were at times. His brown hair brushed his collar as he walked with her, holding back to keep in step with Annie.

"Aren't you late to help with cooking?" He nodded toward her white clapboard house. A birdfeeder was hung at the far end of the porch, which had a peaked black roof, and daisies filled her mamm's flower garden in front of the house. Mamm created a colorful greeting of flora for every season.

She shook her head. "Nee, Eli's helping the Lapps, so I'm helping the boys with milking. What were you doing, cutting tobacco?"

He nodded. "Nice day for it too. The sun was bright, but there was a breeze that kept us cool." He lifted his strong, handsome face toward the sunshine and took in a deep breath.

He was just trying to irritate her, so she ignored his jab. John knew she preferred being outdoors and that she would trade places with him in an instant. When the time was right she would help with the tobacco harvesting and, along with many others, would then prepare the meal after the task was done.

"It looked warm outside to me." She took the milk from him and kept walking. The last of the warm summer days were coming to an end, and soon it would be time for fall harvesting.

They reached the trail that led to John's home on the far side of a stand of tall oak trees. "Not as hot as in the kitchen." He snapped his suspenders and turned onto the trail leading away from her.

"John Yoder…" was all she could say this close to her daed's ears. She watched him continue on down the roughed-out dirt lane thinking of what she would have said if she could. Her gaze took in the many acres of barley, corn, and oat crops and then moved to the Virginia mountainside beyond, where the promise of fall peeked out between the sea of green.

Annie walked up the wooden stairs and into the kitchen. The room was simple and white, uncluttered. A long table and chairs took over the middle of the large room, and rag rugs of blue and emerald added color and softness. For a unique moment it was silent.

"Annie?" Her mamm's voice made her worry again about being late, with a soiled dress and unkempt hair.

Her tall, slender mamm stopped picking up the biscuits from a baking pan and placed both hands on the counter. She let out a breath when Annie came into the kitchen. "Ach, good, you brought the milk." Mamm's tired gaze fell on Annie.

"I was talking with John." She opened the cooler door and placed the milk on the shelf.

Her mamm's smile told Annie she wasn't late after all, so she continued. "He said it was a good day for baling."

Hanna and her brother strolled in, and he grabbed a biscuit, creating a distraction that allowed Annie time to twist her hair up and curl it into a tight bun. A tap from their mamm's hand made her son drop the biscuit back into the basket with the rest.

"I'm so hungry." Thomas's dark freckles on his pudgy face contrasted to his light hair and skin, so unlike Annie's olive-colored complexion, which was more like their daed's.

She tousled his hair. "You are always the first one to dinner and the last one to leave."

"I'm a growing child. Right, Mamm?" Thomas took the basket of biscuits to the table and set them next to his plate.

"That you are. Now go sit down and wait for the others."

Mamm placed a handful of biscuits in the breadbox and brushed her hands off on her white apron.

While they waited for the others to wash up, she addressed Annie. "John walked you out this morning and walked you home?"

"Like he has most every day of my life." Annie's voice almost reached the edge into sarcasm, but she smiled to make light of it. Didn't her mamm know that her obvious nudging turned Annie away from John, not toward him?

Hanna had been quiet, listening, and walked over to Annie. "Should we ask Mamm if we can look in our chests in the attic?"

Annie peered over Hanna's shoulder at Mamm. "Jah, but let's wait until after supper."

Her mamm's brow lifted just as the buzz of her family coming into the room sidetracked her attention from Annie and Hanna. The younger ones were restless with hunger, and the older siblings talked amongst themselves. Frieda, Hanna, Augustus, Eli, Thomas, and Samuel all sat in the same chairs they were always in, and Annie took her assigned seat with the rest.

Her daed sat at the head of the table and waited with watchful eyes until everyone was quiet. When Amos folded his hands, all followed suit, and they all said silent grace.

Geef ons heden ons dagelijks brood. Give us this day our daily bread. Amen. Annie thought the words then kept her eyes closed until she heard movement from the others.

Amos passed the food to his right until it made a full circle back to him.

"We've almost finished with the Lapps's tobacco field," Annie's oldest brother, Eli, informed Amos. He and Hanna had Mamm's silky blond hair and blue eyes, but Hanna didn't have her disposition.

Amos nodded and lifted a bite of chicken to his mouth.

Eli leaned toward Amos. "I can then tend to our barley day after tomorrow."

Amos spoke without looking at his son. "You will work the Lapps's land until they say you are finished. Not before."

The gleam in Eli's dark eyes faded as he took up his fork. "Jah, Daed."

Mamm spoke then. "It's an honor you are able to help them while their daed recovers." She shifted her attention to her husband. "Have you heard how Ephraim is healing?"

Amos continued to eat as he spoke to her mamm. "His back is mending. It's his worrisome wife that keeps him laid up."

"Ach, I'd probably do the same if it were you." Mamm waited a moment until Daed's mouth lifted into a half smile.

He gave the table a smack to stop Frieda from tempting Thomas with another biscuit. "The boy can help himself without your teasing him."

She set their hands in her lap. "Jah, Daed."

He nodded for them to eat again. Conversation was uncommon during meals, so Annie let her mind wander. Harvest season was approaching, and the excitement of upcoming weddings was on everyone's mind. Although the courtship was to be kept quiet, most knew which couples would most likely be married in the coming months.

Annie's mind went to John, the one she knew her parents, as well as his, would expect her to be with. Although she had feelings for him, she wished her spouse would not be chosen for her. It had changed her relationship with him just knowing what their expectations were. He had been her best friend, but she now kept him at bay, hoping for more time before the pressure became too great and they were forced to marry.

She put the palm of her hand to her forehead, resting there with thoughts of who else she could possibly be with from their community. Names went through her mind, but not one appealed to her in the same way John did.

Hanna nudged Annie as everyone began to clear the table. Annie's mind rushed back to the present. She knew why Hanna wanted her attention. She was thinking about the upcoming nuptials too. Their wedding chests gave them promise for their own special day.

"Let's ask Mamm." Hanna's eyes shone with excitement. Annie felt a lift in her spirits at the thought of having the privilege to rummage through their special treasures. She looked at her mamm laughing at her brother's story of his britches getting caught on the Lapps's fence. Her smile faded when he showed her the hole the wire made, which she would be mending that evening.

"You ask her," Annie urged.

Hanna was the closest to Annie's age and her confidante, as she was Hanna's. "After dinner." Hanna got up from her chair to help.

Frieda started the hand pump as the others gathered the dishes and put away the extra food. Once the dishes were cleaned and dried, Hanna and Annie went to their mamm, who stacked plates in the cupboard as the girls walked over to her.

"What do you want to ask me?" Mamm continued with the dishes until the last plate was put away.

Hanna and Annie looked at one another. Annie furrowed her brows to make Hanna talk.

"We'd like to see our hope chests."

"It's a long while from any weddings being published." Mamm placed a hand on the counter and studied them. "Okay, then. But after your lessons are done."

Hanna grabbed Annie's hand, and they walked quickly from the kitchen. "Jah, Mamm," they said in unison. Annie hadn't looked through her chest since she'd given up the doll her mamm had made for her. Since it was her first, Annie had chosen to store it after receiving another from her aunt.

Hanna urged Annie to stop doing homework after she completed hers, but Annie wouldn't go until she'd finished her story. Finally the girls ran up the wooden stairs to the attic. Hanna grabbed the metal doorknob and pushed on the door to open it. The door creaked in the darkness, and Annie held the kerosene lamp up to examine the room before entering. It looked exactly the same as the last time she'd been there.

A chest of drawers held baby clothes, and beside it stood a cabinet full of documents and paperwork Daed kept but never seemed to use. Special dresses and a bonnet hung on the far side of the room alongside a box of old toys her daed and Eli had made.

The girls spotted the chests lined up next to one another, where they would remain until their owners were married. Amos had made each of his girls one in which to keep their sentimental belongings. One day, when they had their own homes, they would have a memory of their daed and the things they held dear during their childhood.

Annie ran to the last one. Amos had lined them up according to age, so Hanna's was right next to Annie's. "You first," Annie told Hanna.

"Nee, you." Hanna moved closer to Annie and watched her lift the heavy wooden lid. "I can't wait." Hanna went to her chest and opened it as well. "Ach, I'd forgotten." Hanna reached for the doll Mamm had made for her.

Annie grabbed hers, and they examined them together, just alike and equally worn. "I loved this doll! I had forgotten how much I played with it when I was a child." The black bonnet was torn around the back, and the hay stuffing peeked out the back of the doll's dress.

"Mine is tattered as well. I'm glad we put them away when we did, or there would be nothing left of them." Hanna glanced at Annie's doll.

Annie placed the doll in her lap and pulled out her wedding quilt, the one of many colors. Hanna's was a box design, and Annie's was circles within circles, resembling the circle of life. She ran her hand across the beautifully stitched material and admired her mamm's handiwork. When she looked up, Hanna was doing the same.

Their eyes met. "Hold yours up so I can see." Hanna's voice was soft and breathy. "It's beautiful, Annie. You're lucky to be closer to marrying than me."

Annie tilted her head and turned the quilt to face her. "I don't feel ready."

Hanna's brows drew together in question. "Why? You've always known you'll be with John. And he is a handsome one." She grinned. "I'll take him off your hands."

Annie tried to force a smile. "Why has everyone chosen my spouse for me?"

Hanna put her quilt back into the chest. "Don't let your mind wander. Just be happy with the way things are."

Annie fell silent, in thought. "Questioning is how we find the truth."

"The truth has already been found." Hanna reached for her family Bible as she spoke.

Annie nodded, humbled, and looked for her special Bible. She moved a carved toy Eli had made for her and a book her mamm had given to her. Finally, at the very bottom, she found a Bible the minister gave her. As she opened it up, she skimmed through the flimsy pages. She went to the very front of the book and smiled when she saw how she had written her name as a young girl. The letters were varied sizes and uneven.

Her mamm's and daed's names were both written under hers, their dates of birth, and a list of her brothers and sisters under that. Births and other dates of additional relatives proceeded on to the next page, including the dates of their marriages. Annie flipped back to the first page and noticed the day of her birth was missing. Only the year was written; the day did not precede it, only the month.

"Hanna, come look." Annie handed her the Bible and searched her sister's face for some sign that she knew the reason for the omission. Annie thought back to the days her family recognized her birthday—one in particular.

Birthdays were often celebrated after church service on Sundays when everyone was already together and they wouldn't take time away from daily chores during the week. This being tradition, Annie didn't think much of the exact date of her birth.

Thoughts of self were discouraged. Everyone was treated equally so as to prevent pride.

On Annie's thirteenth birthday she had been surprised by her family and friends with a party. A cake with thirteen candles was brought out, and gifts were given. Her brother had made her a handmade wooden box, and her sister, a picture of flowers. Other useful gifts such as nonperishable food and fancy soaps made by her aunt in the shape of animals piled up on the picnic table next to a half-eaten cake.

The best gift was from John. He had taken an orange crate and decorated it with his wood-burning tools. It was filled with small, flat wooden figures of every significant person in her life. The time and care he had put into the gift had touched Annie. She treated the present with such care she had thought it wise to store it in her hope chest. Now Annie wished she had enjoyed the box more.

She searched for it now and found the pieces scattered throughout the bottom of the chest. She picked up the wooden figures one by one, examined them, and put them in the box. Although they all looked alike, as no graven images were permitted, she used her imagination to pick out each person. Frieda, Hanna, Augustus, Eli, Thomas, and Samuel were all accounted for, then Mamm and her daed, her mammi and dawdi—grandparents—then John and her. All of the boy figures looked the same as well except for their height, facial hair, and a hat her dawdi always wore.

She'd envision John's figure to be the exception. He had a thick head of black hair and always wore it a bit longer than he should. He could always get away with such things due to his charismatic personality. That was something not encouraged, so not often seen in their community.

Annie ran a finger along the small wooden likeness of John and wondered if she shouldn't dismiss him so readily. As a friend she adored him, but the thought of marrying him annoyed her. But did that feeling come because of him, or was it her?

11

Hanna's sigh brought Annie back to the moment. Hanna looked from her Bible to Annie's. "That's odd, isn't it?"

Annie turned a crisp page and stared at the words again. "I wonder if Mamm simply didn't remember to fill in the day."

Hanna frowned. "It's not like Mamm to forget to do anything like this."

Annie didn't want to believe that Mamm forgot, and Hanna was right in that their mamm never left anything undone, especially when it came to her children. "I'm sure there's a reason."

"The only thing left to do is ask." Hanna closed the Bible and handed it to Annie.

Annie took the black book, its pages edged with light gold.

"Don't you want to?" Hanna grasped her hands together and set them on her knees.

"Jah, I do." Annie stroked the top of the golden pages with her finger. "And then I don't."

Hanna grunted. "Well, that's silly."

Annie stopped and took the Bible in both hands. "But I have a strange feeling." Annie squeezed the Good Book. "Maybe it's better if I don't know."

Chapter Two

THAT NIGHT AS Hanna turned her back toward Annie and fell asleep, Annie lay awake, unhappy that Hanna didn't understand her hesitancy to approach Mamm to ask a question to which Annie didn't know if she wanted the answer. Curiosity plagued her, but so did fear. She couldn't help but think there was a reason they had decided not to tell her, and that reason could only be that it was something terrible. It wasn't until another day had passed that Annie found an opportunity and courage to talk with her mamm alone.

After the evening meal was over Mamm sat mending by the fire. She rocked forward slowly in her chair until it creaked, then swayed backward. She lifted her eyes to Annie as she approached with her Bible in hand. Mamm turned pale then patted the hearth for Annie to sit while she continued to sew.

"What is it, Annie?" She took a sock with a hole in the heel, pulled it over a potato, and then took the needle and began to darn the nickel-size hole together.

Annie was glad her daed wasn't there. It was hard enough to talk to Mamm about this, let alone have Daed in the room. "I wanted to ask you something."

"Go on." She stuck the needle through the sock, closing the hole completely, and then bit at the thread with her teeth.

"When Hanna and I were looking through our chests, I saw in my Bible that there is no day by the month and year I was born."

Mamm slowly lay down the sock she was darning and shifted her eyes to Annie. She didn't speak for a moment but took the Bible and studied the page. Then she called out to Amos, who was fetching his journal in the next room.

Annie furrowed her brow. "Don't you know?" Annie chuckled mockingly at the thought.

Her daed walked under the doorway, missing the beam by less than an inch, and sat in the chair next to Mamm. He looked from Mamm to Annie. "I hope this is to make some plans for Annie and John."

Annie squinted in frustration. If she didn't know better, she would think her daed wanted to get rid of her, but she knew he was a serious man, with plans and goals laid out that he didn't want disturbed. "I want to know the day I was born, that's all."

Her daed lifted his head and then let out a long breath. Mamm sat still and waited for Amos to speak.

Annie's voice rose in frustration. "Why can't you just tell me?"

Her daed leaned forward in his chair and looked directly at Annie, something she could never remember him doing. "You're not our blood, Annie."

Annie's heart stopped for a second and then began to beat wildly. She slowly shook her head. Her mouth fell open, but no words came forth. The concern Hanna thought was an overreaction on Annie's part was turning into reality.

"How can that be?"

"We found you in the north field. A newborn babe." Her daed spoke plainly, with no emotion. When Annie opened her mouth, he held up a finger to silence her. "We had the midwife come. Alma said you were in bad shape, didn't know how you'd survived."

Annie's body was numb, her mind tangled. Words floated around in her brain, but none connected.

She glanced at Mamm, who watched the conversation unfold with heaviness in her eyes. Although she didn't speak, Annie felt her concern. Amos pursed his lips and folded his fingers together, waiting.

Annie's first organized thought was about being taken to the community midwife, unclaimed and abandoned.

"Did you...adopt me?"

"Jah," Amos grunted.

"Who else knows besides Alma?"

"Most of our generation," Mamm answered after a brief hesitation. "But your brothers and sisters don't, or anyone born in their time. Since you are the oldest, there have never been any questions."

Annie believed this, as it was not their way to talk of such things. Still digesting what she'd just heard, she sat silently, not knowing what to say.

Mamm moved forward in her chair. "Annie, you were a gift, given to us by Gott. We were humbled that He would give us the opportunity to raise you." Mamm paused with a deep breath of emotion. "You are one of our own."

Annie's eyes welled. As much as she knew this was true, she felt as if a piece had been taken out of her. Everything she had thought was her identity wasn't. Her voice trembled as she asked, "Why didn't you just put the day you found me in the Bible?"

"You were found early in the morning, long before the sun was up. The coyotes started howling, waking your daed. He took his gun to shoot a coyote and came home with you instead." Mamm gave Annie a small smile. "Alma told us you could have been born just as easily before midnight or early that morning."

"And nothing is recorded in the Holy Bible that isn't pure truth." Amos's voice was heated.

The truth. Did Gott really want her world to be broken because of a few hours unaccounted for? Daed was too rigid. He was no less a hypocrite than the Pharisees, that's what her daed was—a man of the law, living strictly by rules. Guilt from her thoughts stung in her chest. Where did this anger come from? It wasn't really him she was upset with; it was the person who'd abandoned her.

Then the questions started building. "If I'm not who I thought I was, who am I?"

Mamm sat up straight in her chair. "You are Annie Beiler, daughter of Amos and Sarah Beiler."

Amos hit the arm of his chair with a *slap*! "You should be rejoicing that your life was spared."

Annie jumped at the noise. Tears flooded her eyes and ran down her cheeks. Maybe she was Annie Beiler here, but somewhere else she was someone by a different name. "I don't mean to disrespect. I just feel different." How ironic in a place where everyone is the same. But she wasn't now. She would always wonder where she came from and why.

"The Lord spared you, Annie. And He gave you to us. Let's be joyful and rest in that." Mamm's words were kind, but her eyes strained to get her point across.

Amos's eyes flashed as Annie glanced at him. All the words reeling through her mind would have to cease. The words led to questions that only led to strife. They had never planned for her to find out. "Were you ever going to tell me?" It slipped out before she could stop. They had to know she was confused and needed to put the pieces together, didn't they?

Her mother's warning eyes told her she'd gone too far, asked questions when she should be satisfied to have been taken in, loved, and accepted. Couldn't they see it wasn't lack of appreciation on her part but curiosity?

Daed rose to his full six-foot height. He'd never been this upset with her, and the look in his eyes broke Annie's heart. "I will hear no more from this child." He said the words looking at Annie but meant them for her mamm. He was done dealing with her, and her mamm had no choice but to do the same.

Annie turned toward the window, looking into the dark night. She would ask no more questions here, but that didn't mean she wouldn't out there.

Chapter Three

HANNA SAT DOWN on a hay bale across from Annie in the barn as the dusty sunlight shone through the planks of wood. "It's difficult to believe." A cat ran by, and Hanna shooed it away.

Annie thought on that for a moment. It hadn't been hard for her. She'd believed it right away. Did that mean there was something innate in her that knew she wasn't where she belonged? She paused in her thoughts. That was it. That was what bothered her about all of this. She didn't feel she belonged. She was different in a community made for all to be the same.

"It's not hard for me."

Hanna leaned forward. "You don't think it's difficult to believe that you weren't born into our family?" Hanna turned her head to the side, studying her sister.

"Nee, I don't." Annie flicked away a piece of hay off her white apron. She watched it flutter to the ground and become one with the other golden shafts, unrecognizable from the rest. "I don't feel like the same person."

"It's not like you to be so dramatic. I know that much is not the same, but—"

"Maybe I *am* being dramatic, but this place has stifled it from me. Maybe the person I would have been out there would have been in theater." Annie tossed out a hand for effect.

"Ach, don't say such things. You know the celebrity status is vain and selfish."

"Only because I was taught to think that way."

Hanna fell quiet, taking Annie in bit by bit before speaking again. "Okay, let's say you would have been different 'out there,' but Gott put you here with us, with me."

It seemed that Hanna always knew how to go along with her rants to get her back on track. "I'm curious about what my life might have been like if my natural mamm had raised me, but I'm not unhappy that I was raised here." Annie watched the yellow sun rising behind the barley field, glad to be here at this moment with Hanna, searching for answers.

Hanna crossed her arms. "We all wonder about life outside the community, but we weren't called to be there. Plain and simple."

Annie had always felt this way too, until now. "I don't feel curious so much as I do set apart from everything I've always known."

"You aren't apart from us any more than you were yesterday or the day before."

Annie gazed at the sun. It rose quietly and slowly for such a huge and vital part of everyday life. "Then why do I feel so alone?"

Hanna moved closer and put her arm around Annie. She didn't always seem like Annie's younger sister; age-wise she really wasn't, with only eighteen months between them. But Annie had always been the mature one with sound advice and a good heart. Why did she feel this time that the tables had turned?

As they left the barn, Annie saw John through the colorful foliage. He climbed the small hill to their home, pumping his arms as he stepped. When he saw Annie, a grin spread across his face. "Good morning, Beiler ladies."

Annie ignored the unusual sensation in her chest and kept walking with her sister. John didn't miss a beat and slowed his step to walk with them.

"Good morning to you, John." Hanna nudged Annie.

She looked up at him with a tight smile, squinting in the sun. "You're late getting around this morning."

"That's only because you're assuming I just walked out the door for the first time today." He touched the tip of her nose, a familiar gesture.

"Then the question is, What were you doing up so early?"

"Milking so we can help move crop." He glanced at the northern sky. "At the moment it's a whitish gray, but come early morning tomorrow there'll be a storm coming."

"How do you always know the weather?" Hanna followed his gaze as Annie watched the two talk.

Annie wasn't alone in thinking him a know-it-all, an unwanted characteristic in their community, but because this ability was desired and helpful to the farmers, it was overlooked, among other traits. As she considered him, she felt subtle feelings of appreciation instead of the usual irritation for his capacity to help. "How do you know when it will come?" She studied the clouds with them.

She felt his stare as they stood in uncommon silence. "Umm, the color of the clouds, distance, temperature change, wind chill factor. A lot of different things are taken into account."

She nodded in admiration, another feeling forbidden and not one of her normal struggles, but there it was all the same. "Looks like you'll have plenty of help." She pointed to the large black-and-white cluster of men coming down the main dirt road. The closer the men came, the more joined, one after another, until all the able-bodied men in the community were together. Harvest was near, and their livelihoods were at stake if the storm was strong enough to ruin a man's crop. It could not be replaced, only supplemented by his neighbor, and that farmer would have to wait for another year's crop to gain a profit.

John stepped away from Annie and Hanna and into the mass of quiet movement heading to the first field. She watched him go with rapt attention. He slapped his friend David on the back as he entered the group, then looked over as if sensing her gaze upon him.

His smile made a pulse pound in her ears, causing her to let out a small breath of air. Unsure of the reason for her reaction, she began her walk to the house. There would be sandwiches to make and potato salad to prepare, drinks and equipment to bring to the men.

Her mamm was already in the kitchen bringing out the necessary items to make the men their lunch. She would continue to make food, not just for her own but for as many as she could feed, until her supplies were gone. Many others would do the same.

The older boys were already with Amos and the others. Thomas and Samuel would go with Mamm and the girls to take food and then stay with the men until the job was done.

"Annie!" A mother and her young daughter walked up quickly behind her. "Can you watch her for me?" She bent forward and whispered to Annie. "Her brothers and sisters are with my mamm, but she asked to stay with you. She's a bit worried about the storm."

Annie reached out for the girl's hand. "Don't be fearful. Gott will be with us through the storm, just as he told Isaiah not to fear because Gott was with him."

"Annie, danke for watching her." Her mother turned to walk away. "I'll be by later to fetch her."

Annie noticed her grandparents' buggy tethered to the front post as she walked into the house.

Although Dawdi Vernon was too old to be of much help, he came over with Mammi Rebecca to see what was taking place. Mammi sat in Mamm's large kitchen stuffing the sandwiches in bags when they entered the room.

"Sit at the table and hand us the bags." Annie asked the little girl, and she complied.

"Puh! You have enough here to feed the entire community." Mammi frowned.

Mamm let the words wash over her as she took Mammi another plate stacked with sandwiches. "Better too many than not enough."

Mammi shook her head and continued her chore. Annie sat with her and helped make more sandwiches. "Where is Dawdi?"

Mammi answered with a curt tone. *"Ach, bin ins feld glaafe.* He went into the field to see what's happening."

"He probably misses being there with them." Her mammi's hard face relaxed, and she sighed.

"The wagon's here." Little Samuel bounced into the room, cheerful as usual. He stood in front of Annie and snapped his suspenders. "Guess who does this?" He grinned.

Annie's heart warmed. "John, you silly bird." She reached for him, but he turned and hopped away.

"Don't do that, Samuel. You'll stretch out your suspenders," their mamm called after him.

"Stop your yelling," Mammi ordered. "I may be old, but I'm not deaf." Which was contrary to the truth. Samuel approached his mammi. *"Ich bin anschaffe,"* she said, without looking up.

"What did she say, Mamm?" Samuel frowned his confusion.

"She's busy, Samuel. Come help me find more bags." She gently guided him in the right direction with a hand at his back.

"These young ones should still be expected to learn our sacred tongue, or it will soon be lost."

"I think it already is with the upcoming generation." Mamm went to the sink and placed her palms on the counter. Annie saw her take in a deep breath.

Amos's parents were good people but didn't approve of the new ways. They were fearful that Annie's generation would become more like the New Order than what Annie's parents and grandparents were raised with, and this hardened them as they got on in their years.

"Soon we'll live as the Mennonites do," Mammi bellowed.

Many of the Amish men were forced to find employment in the nearby town as land became scarce. Churned butter was rare, and milking by hand was also a thing of the past. Although they still didn't use electricity or plumbing, finances and survival made it necessary to give up some of the old rules.

"We'll always stay Amish, Rebecca. All of us." Mamm lifted her eyes to Annie briefly.

Annie knew her mamm felt her struggling with the information she'd learned. There were many questions she wanted to ask. Did her mammi and dawdi know? But the conversation was over in her daed's mind.

"Jah, it may be so. Let's go. We don't want to keep them waiting." Mammi rose from her chair and went to the door. Before leaving she pinched off the dead buds of pansies in a flowerpot that showed signs of the upcoming fall weather. Then she whispered a prayer for the men before they set out.

Annie fetched their large draft horse while Hanna readied the wagon. They hitched up Otto, and the women and small children rode out to the men. They brought baskets of food and a hay sled to move the haystacks and piles of crop. Other families did the same, and by the time the men stopped for lunch, most of the community had gathered.

After she finished passing out the food, Annie went back to the wagon to consider the whirl of thoughts and emotions that would not leave her be. She moved her gaze over the red, gold, and orange forested slopes of the Blue Ridge Mountains, swinging her feet.

The thud of her left foot on the wheel must have caught John's attention. Before she knew it, he'd swung up to sit beside her, holding a half-eaten sandwich.

"I was wondering where you were." He met her eyes. "So, what is it?"

Annie almost frowned at him, not wanting the intrusion, especially from him. He could read her like a book, and she didn't want to be read right now. "Are you going to be finished with this before sundown?"

He gave her a questioning gaze and took his time to respond. "Nee, we've been to half a dozen farms but finally decided to split up to do double the work. If we had done that from the start, we might be close by now."

Annie stilled her foot. "Whose idea was that?"

His smile gave her the answer she already knew.

"Are you going to tell me what's bothering you?" He stopped chewing. "Or do I have to drag it out of you, like an old mule?"

She bumped into him with her shoulder. "Don't compare me to your old Lou."

"It's actually a compliment. I like old Lou. You're both just stubborn."

"So you like me too?"

"Except when you're so mad you're kicking the wagon wheel."

He knew her too well. She clamped her lips together and fixed her gaze on some little children chasing each other around the wagons.

"Well?" He nudged her with his elbow.

"Jonathon Yoder, don't you know when you're being a pest?"

"Nee, I guess not." Shading his eyes, he watched two young men his age play catch with an overripe pumpkin. It was only a matter of time before one would have pumpkin innards covering his white shirt.

He had the good grace not to look her way. She didn't need any more aggravation, and he was providing exactly that. "I'm frustrated, not mad."

"Okay, but I still want an answer." He took one last huge bite of his sandwich and then dropped a hand to his side.

Annie let out a breath. "Do you know about me? About where I was born?"

"Same as the rest of us, I assume." He rested his hands on the edge of the wagon. "With Alma at your mamm's side."

She sighed, amazed and glad she lived among people who didn't gossip about another's hardship. "I found out that I was abandoned as a newborn and found by my daed." She studied him to make sure he was still looking at her the way he always did—without judgment or accusation—even when she carped about her chores, loved to play baseball, or asked him questions she shouldn't.

His eyes never wavered, just kept their steady probing into

hers. "So you were meant to be here even more than the rest of us." One side of his mouth lifted.

She was surprised for only a second by his answer. But was he right or reaffirming her, knowing she had doubts? "You can't be sure of th—"

"Jah, I can."

Now she was even more frustrated, as if she were talking with her daed. "I have another family somewhe—"

"Your family is here." He gestured to everyone playing, eating, and talking in the field.

"But I want to know things."

"What do you *need* to know?"

"I was adopted and—"

"Adopted by Christ and raised by people who love you. That's more than you may have gotten otherwise."

His words lashed at her, as if he'd thought out every one before she even asked. He showed no patience with her questions and clearly wanted the conversation over.

"Because it's expected? Or because I am truly loved?"

John crossed his arms over his broad chest and shook his head. "Why do you doubt our ways? You never have before, until now when it's the most important."

"What's wrong with questioning if there is nothing to hide?"

"Peace, to live in harmony." He gazed ahead as if to say the subject was now over.

She had gotten little farther with him than she had with her parents. Expecting more, she surrendered to his wishes. "What do I do now?"

"What is there?"

"Find out about my birth family. Wouldn't you want to know?"

"Nee, I wouldn't. And neither should you." He jumped down from the wagon, wiping his hands on his britches, and joined the men to help one another through the storm as the tumult began inside Annie.

~⌒ Chapter Four ⌒~

ANNIE SAT AT the kitchen table trying to read, but her mind kept drifting from her book to a beach with blue water. She wondered what it felt like to have the sun touch her thighs and stomach. While she dreamed about the outside world, she was away from the daily chores, evening mass, and cooking. She had to admit her mamm's food was good, but eating it was much more enjoyable than making it. Was she becoming self-serving in that she only cared about her stomach?

Annie was no larger in size than the other girls her age but more so than the women in the magazine she had seen in town one day—beautiful women with perfect bodies and hair, wearing colorful clothes. She knew this was why she was forbidden to see such things but then wondered why the Amish couldn't learn self-restraint by choosing instead of being told.

"What could an eighteen-year-old girl be so angry about?" her mamm asked. "Come and help with dinner."

"The English would be happy to see their children with a book in their hands," Annie threw back at her mamm.

Her daed stretched out his long legs and set his Bible on the fireplace hearth. "Annie, do not disrespect your mamm." Then he picked up his Bible again and resumed reading.

Annie had so much to say to him that she knew she never could, and questions to ask—so many *whys*: Why didn't you tell me? Why can't I find my birth mother? Why did you decide to keep me?

"Come help me with dinner." Mamm held out a hand to Annie.

Glad to get away from her daed, she followed her mamm without hesitation.

Chicken and dumplings simmered in a large black pan on the stove. Annie followed her nose to the bread in the oven and grabbed an oven mitt to pull out the two steaming loaves. She placed them on a cooling rack and leaned against the counter.

"Daed seems angry with me."

"Ach, he's just a man of few words." Her mamm smiled and handed her a jar of tomato relish. "Will you go to the cellar and fetch two jars of bean salad?" Mamm wiped her cheek with a single finger then poured off the boiling water from the potatoes *grumbeere*. "Make that three. Thomas will eat a jar all by himself."

The damp coolness of the earthen walls gave Annie a chill as she descended the planks leading to the underground storage area. Most of the summer harvest was set aside for winter eating, and because they didn't use refrigerators, they pickled nearly everything.

Annie glanced up at one of the many cabinets filled with applesauce, jam, coleslaw, and pickles. They'd gathered an unusually large number of tomatoes, enough to fill four bushels. They'd been salted and stored in white buckets, and after a week's time the excess water was dumped off, and they were placed in kettles, cooked to the right thickening, and then jarred with spices and sugar.

She took some tomatoes, along with the bean salad, then turned to make her way up the narrow stairs. She stopped and stared down the short tunnel at the end of the cellar. Nothing was stored there, as it was too narrow, but the darkness captivated her, not only this time but every single trip she made down to this underground hole, and she felt the obscurity there. A vacant part of her connected with the uncertainty of what might be in the darkness.

Once Annie turned away, she took each step quickly to the top, almost dropping one of the jars. "Here, Mamm," she said in a breath.

"Are you running from ghosts again?" Mamm reached for the

jars as Annie tried to set them on the counter. One rolled to the edge and fell to the floor with the splintering sound of glass.

Her daed was at the door within a moment's time. He held one hand on the door frame, staring at the runny, red tomatoes mixed with shards of glass. Annie's gaze met his as his eyebrows gathered, drawing lines into his forehead.

"What's gotten into you, girl?"

A name he hadn't called her since she was young, a reprimand she couldn't ignore. "I'm sorry, Daed." She reached for a towel and began to spread the mess into a larger circle of red. Her mind regressed as if she were a young girl instead of a young woman.

A swell of emotion lurched up in her chest and pushed upward, causing a small cry to expel from her lips. Amos grunted and walked to the table to wait for his meal.

Mamm brought over the trash bin and began scooping up the larger pieces of the now-mangled tomatoes. "Go wash up." She patted Annie on the top of one hand and continued to clean the stained floor. Annie stood, looking down at the mess she'd made. She felt disjointed inside as well as out. She couldn't grasp what she now knew. She had to do something. What, she didn't know, but something for sure.

As she washed, her siblings came in one by one and sat down at the table. Feeling the tension, they spoke in low tones, waiting patiently for Annie.

Her daed eyed her as she sat down right after her mamm. They said a silent prayer, and as the food was passed, his stare returned to her throughout the meal. Annie knew there was a "talk" coming but tried to enjoy her meal in spite of it. Were her actions so obvious that her parents knew her thoughts?

Mamm asked Amos if he wanted some of the bean salad, but he ignored her. Annie decided right then that *her* husband would look her in the eyes when she spoke. He'd act interested in what she said, even if he wasn't.

When the meal was finished, Annie and Hanna worked beside

their mamm, washing dishes as Frieda cleared the table. Amos took the boys out with him to gather wood and check the weather. The wind whipped the sides of the house. The wooden chimes Eli had made that hung on the porch clanged and twisted in the snapping gales.

Hanna, Annie, and their mother peered out the window as they finished cleaning up. Annie searched for a glimpse of the men or a drastic change in the weather. From the corner of her eye she could see her sister and mother did the same. By the time they finished, Mamm was almost pacing, attending to tiny, trivial details around the kitchen.

Finally Amos guided Samuel and Thomas through the kitchen door with Eli and Augustus following at his usual snail's pace even now. The door fought against Amos's grip on the doorknob, and the wind caused it to bounce against his boot.

Mamm gathered the younger boys around her. "What took you so long?"

"That wind's fierce." Amos kicked off his boots and placed them in the mudroom, side by side.

"We moved what we could into the barn, tied down the rest." Eli removed his coat and hung it on a rack that held ten rungs and twice that many coats.

"Do you think it'll turn into a tornado?" Mamm helped the younger boys off with their jackets and sent them out of the room with the girls.

"Hope not. All that crop-moving would be for nothing." Amos sat in a chair by the black wood-burning stove. He opened the small door where the logs were fed and rubbed his hands together. Mamm set the kettle on the stove to make tea just as Annie headed toward the door.

"Come here, Annie." Amos's strident voice filled the room.

Annie stopped and turned to her daed. He continued the same motion, warming his hands and leaning toward the hot stove. It was almost as if he hadn't spoken at all. Mamm turned at the waist, froze, and then looked at her husband.

Annie sat in a chair by her daed, placed her hands in her lap, and waited. Amos closed the stove door and studied her. "You need to go back to the way things were."

Not sure of what he was asking, Annie frowned. "What do you mean?"

His stern eyes bore into hers. "Like it was before you found out."

"I can't, Daed."

"Puh, you will."

"It's changed me."

"It doesn't change anything." He forced his words between clenched teeth.

Annie turned her head as a tear rolled down her cheek. She couldn't win this war of words. He wouldn't let her feel, wouldn't let her search for what she needed. "I need to find her."

"You ungrateful child." Her father slowly shook his head.

"Nee, Daed." Annie lifted her hand to his arm. He pulled back and put two fingers to his temple. "Daed, please." Her ears rang as her heart pounded.

Annie stared at her mamm. She had backed up against the counter with one hand covering her mouth. Annie stood and walked quickly to her. Mamm enveloped Annie into her arms, letting her hide just for a moment, until Annie heard the creak of a chair and the footsteps of her daed slowly fade away.

She turned too late; he was gone. Maybe it was better this way, so she could talk with her mamm alone. "I have to try to find out who I really am. You understand, don't you?"

Mamm shook her head once, slowly. "Nee, but I can't stand to see the struggle tear inside you either." She held Annie's face in her palms, and Annie saw the anguish in her eyes. "You're such a sensitive girl. I'd hoped you'd never know." Mamm's head tilted as her hands slipped away.

"This is a path that calls my heart, Mamm. I have to follow where it leads me."

The shuffling noise of Thomas dragging his slippers across the floor caused them both to turn to him.

"I'm hungry." He plunked down in a chair with sleepy eyes and rested his head on his stuffed rabbit that he'd laid on the table. His eyes slowly closed, jerked open for a second, and then closed.

Mamm squeezed Annie's hand. "You'd best get some sleep." She pressed her lips together. "Tomorrow's a new day."

Annie nodded, feeling her mamm understood. She might not welcome Annie's decision, but at least Mamm seemed to know how she felt and what she needed to do. Annie rested in that as she walked up the flight of stairs to her room. *Not only a new day, but a new beginning.*

Chapter Five

ANNIE WOKE TO hear the barn doors thumping together repeatedly. The wind howled against the house as if angry that the building blocked its course. The windows shuddered, weakening under the influence of the high-powered winds.

Annie rushed to the window and watched as ominous clouds from tornado-producing winds clung together. A thunderstorm raced down the fields, causing a burst of thunder from a violent storm. She dressed quickly and ran downstairs.

Amos watched the sky as Mamm gathered the children. Eli coaxed Samuel out from the false safety of underneath his bed.

"Come, boys, to the cellar." At the sound of Mamm's voice both Samuel and Thomas ran to her, with Eli and Augustus following. The girls met them in the hallway, and they huddled together down the stairs as the wind screamed its warning.

Amos stood at the door with coats and blankets. "Stay together as we walk to the cellar. Keep your head down, and follow the feet of the one in front of you," he yelled over the roaring storm. He picked up Thomas and nodded for Eli to take Samuel.

When Amos opened the door, Annie heard a roar as loud as an approaching train. She ducked into the slicing gales, lifting her arms to cover her face. She stumbled against the wind, keeping her gaze on Eli's boots in front of her, while Hanna grabbed her robe from behind.

Samuel squealed, and Thomas cried as the wind slapped their faces with sharp gusts of hard air. Frieda stood straight, pushing against a wall of wind. She tried to place a foot forward, but it snapped back. Annie grabbed Frieda's arm, pulling her close, helping her walk. Augustus followed behind to make sure everyone was accounted for.

The dull sun peeked over the colorless hills, as if hesitant to join the fitful storm. The clouds covered the light, and visibility dropped. Annie tightened her hold on Frieda, unable to see her in the darkness. The others were clinging to each other for the same reason.

Daed and Eli struggled to open the hatch, only to have the wind slap it back down again. John suddenly appeared at another side of the door and without a word helped the other two open the door just enough to let the others enter.

When Annie came close, John placed his hand on her shoulder, shielding her from the unpredictable wind. She ducked under the wooden door, fearing it would snap down on her head. She, Hanna, and Mamm all stood on a stair and held the door open for Daed and the boys.

This time they let the wind push the door shut, and the darkness cut off the light. Annie moved down the stairs, acutely aware of the slanted, vacant area at the end of the cellar. She held John's hand and refused to let go.

Samuel and Thomas sniffled in the dark. The men's boots shuffled against the dirt floor. She stood still and caught her breath.

Hanna pulled away from Annie's side. "I'm going to fetch Samuel." Annie felt her move and listened to the direction she went. She reached for the earthen walls just as a match was scratched and a lamp lit. Daed held the lantern up and moved it around the room.

"Let there be light," Mamm whispered as she drew Thomas in to her.

"Come close." Daed laid blankets on the floor and then pulled their jackets tightly around them.

Annie felt safe next to John and turned to see the courage in his strong face. "I'm glad you're here."

The seriousness in his eyes faded slightly. "I started over the minute I heard that wind pick up."

She wasn't surprised he'd come, and it meant a lot to her that he had.

"Is your family safe?"

"My family went into the cellar in plenty of time." He stopped and listened, looking up to the streaks of light pushing through the darkness from the cracks in the door. "We haven't seen the worst of it yet."

The dimly lit, damp cellar grew colder. Annie shivered, and she noticed the others scooting closer together. John wrapped Annie's coat around her and moved closer for warmth. She nestled against him and tried to shut out the roar of the monstrous wind and the rattle and bang of the door as it jumped and shook under the stronger bursts. Samuel startled the first time but became accustomed to the noise and slowly drifted off.

Thomas eyed the jarred food, and Mamm looked over at him. "Our farm's at stake, and you're worried about your stomach?"

"Sorry, Mamm." He tucked his chin down and after a few minutes closed his eyes.

Their daed leaned against a dirt wall, only moving when a louder sound than usual caused him to stir. Hanna sat next to her brothers. She nodded off once, but the noise of the stubborn wind woke her.

As suddenly as the storm had come, it went, leaving in its wake a calm and unnatural quiet. Amos looked to John, and he nodded. John was the first up the stairs, with Daed close behind him. He lifted the door with ease, looked out, and then motioned for the others to follow. Annie heard Eli groan and scrambled up the stairs to see what the storm had left them.

Annie scanned the fields, which lay barren as far as she could see. Yesterday's hard work had sailed away with the gales, which reached down and snatched the corn leaves, shafts, and husks. Their buggy laid on its side, along with assorted shovels, rakes, and hoes. Some were picked up and tossed a few feet away; others were completely gone. The destructive winds had been selective in what they kept and discarded.

"Thank Gott we moved in our crop." Mamm let Samuel slide down her side.

"The Lord provides." Annie spoke softly, taking in the power of the wind.

John stepped up beside her and touched her shoulder. "Are you okay?"

"Jah." Annie gave his hand a gentle squeeze. "Do you need to go?"

He studied the wind and looked up at the sky, now void of clouds. An eerie stillness hung in the lifeless air. "My daed has four sons to help him." He turned to her. "I'll stay and help Amos."

They walked over to Amos as he examined his farm and then slowly walk toward the barnyards. "Let's check the livestock." The boys followed; even Samuel was at his daed's heels, anxious to see what was left and what was lost.

The east barn was torn down into splinters. Great trees and shrubs had been ripped from the ground, broken off and uprooted, and bark had peeled from tree trunks. Fields were covered with rubble, boards, and timber. Fences lay scattered across the dirt road leading up to their home, which was still standing but with a large hole in the roof. Articles of clothing from the clothesline were matted together or hanging from trees. Grain spilled out from the torn side of one of the granaries.

John walked past the barn to look for hurt or wandering animals. Most had run off when the howling wind came upon them. Others were long gone, and the family could only hope they would find their way back. Only a handful of livestock remained within sight. The storm had chosen an erratic path, leaving some areas untouched while others were stripped bare.

Annie's voice broke the silence. "Does anyone see Otto?" She hated to even hope for him to have made it but couldn't help asking. She scanned the area, but the horse wasn't in view. No one answered, telling her he wasn't around.

A feeling of depression seemed to settle over them. No more words were spoken as they began to pick up debris and haul off broken posts and destroyed tools. The younger ones didn't have the strength to help with the heavy farm equipment, so Annie found a functional wheelbarrow that Augustus pushed around while they threw wreckage into it.

A cluster of men walked down the path, picking up what they could carry along the way. This was the way their community functioned. They would go from farm to farm until every family was tended to. It would take days or weeks to complete the task, but for today they would assess each one's damage and help those most in need first. Hearing their comments, Annie was saddened to hear of the devastating loss.

"Ezekiel lost every one of his chickens, but the tornado didn't touch the rest of his herds."

"Mel's family took cover in a cave when they saw that twister coming. Good thing too, because their house is gone and everything in it."

"I hear the west side didn't get hit at all—not a single farm. Hard to figure."

Annie's sadness changed to appreciation that they were all well, and as she looked out to the farthest pasture, she saw a four-legged creature sure to be Otto. She felt the air seep out of her lungs with relief.

Her daed thought she was too attached to the animal. "He's a work horse, not a pet," he'd tell her when she gave him special attention, so she would steal time with him away from her daed's sight. She rationalized this by telling herself she was caring for one of Gott's creatures.

She clucked to him, and he lifted his huge head toward her. As he made his way over, Annie looked out over the fields. Strange how some were affected and others were left unscathed.

Much like when God puts more obstacles in one person's life than another's. With the new burden she carried she felt like one of the former. One piece of knowledge had turned her whole life upside down. Now she could humbly relate to others with hardships to bear. Now she knew how it felt to be in pain.

As Otto approached, Annie turned and headed to the barn, corralling some of the other wandering horses and animals that were scattered along her path as she went. Once they had been tended to, she made her way into the house to help Mamm. The men would stay in the fields trying to salvage what they could, and the women would prepare a good meal for them before they went out to help.

Mamm stood over the counter cutting up meat into pieces while Hanna cut up vegetables. Frieda was attempting to mix up a batch of dough to make rolls, and Annie went over to help her.

"Need a hand?" She took quick steps over before the bowl of lumpy batter fell onto the floor. When Frieda removed her hands from the bowl, a sticky string of dough trailed along with her.

"Oops!" Frieda stretched her fingers out full of dough and went to the pump to clean up.

Mamm looked over at them. The smile that mishaps usually brought out in her was replaced with hard eyes and straight face. "Hanna, Frieda, will you take this out to the men?" She handed them some cups and a large bottle of water.

Hanna's eyebrows drew together in question. Annie was curious too. They had much cooking to do before the men would come in to eat. Hanna helped Frieda off the stool where she washed, and they went out back with the water.

Annie added flour to the dough to try and save the mushy mess Frieda had made. Mamm picked up the pieces of meat and put them in a large pot that was simmering with broth.

"Annie, are you going to go through with this idea of leaving?" She looked up after she asked and gazed into Annie's eyes.

Annie looked away and answered, "Jah, Mamm. I hope you underst—"

Mamm turned, and they both continued with their work. "If that is so, I will make contact with a family that can take you in." She reached up to the top shelf of the hutch and pulled out an old flour container. Mamm pulled out a roll of cash and handed it to her. "Here, you'll need this."

Annie had not had many occasions to deal with money, aside from the few times they'd gone to town and she'd been asked to pick up something for her mother, which was rare. Paper or a particular spice that Mamm used for fall cooking that she couldn't grow in her garden, or one time when Daed purchased a tool—those were the only times she could remember. They had all they needed.

"I have some, Mamm." She only had what had she earned by selling baked goods at the mud sales they had in town every year. Furniture, crafts, quilts, and livestock were all sold at the spring event. Annie had done well selling a variety of berry breads.

"Not enough. Take it." Mamm shoved the flour-covered bills into Annie's hand. "It's my money to use as I see fit." She quickly put the container away.

"I'll repay you...somehow." She stared at the green paper bills in her hand and felt guilt wash over her. Although she'd thought about the basics she would need to go into the city, she had only considered the emotional cost, not the monetary cost.

"You'll repay me by returning home once this is over." Mamm's voice was level and cold. She was forcing herself to do this for Annie out of necessity, nothing more. But she was helping just the same.

"I know this is difficult, but I'm so grateful you understand enough to help me." Annie stared at her mamm until she finally stopped wiping down the counter and looked back at her.

"It's not just your family you need to worry about. Minister Zeke and the other ministers will be asking questions. You will have to answer to them if you come back." She pressed her lips together and turned to finish her task.

Annie sighed with frustration. No one seemed to believe it would be a short visit, just long enough to get some information. She decided to stop trying; they would just have to see to believe. "Danke, Mamm. And I will repay you."

In just the way Mamm requested—by coming home.

⌒ Chapter Six ⌒

DURING THE NEXT few days Annie became quietly preoccupied with her plans. She knew not to share her thoughts with anyone, but her unusual pensiveness attracted the attention of her sister.

Hanna and Annie followed behind their family on their way to Sunday singing. Hanna glanced up at Annie then back at the dirt road. She kicked a rock, which rolled up next to Samuel, who began a kick-the-stone game with Augustus.

"Are you really going to leave?" Hanna kept her eyes averted.

"I have to, Hanna." Annie didn't look at her, just kept walking. The only sound was the crunch of pebbles beneath their feet.

"What does Daed say?"

"He won't talk with me about it, but Mamm has made arrangements for me to go."

"Where will you stay, and for how long?"

"With a family who lives in Harrisonburg. I'll stay as long as they'll have me."

"Is that where they think you'll find her?"

"That's where the Glicks think it would be best to start."

"The Glicks? That's Amish."

"That's the family I'll be staying with. They left the community when we were young. They were excommunicated."

"Why?"

"Mamm didn't say."

"But she's letting you stay with them?"

Annie stopped and looked at Hanna. "I'll probably be outcast by my family when I leave, so we belong together, jah?" Annie couldn't help but let the bitterness seep out. Her loved ones had drawn a line, and she was crossing it.

"You're willing to let that happen? Is this so important that you're willing to cause this grief to all who care about you?"

Annie paused and looked out over the valley floor and mountaintops. She took in the fresh air and closed her eyes as she answered. "There is a starved place in me, one that can only be filled by finding the truth. I know no one understands that, but no one was discarded by their mamm as a child either."

"There could be lots of reasons why you were abandoned. But it doesn't matter." Hanna waved her hand as if it could be so easily forgotten.

"It does to me. I need to find out." Annie walked quickly to catch up to the rest of her family. Hanna wouldn't talk of this within her daed's range of hearing. But Hanna didn't follow her. Annie glanced over her shoulder to watch her. Hanna kept her distance as she looked out over the endless acres of hibernating fields still scattered and tangled by the storm. Annie followed her gaze and then realized this was the north field, the very one where she was found as a newborn.

What must it have been like that night? My daed on a mission to protect his animals and ending up saving me. When he showed me to Mamm, did she want me? Did he? Would they have admitted not wanting to keep a strange child?

The sound of a rock hitting a tree with a *thunk* brought Annie back. Appreciative of the distraction, she watched her brothers attempt to hit a far-off tree.

Annie followed her family into the home of Jake Umble. Each family took its turn to host a singing, even though most didn't have the room for the hundred or so that attended. There were two churches that met in different homes every other Sunday.

She followed her siblings as they all sat together on a row of benches. Her mamm sat at the far end, and Daed sat at the other end. Annie usually sat in the middle to help keep the young ones from acting up, but today of all days she sat next to Daed. Lost in her thoughts, she hadn't paid attention to where they were seated, but the moment she sat down she felt incredible discomfort. He had made it clear he didn't want her to go, and there would be no forgiveness if she did. Now, sitting next to him, she sat ramrod straight and kept her eyes forward. Annie wondered whether he felt the same tension or only resentment toward her.

The oldest man in the congregation carried the *Ausbund*, a hymnal published in German with nine hundred pages of songs, in a satchel-like box. He silently went to the front of the room and took out the thick book. Slivers of yarn protruded from the old book, which was marked after last week's singing so as to be prepared for today's choices. As Annie reached beside her for her hymnal book, her hand brushed Daed's. He stilled, frozen for only a moment, then continued to open his book to the required song.

Annie's fragile emotions captured her, and her eyes begin to water. She took deep breaths until the tears dried and she was able to sing, forcing out the notes until the song was finally over. Usually one to enjoy singing, she blocked her thoughts and turned so as not to catch a glance from her daed.

The next *Vorsanger* hymn leader stepped up and began the new song, which was always the *"Loblied,"* a hymn of praise. Annie had never felt so void of passion for these dear songs that expressed their faith. The leader belted out the song with a small smile, but Annie felt nothing—no joy in her heart or lifting of her spirit, just words and music that held no meaning.

Because they played no instruments, each person's voice could be heard much easier than when drowned out with music. Her daed's baritone voice filled her ears and tugged on her heartstrings.

A third leader stepped up to sing. He sang the first word and waited for the congregation to join in with him. These men would be the ones considered for the lot when a minister was to be selected. Annie had always thought this man before her would fit the role well but now felt plagued that she didn't consider them all equal, as was expected. She grabbed hold of the

seat in front of her as her knees trembled. She continued to ana-
lyze every detail, tune, and person around her. The room faded,
and her breathing became labored. She tried to hold on to her
senses until the ministers came out from their pre-service council
meeting. Then she could sit and catch her breath. When they finished the song and no one appeared, Annie groaned. Her daed
stiffened but did not look over at her. Annie waited, hoping not
to hear another song announced, and she'd have to stand again.

"Page 492, stanza 25," the leader called out. A *swish* of pages
filled the room.

"Beulah Land," a favorite of most her age, began. It was sung at
a faster pace and kept her thoughts off her overstimulated mind.

Finally the ministers came forth to begin the sermon. When it
was over, Annie had never been so glad to leave. Her anxiety less-
ened once she stepped out of the house and into the sunshine. She
took in a breath of the crisp air and felt more like herself again.

After worship service Amos and the boys went to tending
the animals, while the girls helped Mamm with the cooking.
Although most meals were eaten in silence, this one was pain-
fully so.

Annie went up to finish packing. She'd started days ago to prepare herself, as the time was drawing close. Hanna stood in the
doorway and watched. She met her gaze but continued packing.
Neither of them spoke. Hanna opened Annie's drawer and placed
some heavy black hose in Annie's suitcase. She stared at her for a
moment and then returned to her packing, with Hanna assisting
by her side.

As Annie watched her sister struggle to close the full suitcase,
she tried to understand that Hanna must feel abandoned, much
like she did, but the trepidation Annie felt was something none of
them could comprehend. They lived a sheltered life, away from
where she was going, but she didn't expect them to empathize
with or condone her actions. Annie was going against everything
she had learned up to this point in her life—to be satisfied living
in the community. Once she left, would she be marked forever?

Annie stepped down to the bottom of the stairs to see all of her siblings lined up at the door. As she looked at each one of them, she began to falter. It had seemed so obvious only moments ago, but now looking into their eyes she questioned herself. She sucked in a breath and took the first step onto the squeaky wooden floor and smiled as she walked toward them. She went from Eli, the tallest, to Samuel, the shortest, and then up and down the rest of the way down the line until she reached her mamm.

"Where's Daed?" Annie looked around the room, hoping against hope he'd see her off.

Mamm stroked Annie's hair. "He won't be coming, Annie. I'm sorry."

Annie nodded once. "I guess I shouldn't even ask about Mammi and Dawdi."

Hanna looked away, as did Eli. Augustus twined his fingers together in front of him, and Frieda gazed at her with an apologetic smile. Samuel and Thomas were oblivious, for which she was grateful. No need for them to know how harsh their daed was.

Annie reached for her suitcase, but not as quickly as Eli did. Annie squeezed Hanna's hand as she walked by her. When she stepped outside, Eli stopped and dropped the suitcase. "Morning, John." He looked at Annie. "I'll bring the buggy around." Eli pecked her on the cheek and walked into the house.

She quickly turned to John. He stood at the bottom of the stairs with one boot on the last step. His face was expressionless. "I see why you've been avoiding me."

Annie wanted to look away, but her eyes wouldn't move. Right at that moment she wondered how she could leave him, how she could have stayed away from him these past couple of days. She'd done well to evade talking with him about her plans for a while, but it had become more difficult toward the end.

"I knew if I was around you I wouldn't go."

He took the four stairs to the top and stood only inches away from her. "So you *do* care about me."

She scoffed. "Of course I do."

He grabbed her by the arms. "Then don't do this."

Surprised by his force, she stared into his fiery eyes. "I have to, John."

He let go of her and looked away. "You won't come back."

Annie's emotions jolted. She was so far from that thought; she didn't know how to respond. "Jah, I will."

He shook his head. "You'll see the idols of the outside world, and you won't return."

John's eyes misted, making a lump form in Annie's throat. Maybe she was wrong; this wasn't necessary after all. She could just stay here, where it was safe. She'd lived eighteen years without knowing. Why did she need to know now?

Looking into his eyes, she could make it all go away, all the questions and the raging battle in her heart. She knew it wouldn't last, though, that she'd be miserable if she didn't go. But she would come back. That too she knew was true.

"I will come back, John." She reached up to touch his face, feeling the stubble from his whiskers against her fingers. This was a familiar and safe place, next to him, one that she would remember when she was gone. "I promise."

He reached for her hand and took in deep breath. She knew he was fighting to keep his emotions under control. "I wish I could believe that."

"John, you of all people have to believe me, believe *in* me. I know you don't understand, but maybe you don't have to. Maybe you just need to support me, pray for me, and give me the strength to go so I can come back a complete person."

He touched the tip of her nose with his finger. "You already are complete. I wish you could see that."

So he wouldn't understand. The one person she'd counted on couldn't give her what she needed.

His eyes glazed, as if he knew the disappointment she was feeling. Then he lowered his head and squeezed both of her hands. When he pulled away, he touched his head against hers.

His eyes never opened. Annie stared at him, waiting to see the deep brown of his eyes that had comforted her for so many years.

He turned and slowly walked down the stairs, his dark locks brushing the collar of his white, starched shirt. He stopped at the bottom of the stairs, paused, and then stuck his hands in his pockets.

Annie waited for him to turn so she could see his striking face, but he looked to the ground and took a few steps before breaking into a jog until he disappeared into the thick grove of golden trees that separated them.

Chapter Seven

C OUSIN ABRAHAM KINDLY left his shop to take Annie to the bus station. Their trip to town had been quiet, filled with thoughts about what to expect. She had done all the thinking on the emotional side but only knew what little her mamm did about the outside world and what she would need to get by. Once she was with the Glicks, Mamm felt sure Annie would be in good hands.

The bay horse and black buggy pulled up next to the train station amongst the many automobiles. Abraham pulled on the reins and hopped down from his perch. He came around to Annie's side and grabbed her suitcase. She held Abraham's shoulder as she stepped to the ground.

"I've never been inside." Annie felt intimidation creep in as she scanned the brick and mortar building before her. Traveling by a motored vehicle suddenly seemed like a bad idea. She liked the slow trot of a horse and the open air against her face. But there was no going back now. Not after what she'd put her family through. She had to do this now, or live with the questions for the rest of her life.

She studied the huge machine from top to bottom and side to side. "This is a big change from a horse."

Abraham's large hand rested on her shoulder. "You know how many horses are under that hood? Four hundred and forty-four." He grinned. "You'll be where you're going in no time, with all that power."

His knowledge of something so unimportant in their world surprised Annie. "How do you know that?"

"Couldn't help but ask one day when I saw one of those

Greyhounds roaring down the road." He gestured toward his own stocky horse. "Makes Gracie seem irrelevant, doesn't it?"

"You can't nuzzle up to a bus." Annie tried to smile through her anxiety.

He gave Gracie an admiring grin. "I guess we do have a relationship."

She turned to him and wrapped her arms around his thick waist. "Danke, Abraham." It was easier having him drop her off and generous of him to take time away from his shop.

"Go on, now. Do what you need to do and come home, ya hear?" He forced a smile and gave her a nod.

"I will. That's about the only thing I know for sure, that I'll come home soon." She sighed, hoping the cleansing breath would calm her nerves.

"Maybe that's all you need to know for right now." He winked and watched her go.

Annie sat in the middle of a row of chairs at the bus station. She'd been to the small town of Staunton only a number of times, when she was needed to carry goods or take her mammi and dawdi in for something they needed there, but never for anything to do for herself. She suddenly felt selfish with all the attention drawn around her.

Though it was forbidden, she was curious about some places in the town, but not enough to make excuses to go to them, like some of her friends did. Some of the magazines exposed as much of people's lives as their skin in revealing clothes, and some of the restaurants served alcohol, which made some of the teenagers curious. The more enamored they became with these temptations, the more they drove her away. The things she had seen created a strange feeling in her stomach, as they did now.

"Lord, keep me safe on this journey," she whispered with bowed head.

She tried not to stare as she considered the variety of clothes people wore and wondered what it must be like to have so many choices. She observed one man's arms, which were tattooed from forearm to wrist, wondering how he decided on a green vine wrapping up his arm to his bicep. It reminded her of the jasmine that grew on her mamm's lattice by the garden. Another young man wore earrings from his earlobe to the top of his ear. Even if her community didn't forbid the practice, she knew she wouldn't want any part of that. She cringed at the pain it must cause.

A man and a woman groped one another, their lips locked. Annie hoped only *one* of them would be boarding the bus soon. She'd had enough of an education on public affection for a while.

An unshaven man with tousled hair paced through the station. Annie wondered why another man had on a suit with shiny shoes, and this man searched in the trash cans for food. His long coat was dirty and worn, as were his red high-top tennis shoes. Annie remembered some of the Amish girls wearing high-tops with their plain dresses and looked down at her flat black shoes.

One woman chased after her toddler and gave him two hard slaps to his behind. The boy wailed and screamed. The mother sat beside him with a tense face, trying to ignore him. Annie wondered who suffered more from the disciplinary action—the mother or the child.

An elderly lady slowly walked over and sat near her. She put her purse in the chair between them and took off her scarf. "I've always admired those bonnets you ladies wear." She gazed admiringly at Annie's kapp.

"Danke." Annie paused when the woman smiled. "I mean, thank you." She noticed the purple scarf she'd removed from her puffy hairdo and then folded neatly in her lap. "That's a pretty color."

The woman's eyes lit up. "You don't wear color?"

"We wear some dark colors." Annie smiled at the lady's interest.

"Really?" She chuckled. "Soon enough you won't be able to tell a Mennonite from an Amish."

Annie thought on that for a moment. The woman might be right. Wouldn't that put a wrinkle in Mammi's bed sheets? She had known Mammi and Dawdi wouldn't come to see her off, but she was disappointed her daed hadn't told her good-bye. She'd never forgive herself if something happened to him while she was gone. He would probably never understand why she'd left.

"I didn't offend you, did I?" The woman put a hand on Annie's arm.

"No, it's our faith that matters most. And we do agree on that."

"Well, that's what I've always thought."

"Some of our rules are not the same. But we appreciate our similarities more than our differences."

"Smart girl." She smiled and reached for her bag. "Are you riding on this bus?" She nodded toward the window into the huge garage that housed the buses.

Annie noticed the Harrisonburg name on the side. "Jah, I am." She made a mental note to try and curb her Deitsch tongue.

A man wearing a shirt with the Greyhound logo stepped down from a bus and yelled to the crowd. "Now boarding for Harrisonburg, Virginia."

The lady scanned the room and all the people heading for the bus. "Looks like it might be crowded. Maybe we can sit together."

Annie nodded. "My name's Annie."

The lady held out her hand. "Mine's Delores."

She took the woman's warm, wrinkled hand in hers. A common gesture, but the Amish handshake was a single, firm pump.

"Do you have friends in Harrisonburg?"

Not wanting to share her story, Annie nodded. "Do you?"

"My grandchildren, whom I miss terribly."

"It must be hard to be away from them."

"Yes, yes it is." A grim shadow fell over Delores's face as she turned her head forward to follow the line to the garage.

Annie thought about how hard it must be not to have all the generations of family together. As much as her grandparents were difficult to be around at times, she couldn't imagine them not being next door. And she still dearly missed her mamm's mamm as well. She didn't live far, but it was far enough that it took all day to get there, eat a meal, and come home again.

By the time they got on the bus, few seats were left. They took the last two that were together and settled in and talked for a short while before Delores fell asleep.

Annie couldn't. There was too much to see. The acres of crops soon turned to pasture, and then houses were everywhere, one on top of another, with small yards crowded together as far as she could see. She'd always figured they must be very compatible. How else could they live that close together? Drops of rain hit the window and bounced off the leaves of a row of maple trees they drove by. The moisture would keep the foliage green a bit longer before autumn would alter its many colors in the valley.

Annie tried to enjoy the ride and not think about what her family was doing. She was homesick from the minute she stepped onto the bus. She knew thinking of home wouldn't help, but when she shut her eyes, its images flooded her heart.

They'd been fishing all morning, and not a single fish dangled from the string. Annie yanked in her line and threw the pole on the grass behind her. She felt regret when John laid his rod on the bank beside him and waved her over. "Dig, right here." He pointed to a muddy spot next to the water.

Annie squinted up at him.

"It's just like making a mud pie."

The dirt became soft, and she scooped out a large handful. He touched her nose and stuck a finger in the middle of the pile. Out popped a pink worm, fat and lively as it made its way out of the brown earth in her palm.

John took her pole and then the worm, which he stuck on the hook and then set in front of her. "Now give it a good spit."

Annie caught his eye to confirm his request. He nodded. She swished the saliva around in her cheeks and puckered, then forced the liquid from her mouth. She missed and frowned at John.

He chuckled. "Try again, and aim."

She did and hit the worm.

"There, now you'll catch a fish."

She tossed her line right after he did. "You think so?"

"Maybe even Charlie."

"Really?"

Charlie had been caught a handful of times but always returned to the pond. When John had said Charlie was as old as the hills, Annie had looked at the valley and then the rolling mounds and wondered how old that was.

She did catch a fish that day, and she spit on her hook every time she went fishing afterwards.

The cry of a toddler drew her back to the present. The woman with the young child had no rest. The little one was in charge of when he ate, got his toy, and left his seat to explore. Annie had never seen such a small person with so much control over someone older.

The couple she'd noticed earlier ended up together on the bus and found their place toward the back. At first Annie was merely uncomfortable by their show such affection, then her worry grew as she watched the boy's anger when the girl tried to stop. After witnessing the display, she appreciated John and the respect expected in courting.

As they drove through town, Annie noticed a lot of young adults, many carrying backpacks or tote bags and wearing English clothes. Delores, her seat partner, yawned and stretched. Delores took the scarf out of her bag and tied it around her head and then followed Annie's gaze.

"Do they attend James Madison University?" Annie asked.

"That, or Eastern Mennonite University. You can't tell them apart much anymore." She turned to Annie. "That family you're staying with sounds real nice. I'm sure they'll take good care of you. If you need anything, here's a number where you can reach me." She squeezed Annie's hand, slipping a piece of paper into her palm as the bus came to a stop. They silently disboarded then

was on her mind, and she didn't need a reminder of it. But she wasn't there to be friends with these people. She needed to stay focused and find what she'd come for. She sighed inwardly. It might not be as easy as she'd thought.

They drove through an older neighborhood with small houses sitting on tiny lots. Rudy parked by a home with a huge oak tree in front. Its leaves of red, orange, and yellow reminded her of home.

Rudy noticed her admiring the tree and walked over to it. "Enjoy it. It's the only one on the place."

Annie pointed. "These are your initials."

"My first crush."

"So you cut into trees to show your affection?"

"You probably have too much sense to do something like that." He took her suitcase, and they walked through the garage.

"No one knows who they will end up with, and it's all kept secret until an engagement is announced."

"How do you keep it a secret?"

"We're a little more discreet than carving our initials into places where everyone can see."

"So, do you have a guy back home?" He stopped at the door to the house.

"Not really." She didn't know if she was lying or telling the truth. She didn't know whether John would wait for her or accept her back after leaving. Maybe none of them would.

"Aren't you at the age everyone marries?"

"Jah, but some wait."

He turned to her before opening the door. "I guess your business here is more important." He paused and studied her. "Or maybe you're one of those who wait?"

She didn't feel that deliberate about anything in her life right now, not until she found out about the missing part of her. But Rudy Glick seemed to be an intelligent young man, and the last thing she'd let him do was outsmart her. "Jah, I s'pose I am. And I wouldn't be here if it weren't important."

He paused, taking in her comment before opening the door.

The television was blaring in one room, music roared from upstairs, a dog bounded toward her, barking, and above it all Rudy yelled out, "She's here."

Chapter Eight

SLITS OF SUNLIGHT inched over the hills as John made his way to the house for breakfast.

The animals had been fed and the cows milked, and the processed milk was in cans ready for the truck to pick up to take to the local dairy. Any other day Annie would be just a pasture away. She'd have helped with the milking and prepared breakfast with her mamm and then gotten the children off to school. It was Monday, so she'd do the laundry, and there was always the cooking and washing dishes. And, due to the season, she would work in the garden to gather the last of the herbs and vegetables before the first freeze. Since it was the beginning of fall harvest, Annie would be in the fields tending to the barley crop, just as he would be doing.

It had always been comforting knowing she was just a field or two away doing the same chores he was, almost in sync, as if they were one. Just the way he imaged them once they were married. He chuckled that he'd fallen for an oldest girl. They were almost like second mothers helping their mamms raise their siblings and skillful at the duties to run a home.

John stopped and looked across the way toward the Beiler acreage. Although it hadn't changed in the few short days since Annie had left, it seemed lonely and cold. He shoved his hands in his pockets as the chill and wind made him shiver. He planned to keep himself busier than usual over the next few weeks or however long it would be until she returned. He tried to keep from being impatient or judging her, but it was difficult sometimes, especially when he was alone.

As soon as he walked in the door, the commotion began.

"Gabriel, let Robert be." His mamm and only sister, Mary, made lunches for the youngest two boys to get them out the door for school.

John rested a hand on Gabriel before they got riled up with one another. "Off you go," he told them in a firm voice. The two boys responded and made their way out the door with Mary, leaving him and his brother, Isaac, to have a quiet breakfast.

When his daed sat down, his mamm brought out the sausages and placed the dish on the table with the eggs, bread, and coffee.

John took a bite of sausage. "I noticed some weevil in the northwest alfalfa field. Soil nutrients must be out of balance."

His daed frowned with discouragement and waited for John's advice on the harvest.

"The rotation may finally pay off this year. The increased grazing pastures have improved. The soil's rich for planting in the spring. Isaac, pass the bread."

John's brother surrounded himself with the platters of food. He was heavier than most for his sixteen years of age and became reticent at mealtimes. He tore off a hunk from the warm loaf and handed the rest to John.

"What's the weather supposed to be like for the week?"

It pleased John that his daed checked the forecasts but depended on his guidance more.

"The tobacco will be ready soon, but I do have a *gut* feeling the barley fields are ready. The sun's beginning to hide a bit more, so today is as good as any." They all knew those three days of sunshine were necessary to cure the barley in order to store it properly for the winter. His daed nodded, and Isaac didn't disagree, so the next few days would be busy even into the night, with rests to grab a bite to eat at lunch and dinnertime.

"I hear some upstate are buying their corn from one of the seed corporations. They say it's near half the price the Doeblers charge." Isaac shoved a mound of scrambled eggs in his mouth and scooped up more with his fork.

John shook his head. Fortunately Isaac lived a life where

physical work was required; if not, his body wouldn't be able to handle his appetite.

Elam looked over at Isaac. "We farm the way we do because it supports the community. That includes people as well as land and wildlife."

"And also, buying from the farmers helps preserve genetic diversity of the corn," John added, but not to Isaac's liking.

"How do you know?" Isaac actually stopped eating long enough to shake his head at John.

"I just take notice."

John's interest in the weather and the advantage it made with the crop was taken by many as boastful instead of helpful. Isaac was one of those people. In his struggle to find a balance, John had decided to only offer his knowledge when asked, which his daed always did. Sometimes it was not enough for Isaac.

"Well, then, that's more important than saving a few dollars," Isaac stood. "I'm finished, so I'll meet you two slowpokes outside."

John chuckled and looked at his daed, who was grinning. "Guess we should stop eating so much and get to work like Isaac."

Elam and John stepped out the front door just as Hanna rode up with Amos in a wooden wagon, pulling three mules that were tethered to the back—just what they needed to add to their team to keep their three wagons in motion. Their neighbor, David, was the eldest of four brothers and had come to help. With their muscle they had the needed manpower. The additional mule power would even things out.

"Morning, Amos, Hanna." David stepped closer to the wagon and shook Amos's hand. He jumped down from the wagon, and they began a conversation about the weather.

Hanna jumped off too and walked straight to John, who was untying one of the mules. "You'll want to stay clear of that one's back hooves."

"He's a kicker, eh?"

John took the lead rope and turned so they were hidden behind the mule. "Hanna, I'm glad you stopped by."

She smiled and stepped closer. "You are?"

He nodded, "Jah, you'll be doing a lot of what Annie usually does."

Hanna tilted her head. "I suppose so."

"Helping your mamm with all the extra chores." He continued as if he hadn't heard her, thinking of the void he felt for Annie. "Filling in for her."

She brightened suddenly, almost glowed, as if something had shot off in her mind.

John noticed but couldn't make sense of it. "Have you heard whether Annie made it safely?"

Hanna stopped beaming, but still there was a gleam in her eyes. "No, John. I haven't."

John looked out at the field of barley they would soon be cutting and stripping for a good part of their days. It hadn't been long since Annie had left, but he knew she was around modern communication and that Abraham could get the call at his shop in town and let them know she was at her destination. He'd never wished for the use of such things, but in this case he'd make an exception. If she wanted to be left alone during the rest of her time there, that was fine, but he at least wanted to know this much.

Hanna touched his arm, and he turned his attention back to her. "I'm sure she's fine, John. We'll just have to make do without her for a while. You know how she is when she gets something into her head. There's no changing her mind."

He grinned and grunted his understanding. That much was true. Annie Beiler wouldn't stop until she finished what she set out to do.

Chapter Nine

THE LITTLE BRICK house didn't prepare Annie for the energy inside. Rudy introduced her to his family. His daed, Levi, a stocky construction worker with gentle eyes, rose from his chair to meet her, unlike his daughter, Essie, who narrowed her eyes at Annie, arms crossed over her chest. Annie walked into the small kitchen to see Rudy's mother, Elizabeth, cooking a scrumptious meal that smelled of cinnamon and spices.

Elizabeth stirred a sauce in a flat pan and reached for the lid from an overflowing pot just as the timer went off. "Oh, Annie, I apologize. I'm running late with dinner."

"Let me help." She walked over to the timer and studied it.

"It means the rolls are done in the oven." Elizabeth placed the lid on the counter from the pot as the sauce began to bubble. "I didn't time things too well, especially with you coming in."

Annie took the rolls out of the oven and set them down on a pot holder. She went to the stove and turned down the heat to the sauce. "Maybe that will help."

Rudy walked in and grabbed an apple. "Looks like you're a natural," he said with a smirk.

Annie shrugged. "I'd like to help out while I'm here."

"That's good, since Essie doesn't." Rudy rubbed the apple on his sleeve and took a bite.

Essie sneered as she walked into the room. "I suppose you're going to tell me you like doing chores." She pushed one foot out and leaned back.

"Leisure and chores don't compete. They're both a natural part of life."

"Give me a break." She shook her head.

Annie felt as if she were speaking in another language. "I try and do everything with the same mind-set. It's one's spirit that makes the difference."

"There's some truth in that." Elizabeth gave Essie a look before turning back to her sauce.

Levi returned and sat at the table. "How long will you be staying with us, Annie?"

"I'd like my room back as soon as possible." Essie glared at her brother. "I didn't appreciate you just dropping our 'guest's' suitcase in my room." Her voice dripped with sarcasm.

"She'll stay for as long as she needs to, Essie." Levi lifted his chin a notch.

Annie didn't know when to speak, but with the first bit of silence since she'd walked in the door she thought she'd clarify her plan. "I just need to take care of some things, and then I'll be on my way."

"You're welcome here, Annie." Levi took a drink and set the glass on the wood table.

She glanced at Essie. "I'll just see how things go."

Essie grunted and left the room.

Rudy stepped forward. "Ignore her."

"It's fine," Annie said, trying to put aside her doubts about sleeping in a room with someone who held such anger toward her. She hadn't come with a timeline in mind; just whatever it took to try and get the necessary paperwork done and possibly make a connection. But maybe that was asking too much.

"If you want to unpack, I can kick Essie out of her room for a while." Rudy gestured toward the stairs.

"I'll wait until later." She continued to help Elizabeth with dinner. Annie could look Elizabeth in the eye when they talked, which felt strange after looking up to her tall mamm.

Levi called them to gather as Annie set down the steaming glazed carrots on the table. "Rudy, bring over another chair for Annie," Elizabeth requested and then sat across from Levi.

Rudy set the chair next to his and sat down. Annie folded her hands in her lap while they waited for Essie. "You have a nice home."

Levi shrugged. "It's not surrounded by a hundred acres like your daed's, but it's home."

The television droned the evening news. She tried not to watch but was fascinated with the constant talk and pictures moving quickly from one topic to another. People spoke in irregular tones and smiled while telling of unfortunate events. Their lack of emotion bothered Annie. She didn't understand how a person could inform people of tragedies without expressing sympathy.

Levi called out to Essie for the third time and nodded to Elizabeth to bow her head. Essie appeared and slid into her chair, her expression daring anyone to protest her tardiness. As they all prayed in silence, Annie sensed Essie staring at her instead of bowing her head like the rest of them.

"Don't make us wait, Essie." Levi told her as he took a bite of his pork chop.

Annie pushed the cinnamon apples around on her plate while they argued. The aroma caused her empty stomach to growl, even though the tension in the room made her feel queasy.

Essie's fork clattered onto her plate. "If you're gonna start on me, I'm leaving." Her blonde curls twitched with her frustration as she tossed her head.

"Eat your food, Essie," Levi said and then took a long drink from his iced tea.

The meal couldn't be over fast enough. The parents tried to have a conversation, but Essie's alternating rude comments and sulking made the dialogue drag or cut short. Rudy continued to eat in spite of it all and left the table as soon as he finished.

Rudy placed his plate in the dishwasher, which Annie admired but refused to use. She helped Elizabeth rinse off the dishes and clear the table, but then asked to unpack to avoid using the machine. She wasn't sure of the rules she should follow but thought it best to just do what she did at home and no more.

Annie's day had been a long, unpleasant, and uncomfortable

one. As she got ready for bed, she told herself tomorrow could only be better. At least she hoped so.

Essie's room was a plethora of posters, pillows, bright colors, and noise. Annie couldn't imagine where Rudy had put her suitcase, let alone where she would sleep. She was sitting in an overstuffed chair with her handbag on her lap when Rudy came in.

He scanned the room. "Worse than the last time I was in here."

"I can't believe that." Annie was still taking in all the pictures on the walls and lyrics of the song playing. "Is this normal?"

"No, come look at mine." He motioned with his head to the hall and walked to his room. "See, pretty boring compared to Essie's, but I'm able to think."

White walls and a black bedspread with big fluffy pillows calmed her. A picture of the Eiffel tower, a huge bridge that went over an endless body of water, and a calendar were the only objects covering the walls. Plain.

Annie sighed. "This is much better." Annie gestured to the bridge. "Where is that?"

"Somewhere in Australia. Biggest expansion bridge made." He stared at it as if seeing it for the first time.

"This is what you're going to school to do?" Annie really wanted to sit on the comfortable-looking bed, but her upbringing prevented her. She switched her weight to the other foot.

Rudy pulled out the chair by his desk. "Here."

He sat on the bed across from her, and Annie suddenly felt uncomfortable in his room with him alone.

"The door's open." He gestured toward the wide open doorway. "Like I'm going to make a move on an Amish girl," he teased, reading her mind.

Annie blushed and took a seat. She glanced at the desk and noticed the numbers and formulas written on a page, a draft of a building on another. "This looks fascinating." She turned her head to get a better look.

He turned the paper so she couldn't see them. "It's nothing."

Annie widened her eyes. "Was that a home? It was as big as a barn. Bigger."

"Dream home." He grinned and shrugged. "You look tired."

"I have some papers to read." Exhausted from the ride, but even more so from all the draining emotions, she'd like nothing more than to sleep. "I should unpack." She stood to get her handbag.

"I have a night class, and everyone else has commitments, so do whatever you want."

Curious she asked, "What kind of commitments?"

"Dad's working some overtime, Mom's quilting tonight, and Essie should be studying too, but she'll turn on the TV when Mom and Dad leave."

Quilting sounded so familiar it hurt. "Essie has no rules?"

"She has them; she just doesn't follow them. You might want to stay clear of her."

Before she could ask why, he took a book from the desk and left, shutting the door behind him. She looked from the door to her handbag with all the paperwork she had for her search. She sat on the bed and went over them, then laid her head down just for a moment, and when she woke up, it was morning.

Chapter Ten

JOHN SPLIT THE stalk from the top to within a few inches of the ground and then cut the tobacco off at the bottom and placed it on a stick. As he ran the lath through the split, perspiration dripped down his forehead. He wiped his eyebrows with the back of his hand and placed an armful of tobacco across racks made for hauling.

The wagon was full, which was what he'd been working for. "Amos, I can take this load in." John pulled off his gloves and shoved them into his back pocket.

"*Gut.*" Amos almost smiled. "Good of you to help us, John."

Eli scoffed and turned away. John understood Eli's frustration but didn't mean for it to be this way; he just wanted to help and be close to the Beilers. Eli was the oldest son and would normally be doing the hauling, along with other tasks that John was doing.

"I always help you with the tobacco crop, Amos. And you're good to let us borrow your mules in return." It was no lie, but they both knew he was there for more reason than the crop.

"I thought you might not want to be here this time." Amos never met his eyes. He always seemed distracted or bothered by conversation. And he never mentioned Annie.

"I wanted to, *especially* this time." John took a chance and asked what he wanted to know. "Do you hear from her?" He looked at Amos now, searching for any sign that might tell him something, anything about her.

Lord, let her be safe.

He had prayed for a hedge of protection to surround her, and he was a believing man, so he had to know that she was okay.

Amos took his time to answer, waiting and walking beside John to adjust the horses for hauling. "I don't speak of her, John."

Just like Amos to not so much as flinch or give a substantial answer. John laid a hand on Otto, Annie's favorite horse, and tried to refocus.

Amos walked away, which surprised John, but it didn't let him down all the same. Amos was dismissing her before she had even decided whether to return. Annie's fate was sealed in Amos's mind, but John prayed she would come back as quickly as she left. He tried not to be selfish in his desires, but the thought of her finding a life without him was more than he could bear.

Annie wouldn't be afraid. She was one who trusted in the Lord in all things, even better than he did. And she also was one of the few who didn't have a curiosity about the outside world, as so many her age did. John had been curious from time to time, but Annie had drawn him back to their simple ways with reminders of the temptations that never cease once you indulge.

She'd say, "Not that I think you'd fall onto the wrong path, John Yoder. You're just not that way." And her belief in him had made John live up to her expectations. John stepped up onto the wagon and pulled himself onto the bench. Amos's response had given him hope that Sarah had heard from Annie.

As John pulled up to the tobacco barn, Augustus came over to the wagon. "Another one already?" He reached over into the wagon and began to feel the leaves. He bent a brittle leaf between his fingers. "Good color."

"Just a touch of yellow," John added. "Is your mamm in the kitchen?"

"Jah, making honey bread." Augustus handed a bundle to Thomas, who struggled to see over the tall leaves. The two of them began to unload, with Samuel doing what he could, which wasn't much.

"I'll be back." John made his way quickly to the house. He wasn't one to stop for a break without the others, but this wasn't about him, and he needed privacy. He knocked twice and eased the squeaky door open.

Sarah turned, gave a slow smile, and went back to kneading the hard dough that she had left unattended so it would dry out just enough to develop a top layer of crust.

"Would you like a drink, John?"

"Jah, danke." As he walked across the wooden floor, his boots thumped. He took a glass of water from her. She was unusually quiet, serious about her work, not the talkative woman he knew her to be. He might be wrong to ask, knowing she wasn't herself, but couldn't stop himself.

"Have you heard from Annie?"

She kept pounding away at the large mound of dough, unfazed. Sprinkling some flour, she dug her fist into the white dusted bundle and then wiped off one hand and pulled on the handle of a cupboard. Reaching to the back, she took out a letter and handed it to him. Without a word, she started again with the bread.

The crisp paper crinkled in his hands as he opened the brown stationery with small crushed flowers in the corners, a gift Frieda had made for Annie last Christmas, only one page. Leaning against the counter, John became engulfed in her world, and finding what he needed most, he was satisfied.

> *Abraham,*
>
> *I'm writing to you because I didn't know whether anyone else would accept my letter. Please let John and everyone else know that I am with the Glicks and am fine. I am going into the city tomorrow to talk with the Inter-County Adoption Board to help me start a search. The Glicks's oldest son, Rudy, will help me, as I am lost in this place of speed, crowds, and complicated "conveniences." I hope to find answers and be home soon. I love and miss you all.*
>
> *Annie*

When he finished, Sarah faced him with tears trickling down her cheeks. She wiped one side of her face with the back of a powdered hand. "She mentioned you."

John handed the letter back to her. Sarah took it with a shaky hand and replaced it in the back of the cupboard.

"I wondered how she could leave me. It sounds selfish to say that, but I know I could never have left her." He looked out the window to see Amos talking with the boys as they unloaded the last of the bundles.

"I know." She knuckled her fists and started kneading again.

Hanna popped in through the back door in a huff. Her wide eyes rested on John. "Well, it's good to see you again, John Yoder."

Hearing his names together reminded him all too clearly of Annie, and if he wasn't mistaken, Hanna's tone was much the same as well. "Hanna." He gave a small nod her way and then turned to Sarah. "I should get back to work." He pulled his gloves from his pocket and took a step forward.

Hanna latched on to his arm. "I don't see you for days, and then you leave the minute I lay eyes on you." She walked him two steps back to the table and lifted the glass he'd used. "We have lemonade, don't we, Mamm?"

Sarah shook her head, squinting as she went about tearing the dough into quarters to put into pans.

Hanna must have known she'd misspoken when John looked to the floor, knowing it was Amos's favorite drink and that Annie usually made it.

"Well then, tea. Sweet tea, if you like."

John caught her arm as she walked past him to the cooler. "The water was enough, Hanna."

As he took a step away from the door she spoke again. "Have you heard from her?" She anxiously rubbed her hands together, waiting for his response.

"No. Have you?" He suddenly felt hopeful, thinking Annie might contact Hanna as well.

Hanna crossed her arms. "None of us have. It's like she's disappeared."

Sarah stared at Hanna, hard, saying nothing about the letter in the cupboard. "She's doing something no one here approves of, Hanna. That would lead a person to be hesitant to reach out."

"Jah, Mamm. I hadn't thought of it that way." She walked over to John and circled her arm into his.

Sarah turned away as if she hadn't seen the captured opportunity and then glanced at the cupboard with the letter. She grabbed the envelope and squeezed it, her face taut, as if she could break down. Then she released it and shut the cabinet door, holding her hand there as if to keep everything in and let nothing out.

Chapter Eleven

NOTICING THROUGH THE haze of sleep that she still had on her shoes, Annie bolted upright. She put both feet on the floor and rubbed her face to wake up. Waking in a strange room confused her, made her feel out of place and alone. She looked to the tan blinds over the window and saw streams of light peeking through. She couldn't remember the last time she'd woken up after daybreak. And then the memory came back to her...

"Just take one more bite." Mamm held a spoon of chicken soup to Annie's lips and parted her own as if she were taking the spoonful. Annie's body trembled with fever as she used every ounce of energy she had to chew and swallow the small bit of nourishment.

Annie turned her head away, letting Mamm know she was done. "One more?" Mamm pleaded.

"Nee." Annie closed her eyes in hope of sleep, only to hear the sket sket *of Thomas's slippers on the wooden floor of her bedroom. Annie opened her eyes into slits.*

He held his stuffed bunny that Mamm made him—his one prized possession—against his chest and stared at her in silence. Annie closed her eyes again but could hear his breathing next to her. Then she felt the soft bulge of the bunny against her cheek and heard the sket sket *again until the door closed.*

Looking around the room, she saw her handbag and the shirt Rudy had worn yesterday on a chair. Annie felt uneasy with the thought he'd come in when she was sleeping but very grateful that she'd slept in his bed instead of in Essie's room.

His bed.

Annie thought of how her daed would react to such behavior. She shook away the thought. She would have to endure the unfamiliar if she was to accomplish what she came here to do.

She squared her shoulders, preparing to face the Glicks, and then found the bathroom and washed up before going downstairs. Essie took one last bite of cereal and grabbed her backpack. "My room wasn't good enough for ya, huh?"

"I didn't think you wanted me in your room," Annie replied, to her own surprise.

"Whatever." Essie hiked the bag over her shoulder and walked through the door to the garage door.

"Don't mind her. Are you hungry?" Elizabeth set a plate of eggs, sausage, and toast on the table with a glass of juice. Annie eyed the clear glass of orange juice and drank it down quickly.

Elizabeth handed Annie a piece of paper and sat down next to her. She drank her coffee as Annie read the information about the Harrisonburg Department of Health registry and an adoption search agency by the name of Dream Maker.

"Here are the directions to the county building. You should start there first to see if you get anywhere. If not, there are always the adoption search specialists."

Annie nodded and pushed away the plate of delicious food. Her insides gelled at the thought of what she was actually going to do. She wanted this, but now she was thinking of what could come of it. What if she found only dead ends? She couldn't predict the reaction her birth mother would have toward her. And how long could she live in this tension-filled house?

"Danke for your help and for letting me stay with you. I know it's an inconvenience to have a stranger in your home."

Elizabeth touched Annie's hand. "It's not you, Annie. Our family's had some things happen, but don't think any of it is because of you." Her smile was worn and sad. She took a deep breath and carried on in the kitchen as if she hadn't said the last of her words.

"Rudy will be home from his first class soon. He'll take you." She stood. "And I'm off to work."

Annie moved back in her chair. "You work?"

"It's not much—a secretarial position at the church—but we need the paycheck." She grabbed her jacket and purse. "College is expensive. But I wouldn't have it any other way for Rudy. He'll make something of himself."

"I don't doubt that, Mrs. Glick." Annie turned her attention back to the papers after Elizabeth left her alone with her thoughts. There were numbers to both places, and she was tempted to call but didn't feel comfortable using the phone. She tapped her fingers on the table and debated. Just then Rudy walked in.

He sat down next to her and noticed the papers. "So, I'm supposed to take you somewhere?"

"Actually, I'd like you to make a phone call for me."

Rudy shrugged. "Sure. You're okay, then, with my knowing about this?"

"When your mother told me you were taking me around today, I figured you'd find out." She really didn't trust him, or anyone here for that matter. Although Levi and Elizabeth were kind, they were both busy with their own lives. And there was absolutely no trust with Essie or even Rudy.

"So you're looking for your biological mother." He wasn't asking; he knew. So what was he waiting for her to say?

Annie nodded and flipped through the papers in her handbag with her fingers.

"What happened?"

As she pulled the papers out of her bag, she searched his eyes, not knowing if she should entrust her information to him, but then she realized she really didn't have a choice.

"She abandoned me right after I was born. My daed found me in one of his fields." She looked away at first and then decided to stare directly at him. To her surprise, his eyes were fixed on her. A strange sort of connection passed between them.

"So you don't fit in, either?" He slowly shook his head.

Annie balked at the arrogant assumption. Few words angered her, but his did. She took a moment to figure out why. She had learned in the short time she'd been with the Glicks that a deep bitterness poisoned the entire family, although she had determined it wasn't so much her being there as what they had gone through with her community years ago. Why would she expect anything different from Rudy than this sort of comment?

"Why do you want to know who your real mom is? Do you think that will make them accept you?" He laughed cynically. "They'll never look at you the same again."

A pang went through her chest and into her heart. Her shoulders tightened as she realized what he said was true. She reached up and rubbed around them at the base of her neck.

She'd not only been one of them, but she was also looked up to and appreciated for not engaging in the rebellious acts of *rumspringa*. Annie was the one the mamms called on to watch their children, and Alma used to ask her to assist her with deliveries. Others would ask her to recite a Bible verse they'd forgotten or help them understand a certain passage. She was more than accepted. She had found her identity solely in being Amish and following their ways.

"Are you okay?" Rudy reached for her, but she moved away. She was embarrassed that her pretenses were down. She was vulnerable and lost.

He threw up his hands. "Whatever." He turned away.

"Maybe it was too much to ask to come here." Annie's words tumbled out before she could catch them.

He jerked around to face her. "Ya think? A member of the group who threw us out?" He ran his hand over his face as if he was trying to stop but couldn't. "My parents can deal with it, but me…I got a problem with it, myself. And Essie…well, I don't need to explain anything there."

Annie had never felt her body temperature rise from anger, but at this moment she felt as if she were a kettle about to blow. "Then I should go." She stuffed her papers back in her handbag with a level of unrighteous anger she'd never before experienced. Rudy struggled with his emotions. He walked to the end of the room, turned, and walked back again.

"You can't go."

"How can I stay?"

He put his chin down on his chest, looking to the floor with his hands on his hips. "How bad do you want to find out about this?"

Annie pursed her lips in unbelievable frustration. "I've come this far."

"Then stay." He clapped his hands together as if to say it was decided.

"But I won't if you can't forgive and move on. I won't be a constant reminder of your past with my people."

Rudy's eyes glazed. He looked blankly past her and into the other room, as if he could see the ghosts haunting him. "Don't talk to me about forgiveness, and I won't blame you for what *your* people did to us."

An awkward silence permeated the room. Annie's instinct was to run far away from this family that couldn't deal with her presence because of the pain they had experienced.

Then Rudy did something totally unexpected. He bowed his head...and prayed.

Chapter Twelve

HAAA." DAVID PULLED once on the lead rope to calm the mare. Her blond coat was wet with perspiration that left trails of water down her sides. The weather was not warm enough to cause the horse to sweat, but it was obvious by the way she was dancing around that she didn't like to be shod.

"You need to get yourself a new place to tie off your horses." John smiled as he took the lead so David could tend to the preparations necessary to fit her for a new set of horseshoes.

"Lucy here ended up making it through the first time in fine shape after a toe-to-toe. I wish she'd remember that and stop causing me so much trouble," David explained as he tethered the horse.

"She's a giveaway from some Englishers that came through here a few months ago. Said she was too much work for 'em." David glanced at John.

"Is that so?" John at least understood David's excuse to have him there. There was no hostility between them; they'd just never spent much time together. But by the way David was staring at him, John figured there was something more. Since Annie had left, people had been acting strange. There was more drama and gossip, and John wasn't partial to either and made a point to stop talk before it started. He had a bad feeling this was going to one of those times.

David stroked the horse's side in a slow, smooth motion. He'd made a name for himself tackling the tough cases when a horse wouldn't cooperate. His daed was the general "blacksmith" in the community. Although others could shoe a horse, the tough cases always ended up with David.

"Jah, said she was"—he looked up in thought—"unbreakable, that's the word they used."

John eyed David but kept a firm hold on the lead rope. The horse was high spirited, but John had a hard time believing this was one David couldn't handle. In order to save time he thought he'd get to the point. He had his own chores to do, and time was a wasting. "Is that why you asked me to come over this morning?"

David shrugged. "That among other things."

He walked inside his shop filled with brooms, tools, and horse-shoes hanging from the walls. The anvil he used for forming the metal shoes stood by the contained embers of hot coal. A metal stall was available for a rambunctious horse, but to use it on Lucy would only make her more nervous. David rolled out a cart to where John stood with the horse and then put on a heavy apron over his black pants and plain shirt. He calmly stroked the leg he was about to work on, and when Lucy was quiet, he slowly put pressure on her ankle so that she would lift her leg. He had a nice touch and didn't show any fear. If horses felt the fear of another, it created even greater anxiety.

"What other things?" John had an idea but didn't know why David brought it up. The situation with the Beilers wasn't something John wanted to discuss, especially with someone he didn't know well enough to trust.

"I'd wondered whether anything had changed between you and Annie with her gone."

"It's hard to tell when someone's far away for a long period of time, and I'm not naive enough to think she's not taking in all there is to see." He stopped and thought about that for a moment. These were things he hadn't let himself think about, but now that he was, he supposed he should be prepared for anything. Although he knew how he felt about Annie, he didn't know whether she felt the same and if the rest of the world might be exciting enough for her to turn toward another beau or way of life.

"Why do you ask?"

"You know the Beiler family better than anybody, and I'm thinking of taking Hanna to Sunday singing."

David began the process of removing the horseshoes. First he removed the nails and cleaned out the dirt. Then he used a special tool to cut down the hoof about a half inch all the way around. John had shod his family's horses, but the ease and precision with which David worked was much to be desired.

He took the shoes over to the coals and let them set for a few minutes, then took one out using a long metal rod with pinchers on the end that held the shoe on the anvil. He hammered away until the horseshoe was back in good shape, and then he stuck it in a wooden tub full of water. John backed away when the cloud of steam rose. Then David took the next one and repeated the process until all were pounded down and ready to be refastened to the horse's hoof.

As he worked, John thought about Hanna and David. Their personalities were similar, and though Hanna was a bit younger than David, they seemed a good fit. "They're good people," he said. "Amos is tough on the outside, but he's a good man. Mamm is much the same but makes a body feel welcome."

David used a small blowtorch to raise the surface on the bottom of the shoe to create traction. He dunked them in the water again, making clouds of steam rise around and twirl up as the water hissed.

"You don't have a problem with me taking Hanna?"

"No, why would I?" John's thoughts wandered as he tried to figure why David would care what he thought about Hanna. The mare sidestepped, bringing John back to the job at hand. He gently pulled on the rope as he stroked her side. "Easy, girl."

"You got her?" David took a step back and waited.

When the mare calmed, he placed a shoe on her hoof and drove the nails in until the point came out at an angle through the side. He pounded the nail back to stabilize it against the hoof. The excess was cut off, and he filed it down until it was smooth.

"Just making sure. I wouldn't want to start something that

would cause any more problems. The Beilers have enough on their minds without adding to it."

John took that for what it was worth and not a penny more. It seemed David was fishing for him to take the bait, but maybe he wasn't giving him the benefit of the doubt. If he was being genuine, John was being a heel.

"I'd have to agree with that." He untied the horse and walked her around to ensure her new shoes fit properly. "I've got to say, you're as good as your daed at shoeing a horse."

David nodded and stared at John like he was sizing him up. Something seemed to be missing from this conversation, but John had found out all he could without asking outright. He was sure he'd find out soon enough.

⚬ Chapter Thirteen ⚬

WITHIN A COUPLE of weeks they were working together making contacts and doing research. Rudy went about making phone calls, one leading to another. While he was on hold, he asked Annie questions about other avenues she might take if one fell through. Annie now worried she was getting her hopes up. She made a list of steps that, when completed, would mean she was done.

One morning, to her surprise, Rudy walked toward the door without a word. Unsure whether he was leaving or taking her with him, she waited.

"Okay, let's go." He grabbed his keys, and she followed him to the car. The silence during the ride was uncomfortable, and with no idea of how long she would be in the car with him, she looked out the window, distracting herself with watching people as they drove downtown.

One woman had a child in a contraption strapped to her back, much as the Indians used to do. Another man was digging in the trash on a street corner. Annie wondered why there were so many of those men in the city. Didn't others offer food to people who didn't have any?

Rudy parked on a busy downtown street and walked her to the Department of Social Services. People turned to stare as they walked through the sterile halls. When Rudy asked a security guard for directions, though he answered Rudy, he kept his eyes on Annie throughout the conversation. What must they be thinking? That they were a couple?

As they stood in line, Rudy kept looking at his handheld phone. It rang a couple of times, and he made some calls. Annie wondered if he was purposely ignoring her or if this was his normal routine.

A couple of teenagers walked by and snickered at them. Another joined the teens and laughed out loud at comments that Annie could only imagine.

Rudy watched the whole scene with the phone by his ear, having a heated conversation with someone on the other end of the line. "Jerks." He shook his head at the teens.

Annie didn't want his pity or even his encouragement. She had decided to concentrate on completing her purpose here with as few emotions as possible.

"Maybe you shouldn't dress Amish in a secular community." Rudy turned to see her reaction.

No doubt it would make their time easier when she was in public, but she continued to feel pressured to do things here that weren't comfortable for her. She just had to decide which way was the *most* uncomfortable.

The woman at the window called to them just in time. Annie quickly stepped forward so she didn't have to answer Rudy. "I need to fill out a form to find information on my birth mother."

The woman took in Annie's plain clothes and then all but froze when Annie told her why she'd come. She thawed after a moment and reached for some paperwork. "Once this is filed, we can search to see what information we have on your birth mother."

"When will you know?" It had to be soon. She couldn't put out the Glicks any more than she already had. And Essie and Rudy treated her like a chore on their lists.

"It depends on how much you give us to go on." The large woman tapped her pink fingernail on the counter, waiting for Annie to complete the form. When Annie handed it back, she glanced at the information. "I can tell you already this isn't enough. Come back in an hour, and I'll show you how to get more information."

For the first time since she arrived, someone who could help her was actually offering their time. "Danke. Thank you."

"You're welcome," she said, and then added, "There is a twenty dollar processing fee."

Annie pulled out her knitted money pouch, and as she handed the woman a twenty-dollar bill, she noticed how Rudy watched her. She still felt bad that Mamm had given her the money she saved, and when she saw the specks of flour on the bills, she felt guilty all over again.

When they were almost to his car, Rudy asked, "Do you have enough money for all this?"

She ran her hands over her arms, thinking about his question. Having seen how she handled her money, Rudy had to be aware of her limited funds. "I just want you to know that this can cost a lot of money."

Annie nodded and turned to walk again, embarrassed by his discovery about her lack of funds. She hadn't thought anyone would find out this soon.

"I know you want to keep things private. But you've got to—"

"Rudy, stop being so logical and *feel* for a minute." For a moment she wished she were alone, that no one knew her or why she was here. "I have some money. Maybe it's enough; maybe it's not. And I don't have a choice with what I wear." She let out a long, weary breath, feeling more tired than after a full day's work on the farm. "But I have to do this. So please don't continue to point out the obstacles."

When she turned to continue to the car, she saw him shove his wallet back into his back pocket. The gesture both surprised and confused her. So far the only feeling she'd gotten from him was that this was something he was supposed to do. The thought that he might actually want to help gave her a slight bit of hope, but then she thought he could also just be trying to get rid of her faster.

On their drive home Rudy stopped on campus to get a syllabus for a test he had later that week. He hopped out, but when Annie didn't follow, he opened her car door. "Aren't you coming?"

Annie scanned the area, met one girl's eyes, and turned away. "Nee, I'll wait here."

Rudy crouched down and held on to a corner of the window for support. "If you're not comfortable walking through campus, I can come back later." But he acted put-out with the offer.

Annie let out a breath. What was worse—walking through a Mennonite campus or spending time alone with Essie? "I'll wait." And she did, for what seemed to be a long time. She fought to keep her mind steady and prayed for a vacant space. She needed a fruitful void, some place to let the Spirit come in to keep discouraging thoughts out.

On the drive home Rudy stopped at a strip mall and parked the car. "You want to go in?"

Annie scanned the huge cement building, countless cars, and people everywhere. "Nee, you go."

"Wait here. I won't be long." He gave her what appeared to be a small smile and stepped out of the car.

But it was long, and Annie was almost angry by the time he got back. She'd never felt like such a burden. Tomorrow she'd figure out how to take the bus, like Essie did. She unlocked the door for him, and he handed her a bag as he slipped into the seat. "Here."

Annie opened the bag to find an ankle-length denim skirt and bright-yellow shirt. She shut the bag. "I can't."

He put the car in gear and started for the agency. "You're not on the farm, where you wear farm clothes. In Harrisonburg you wear street clothes," he said, as if it were a written law.

She peeked into the bag and admired the blue etching around the collar of the shirt, imagining what it would look like on her. She shook her head. "I don't know."

"It doesn't mean you've changed into an Englisher, Annie." He chuckled.

She hadn't heard him laugh. It was nice to see his eyes sparkle and his smile, even if the reason wasn't in her favor. "Why did you laugh?"

"Because you're the most Amish person I've ever known."

Annie took that as a compliment and looked at the clothes without intimidation.

As they walked to the same window they were at previously, Annie noticed the first lady they'd talked to was gone. Annie's stomach rolled, hoping she hadn't left for the day.

Rudy went up to the window and asked for the woman by name. The lady at the window directed Rudy to the door at the side and buzzed them in. The dull white walls and dirty tile floors were no better in the back area. Annie felt an instinctual urge to clean the place up a bit, or maybe a lot.

"Come this way."

They followed the pink-fingernailed lady into a small office. She sat behind the desk and gestured to two chairs on the opposite side. Her nails clicked on the computer keys as she spoke. "The first objective of an adoption search is to discover the names of the birth parents who gave you up for adoption. I see you've written the name of a hospital and the agency who handled your adoption. That's a start, but the more we have, the quicker we'll find information. Do your parents or anyone else in your family have any insight that may be helpful?"

Annie's skin crawled at the thought of asking her daed for anything about the adoption. He wouldn't want to know she was inquiring for information

"No, they don't know anything." She looked down as she answered, not wanting to answer anymore similar questions.

"Can you ask them to contact government officials for documents, such as an amended birth certificate, petition for adoption, and the final decree of adoption?" She stopped typing and looked from Annie to Rudy.

Rudy spoke before Annie had to. "No, we can't ask them to do anything." He held Annie's stare until she nodded her understanding then continued.

"With the information you've given me, we'll search for non-identifying information. It will be released to you and may include clues to help you in your adoption search. The amount of information varies depending upon the details that were recorded at the time of the birth and adoption." She stopped talking and typing, corrected something on the screen, and went on.

"Each agency, governed by the state law and agency policy, releases what is considered appropriate and non-identifying, and may include details on the adoptee, adoptive parents, and birth parents such as"—she cleared her throat and pushed the keyboard aside—"medical history, health status, cause of and age of death, height, weight, eye and hair color, ethnic origins, profession, and religion. Do you have any questions?"

"What else can we be doing while we wait to hear the results of your search?" Annie moved to the front of her seat with paper and pencil, ready to write down anything that this woman said she could do.

The lady pulled out some papers from a file on the desk. "There are some registries you can plug in to. I'll make a copy of this sheet for you. There's one that matches people who might be looking for each other. Another is more of a support group, but they also help each other with information concerning new laws, search techniques, and other up-to-date information they've learned from their own personal experiences. There's also a service that will help you search, for a fee, but I've heard they're very successful."

Rudy put up a hand to stop her. "What do they do that makes them successful?"

"Many states, including Virginia, have instituted intermediary or search consent systems to allow adoptees and birth parents the ability to contact each other through mutual consent. The Confidential Intermediary Program is given access to the court or agency file and, using the information, attempts to locate the individuals."

"What happens if they find them?" Annie asked.

"The person found is given the option of allowing or refusing contact with the searching party. If the person located agrees to contact, the court will authorize the CIP to give the name and current address to us, and we will contact both parties."

Annie caught her breath at the thought. "And then what?"

The lady smiled to one side. "Then one of you makes contact, or not."

Annie frowned. "What do you mean by 'or not'?"

"Sometimes people just want to know that the person is out there, but once they get the information, they never connect." She shrugged.

Annie let that sink in but still didn't understand why a person wouldn't want to communicate with part of her family. "Danke. I appreciate you taking the time to explain all of this. It's very complicated."

The lady smiled. "You're the first Amish I've had ask for this sort of assistance—any assistance, for that matter. I'm sure it's a very unique situation, so I wanted to help."

"Praise Gott." Annie whispered so softly neither Rudy nor the lady noticed. "What's your name?"

She stuck out her hand. "Sarah, Sarah Webb."

The same as her mother's. Annie's eyes filled, and she blinked rapidly to keep her tears from spilling. She shook her hand. "Danke, Sarah Webb."

⌒ Chapter Fourteen ⌒

SAWDUST SWIRLED AROUND John as battery-powered saws cut through long boards that would be the tall sides of the barn. He was one of three men carrying them to a group that placed the planks side by side, ready to be hammered into the frame they'd built that morning.

Another dozen boys wearing carpenter bags filled with hammers and nails would help pound nails into the board connecting with a beam. The men would follow behind them to make sure they finished the job correctly.

A third group spread out on the roof, placing tar paper on top. The scent of freshly cut wood filled the air as each man and boy worked at his task while the women prepared the food. Not one person stood idle; it was a swarm of busy activity, and John relished it. He secured the walls into place and then climbed down to fasten the boards of the roof.

He couldn't count how many barn-raisings he'd done and dreamed of the day it would be his time. He had chosen the land and the direction the barn doors would face, leading out to the largest field of *welschkorn* his daed owned. Being the oldest, he'd pick his section of the property, leaving his younger brothers equal amounts.

Annie wanted a view of the hills, but he'd disagreed and chosen the valley. Now it seemed unimportant, and John wished he would have at least listened to her opinion before deciding. He wished a lot of things were different. One was telling her how much he appreciated her coming out to the fields during harvest or a barn-raising to bring him her lemonade. Some of the other girls did the same for their beaus, but no one made lemonade like

Annie, or had her way. She put in extra lemon—not too much, to make it sour, but enough to give a good tang to quench the thirst. And Annie was not only appealing to look at; she was also mature and steadfast in her faith.

Another regret was waiting to ask her to court for the upcoming wedding season. When he thought back on it, they'd actually courted most of their lives. Because of this it was difficult to make them officially a couple, because they already were in his mind. Then, when Annie had found out about her birth mother, he'd felt sure he should wait, but he'd never regretted anything more in his life. Maybe affirming their intentions would have kept her at home or ensured her return.

Irene, the woman whose barn was being built, called to everyone. "*Komm esse!*"

They all stopped what they were doing. Tool belts unsnapped, the buzz of saws ceased, and hammers were silenced. All the men walked over to the dozen tables set up, lined with long benches. Soap, towels, and three tubs of water were set up to wash with before sitting down. The hot, sweaty men sat side by side, passing the food as quickly as they talked of their progress on the barn. The women bustled around, adding more dishes of potato salad, chicken, and Jell-O salad for the young ones.

Hanna came up beside John. "Save room for my pumpkin pie," she said as she set the huge orange pastry in front of him. The chatter dulled as the men stared at the monster pie.

"This looks really good, Hanna," David commented, and rightly so, as he had taken Hanna to singing in his buggy for a second time now. David took the knife to cut a slice.

Hanna grabbed the knife from him. "I'll serve." She cut two pieces and handed one to David after handing John a piece.

David eyed John, who ignored him, but John knew he could no longer put off having a conversation with Hanna. He needed to find out what she had going on in her head. This wasn't the way things were done. The fact that Annie was out of sight didn't mean she was out of his mind. Sometimes he thought he reflected on her even more than before. Maybe he'd taken her for granted, always having been there, and he secretly assumed she would be all his life. He'd never actually said the words to her.

The conversation picked up again, but John ignored the pie. Silly as it seemed, he didn't want to appear as though he was partaking in the intense attention Hanna was giving him. Still, as he sat and watched the others eat, laugh, and talk about the chore ahead of them, he wondered if he was being overly sensitive.

"What do you hear from Annie?" David glanced at John as he asked. The others remained silent, waiting for John's answer. "She has had a safe journey." That was all he could say, because that's all he knew. And no one had asked up to this point, so he hadn't had to think through an answer.

David nodded, as did some of the others. The awkward moment passed quickly when David reached for his slice of pie. "I've been waiting for this." He smirked at John and then stuffed a large bite in his mouth. "Have you ever had one of Hanna's pies?"

John took his meaning to be that he knew Hanna, and she knew him, and not to interfere. But again, he could be reading into things that weren't there. His guilt played games with him, making him insecure, something he was unfamiliar with.

"Nee, I don't believe I have." He took a long swig of tea, now diluted from melting ice. Although no one else was finished, John stood, ready to get back to work. Anything to get his mind off the Beiler girls.

Chapter Fifteen

LEVI TOLD ANNIE that Essie would give her a ride to the library the next day. Annie knew Rudy would probably be more help on the computer and microfiche, but she didn't feel that much more comfortable with him than she did Essie.

As she descended the stairs, she heard the tap of a coffee mug hit the kitchen table and the clip of Jake's paws on the wood floor. Levi lowered the paper when he saw her. "You're up early. The library doesn't open for a while yet."

"It's just habit. I'm used to getting up to do chores." She sat with him and glanced at the headlines. A murder, something about the stock exchange, and sport scores seemed to be the most important events going on in the town of Harrisonburg.

"How's Rudy's room working out for you?" His gentle eyes crinkled as he asked.

"It's very kind of him to give up his room for me." She looked toward the brown plaid couch. "I just hope he's sleeping all right."

"He's fine. He has the dog to keep him company." Levi folded the paper and laid it in front of him. "How is the search going?"

With the way he gave her his undivided attention and studied her face, she felt he really cared, and she answered without hesitation. "The city search didn't find any matches. I went back down and filled out the paperwork for them to run a state search, so maybe they'll find something."

He gathered his eyebrows together. "Did Rudy take you?"

She shook her head, hoping it was enough of an answer. The frown on his face told her he wasn't happy with the situation, so she continued. "Elizabeth dropped me off on her way to work, and I took the bus home."

His lips turned down. "I don't want you taking the bus, Annie. You're my responsibility while you're here."

"It wasn't bad. After taking the bus here from home, I didn't feel too uncomfortable." She lied. Nothing about this place was comfortable, especially the transportation. She had developed a whole new appreciation for her four-hoofed friends back home.

Levi rubbed his callused hands together. "It *is* a straight shot from our house to downtown." He let out a breath. "But I'd feel better if Rudy took you. He has time in between classes, so he can make it work."

Annie didn't want Rudy to take her anywhere unless he offered, and she didn't think that was going to happen. And Essie was out of the question. She didn't know of a person who made her more uncomfortable or out of place. "I hate to make him, though. I'm sure he has other things he'd rather be doing."

Levi looked up abruptly. "Maybe so, but his first obligation is to you."

"Okay, then. No more bus." She didn't mean that either but knew Levi wasn't going to give in. He and Elizabeth meant well, but their children didn't share their concern or hospitality.

He smiled, the same smile Rudy had the other day. "Something will turn up. You'd be surprised these days what they can find with even the smallest amount of information." He glanced at his watch and scooted his chair out. "I'm off to work. Elizabeth will be down soon. She overslept a little. She's a bit under the weather."

Annie's back straightened. "Ach. Well, does she need anything?"

"No, a hot shower and she'll be fine. Probably just allergies." He stopped at the garage door, keys in hand. "Good luck today, Annie."

Annie thought about allergies as she searched for tea to make for Elizabeth. She couldn't think of anyone she knew who'd ever had them and wondered what the cause was. Or maybe they'd had them and didn't know it. Whatever the case, Annie couldn't find the tea and didn't want to pry into any more cabinets than she already had.

Rudy's head popped up from behind the couch. "Morning."

Annie started the fire under the kettle. She rationalized using the gas stove to assist someone who was ill. It was her only way of heating the water. "Good morning, Rudy. Can you tell me where the tea is?"

He pointed to the pantry, and she found it as soon as she opened the door. He scratched his head and put on a T-shirt that draped over his sweatpants. "What are you doing today?"

She took advantage of the opportunity, hoping he would see her need for transportation without having to ask. "Since we haven't found anything on your computer, one of the sites suggested going to the library to find records."

"Essie can take you after she drops me off at my morning class." He reached for the coffeepot. "It's not the best solution, but we only have one car between us."

Annie handed him a mug of tea and made one for Elizabeth. "That's fine. I've taken too much of your time these past few days."

That much was true. He was diligent about his classes and studying, and she knew her schedule was stretching him. He was quiet too long—long enough that Annie thought she'd upset him.

"If things fall through with Essie, let me know." He set down his cup. "I'm gonna shower."

Annie nodded and held her mug with both hands for warmth. She watched him climb the stairs and soon heard the shower running and Essie's loud voice complaining that she needed the bathroom.

A few minutes later Essie came into the kitchen. She looked past Annie and opened the refrigerator. "What are you looking at?" She took out the milk and poured some cereal.

"When will you be ready?"

Squinting, Essie slowly lifted her head. "You're joking, right?"

She took a huge bite of cereal. Drops of milk splashed from her lips into the bowl.

"Rudy said you could take me after you drop him off." Annie shifted her weight, hoping she'd say yes and avoid a standoff.

Essie took a couple more bites of cereal, crunching loudly. "Okay, but not in those clothes." Essie pointed at her with her spoon.

Annie looked down and thought of the clothes Rudy bought for her. It seemed to be the only solution. "Okay, I'll go change."

Rudy drove to campus, got out, and let Essie get into the driver's seat. He leaned into the window of the car and looked directly at Essie. "No speeding or tailgating. Go straight to the library and come back here. Got it?"

Essie bent the rearview mirror and applied some more makeup to her already pretty face. Annie wondered why she bothered coloring herself. "Got it." She snapped the lid on her makeup case and reached for the wheel.

"Keep your cell phone on," Rudy yelled as she pulled away.

As soon as they were out of sight, Essie pushed on the gas pedal. Annie hadn't felt unsafe in a car until that moment. She grasped the armrest as the speed pushed her back into the seat.

She thought about telling Essie to slow down but knew it would probably only make her go faster. When she looked over at her, a thought flashed through her mind. Maybe Essie had no intention of helping her; maybe this was all about gaining her freedom.

Annie sensed danger, but no one was around to protect her. She closed her eyes and prayed for strength.

The swing weighed heavy around the thick tree limb, creaking with each sway forward. Annie pumped her feet to go faster, even though the power was coming from her dawdi's strong arm. With each gentle push he said a letter of the alphabet in English, and she would say it in Deitsch.

"A." His gruff tone scratched out the letter.

"Ah." Annie's tiny voice answered.

"Say 'B.'"

Annie swung her bare feet out in excitement. "Vee."

"Gut. Now say 'C.'" Annie paused, trying to remember the pronunciation. Her feet stilled. Suddenly she remembered and pulled on the coarse rope, lifting herself up slightly in the swing as she blurted out the word. "Tsay," she squealed, just as her dawdi pulled the wooden seat, causing her to fall onto the pebbled dirt.

She landed on her hands and knees. Her cry brought Dawdi quickly to her side. He lifted her to his chest, shushing her, and stroked her head. "Shhh." His warm breath enveloped her neck, wrapping around her heart, as the blood ran from her bruised knees and palms.

"Essie! Stop the car." The words flew out before Annie knew she was saying them.

Essie startled at her demand and slowed down. "What's your problem?"

"I'm not used to cars, Essie, especially fast ones." Annie told herself to breathe.

"This engine has a few more horses in it than you're used to." Essie crossed her arms to let Annie know she was inconvenienced by the wait.

"I do miss Otto."

"Otto? What kind of name is that?" Essie cringed.

"It's short for automobile."

Essie actually laughed and gazed out the window, maybe to keep Annie from seeing her reaction. "You ready now?"

Annie really didn't want to go anywhere with Essie, for a number of reasons. "Is there a library at the college?"

Essie snorted. "Of course there's a library."

Annie stared at her to get her to understand the question more specifically. "One that I could go to?"

Essie looked her up and down. "Dressed in those normal

clothes, you could." Essie smiled at Annie for the first time since she'd been there. "Great idea."

Essie turned the car around and headed back to the campus. Annie closed her eyes and counted to ten. When she opened them, they were back where Essie dropped off Rudy. "Here ya go."

She couldn't get rid of her fast enough. Annie was obviously cramping her style. Tired of Essie's antics, Annie didn't say a word; she just shut the door and set off to the find the library.

After asking a couple of students, she finally found her way to the building she was looking for. The library was overwhelmingly large, with cement pillars in front. She watched as people walked in and out repeatedly. Then she took in a breath and marched forward through the revolving door and stopped when she got inside.

Rudy had given her a card to use if she needed. As she dug around to find it she came across the slip of paper Delores, the woman she'd met on the bus, had given her. She was tempted to call but didn't want to bother her. But Annie seemed to know she would find comfort from the older woman, much like she would from her grandparents.

As she approached the phone on the wall, she hesitated when she read what coins she needed to make a call and then shoved her hand in her bag again and pulled out some quarters. Slipping them into the slot created a buzz in the phone. That meant it was working; she knew that much. After she punched in the numbers a child answered the phone.

She asked for Delores and let out a sigh when Delores responded with delight.

"How are things going, dear?"

Her gravelly voice was a welcome sound, but at that moment Annie didn't even know why she'd called; she just wanted to hear her voice.

"Slow, but I suppose that's to be expected. How are you and your grandchildren?" Talk of family felt good and familiar to her.

"Everyone's well except for Michael. He's the middle one,

and well, you know how those children are that are in-between. Seems to always need attention." Delores laughed. "How is the family you're staying with?"

Annie tried to find the right words. "It's been difficult. The parents are fine, but their daughter doesn't seem to want me here."

"Well, she'll come around, or she won't, but don't let her ruin your visit. Where are you now?" She was so enthusiastic, Annie wished she could be with her now, getting encouragement.

"I'm at the library here at the college." She looked around and watched as some students operated a machine resembling what Rudy had described as a microfiche. "I'm researching for something that I can't find. So, I don't know if it's beneficial to be here." Annie heard herself and realized she was being negative. Just to be doing something was better than sitting and waiting. "It's such a big town."

Delores laughed. "It's actually a small town, honey. You keep the faith, Annie. You never know what you may find." As Annie continued to listen to Delores, she realized she was trying hard to cheer her. It must be obvious in Annie's voice that she was discouraged.

A strange voice came on the phone telling her to deposit more coins. Annie dug into her bag to find more change. "I think it might be more the place I'm staying than the reason I'm here. I'm glad you helped me see that." Annie didn't want to lose the connection. Delores seemed to be the only person she could talk with that understood.

The phone made a beeping noise and then went dead.

Annie heaved a sigh. "Danke, Delores."

Chapter Sixteen

AT HANNA'S REQUEST John walked up to the Beiler barn to help her get ready for the annual two-day quilting party. His stomach churned with each step, his reservations growing. The quilts were to be made for upcoming weddings in the Shenandoah communities. It was the biggest event of its kind among the Amish, and more than three hundred postcards had been sent out.

He'd helped out a dozen times before, but this was the first time that Hanna had pointedly asked for him to be there.

In the past all the activities he'd helped the Beliers with were because of Annie. Now they continued because of Hanna.

He had to admit he appreciated being with the family he knew so well. He'd come to accept the attention Hanna gave him too, but nothing could fill the void Annie had left—no one other than Annie herself. He stopped a few feet short of the barn, feeling the hustle and bustle of energy. The family was performing their tasks, just as they'd always done, but without one person, and he wondered whether they felt the same emptiness he did.

"Are you just going to stand there?" Hanna stood in front of the barn door with her hands on her hips, a stance that was becoming more common.

He pressed his heavy boot into the brown grass and felt her hand touch his elbow to guide him. "I would have come earlier, but I needed to do some extra chores so Mary and the boys could get ready."

"There's still plenty to do with us hosting this year." Hanna beamed as if she were hostess and he, her escort.

"John, want to help me with these quilting frames?" Eli walked ahead of him to half a dozen frames, and they began to place them throughout the barn.

The huge building had been emptied of horses, buggies, and tack to create one big open room. The dirt floor had been raked through and evened out to create a level, solid flooring for the ladies to walk on and set their chairs on. Tables had been set up for refreshments and sewing materials.

John grabbed a frame and followed behind Eli to spread them evenly through the area. Hanna watched for a moment and then huffed out a breath before turning on her heel and leaving.

John steadied a frame on the dirt floor. "How many are coming?"

"Mamm said over a hundred Nebraska Amish will be arriving on a bus today, and another hundred and fifty throughout the weekend from around here." Eli kicked a clod of dirt before setting down another frame. "That's not including all the kids."

Sarah brought the boxes of thread from the house and laid them on a table. "This, combined with what the others are bringing, will add up to fifty-five hundred yards of thread." She lifted the box on the top to reveal the quilt tray. "And two hundred and twenty trays." She put her hands on her hips again and admired the colorful thread and patches of quilt.

Frieda squealed with excitement as she touched the spools of thread. Her brown hair and eyes resembled Annie's when she was younger and brought back memories of Annie.

Right at that moment Hanna pulled him away to help her with more chairs.

As they made their way through the house, Hanna stopped and turned, looking him in the eyes. Her strong gaze fell on him, with a smothering affect. "John Yoder..."

He let out the breath he was holding and prepared himself for what was to come. By the way she was staring at him, he expected a confession or a question he didn't want to answer.

The blue of her eyes sparkled into what looked like silver around the edge of her pupils, radiant and alluring.

"I was wondering if you could take me to worship on Sunday."

When he didn't reply, she continued. "We'll have women here from out of town, and Mamm will need to take them."

John knew their neighbors, the Zooks, were hosting the worship that Sunday and were within walking distance, but he didn't know how to say no. "Jah, and your brothers and Frieda too?"

Hanna stepped back. "I don't think they'll need a ride."

John tilted his head. "To make more room?" He squinted, watching her put her hands behind her back and slightly sway from side to side. "It'd be nice if it were just the two of us." She bumped into Amos as he came around the corner and stopped.

"Do you two have a reason for being in here?" His voice was steady and direct.

Hanna quickly moved to the other room to grab a chair. "Gathering chairs, Daed."

He stared at John, studying him, and then turned and left. John touched Hanna's arm as she brushed by. "I don't think Amos wants us together, Hanna."

She set down the chair only for a moment then picked it up again. "He just doesn't want us to be alone." She smiled big and wide, as if she'd just told a secret.

John watched her leave as he collected his thoughts. Amos came back through, a chair in each hand, and stopped in front of John. "Glad you still come around to help, John. But you don't need to since things have changed." With that, Amos left as quickly as he had come.

John thought he understood his meaning but wondered whether he had read more into their words than he needed to. His mind was tangled with thoughts of Annie. He ran a hand over his face and collected himself before entering the barn again.

Groups of women poured in carrying baskets full of needles and thimbles. Some had swatches to sew into a specially made quilt for a bride or newborn babe. They each took a seat around a frame and got adjusted for a full day of sewing, eating, and fellowship.

As he walked past a group of women from his own community, he heard some of their conversation.

"Annie left…"

"Did you hear…"

"Poor Sarah…"

He stopped to quiet their tongues and said hallo. An older woman with salt-and-pepper hair gave him an empathetic gaze.

"How are you holding up, John?"

"I'm doing well, Mrs. Smithson." He leaned into the circle.

"I'm so sorry, John." Another patted his hand.

"Ladies, everything's just fine, really." He stood tall, and they all stilled for a moment. "Enjoy your quilting." As he walked away, he heard hushed tones but didn't want to try and decipher what was being said. He noticed more heads turning his way as he left the room but held his head high and kept walking.

John decided this was a good time to get some air and took a wagon to fetch more chairs from his home. When he got back the barn was full of women side by side chattering and stitching. When he passed by the group Hanna was with, she caught his arm.

"Ladies, this is John Yoder." She beamed at him and then turned to see the ladies' reactions.

They all fussed over him as he nodded to them. "Hallo, ladies."

"What a bright smile."

"How polite."

"Why, you're about my daughter's age."

Hanna stiffened and took his hand. "He's spoken for."

John pulled his hand away and gave Hanna a quizzical look. He hoped she meant Annie. "Nice to meet you, ladies."

He walked as fast as he could through the mass of women, only to be stopped again by Eli. "I got the last of the chairs, but that still might not be enough." They glanced over the many bodies taking up every inch of space in the building. "Have you ever seen so many women?" Eli gawked.

"Nee, can't say that I have." As John searched the room, his eyes met with one woman in particular. Her clothes were fitted, unlike the clothes of their order, which showed no shape underneath their black dresses. The material looked slick and shiny, and her shoes were black with thick heels. She stood and walked over to a table and poured a cup of coffee. She had a different style and carried herself in a way he'd seen from the English, not the humility of his world.

Eli leaned toward John. "Her daed is a rich farmer."

Slightly embarrassed by his interest in the young woman, John motioned to Eli. "Let's get more chairs from the wagon. I need to get some chores done." As he walked by the young lady, she lifted her eyes to his and smiled. His heart jumped for the first time since he'd told Annie good-bye.

⟿ Chapter Seventeen ⟾

ANOTHER MONTH CREPT slowly by as Annie awaited her answers. She grew impatient, though she had to admit that the weeks of waiting had forced her into a quiet bonding with the Glicks. Adjusting to life with them hadn't been easy, thanks to Essie's hostility. She was also still unsure of which conveniences to indulge in. And the way people depended on themselves and not the help of others made her feel even more alone.

Scattered thoughts ran through her mind. *What will happen if I find my mother? Will I know myself any better? Will it have been worth the price I've paid?* And what was happening with Rudy? He was very helpful, which she appreciated, but maybe too much. The closer she became to Rudy, the more she missed John. Was it out of guilt, or was there was something more?

He consoled her when they reached their first dead end and encouraged her to try other avenues. Each time they heard the same answer: access denied.

Essie spent most of her time watching TV, Elizabeth and Levi worked, and Annie read. When Rudy was home from school, he helped Annie search on the computer or took her to various institutions that had potentially useful information.

Rudy insisted on taking her to the adoption search agency to start an investigation. Although Annie wasn't comfortable with the financial situation, she was grateful they were doing everything they could. When they received another negative response, Annie showed the first signs of giving up, but Rudy kept on and found another registry to do a search.

When they entered the building that first day, Annie tried to keep her spirits up, more for Rudy's sake than her own. After all, he'd been the one to arrange the meeting. They were ushered into an office just off the hallway.

The name plate on the woman's desk announced that she was Mrs. Jean Cook. She stood as they entered her office, didn't offer to shake hands, and then sat again, quickly and businesslike. She nodded to two chairs across from her desk, where Annie and Rudy sat. On the wall behind her hung a fancy arrangement of framed papers that claimed she had experience and a license for her profession.

As Mrs. Cook settled into her own chair, she flipped through a file on her desk and then gave Annie the once-over. "I'll be honest. We don't usually deal with people from your community, Ms. Beiler."

Rudy leaned forward in his chair. "That sounds biased."

"I don't mean it that way. They have a different culture, very few records to give us any leads. They don't pay many taxes or have medical insurance." She spoke as if Annie were not in the room.

"I'd never even considered her being someone from our own community." It was unfathomable to Annie, but then, all of this was.

Mrs. Cook continued. "And as far as a mother outside the community, unless she went to a hospital after, or an ob-gyn, there would be no record of her either. The chances of her registering so she could be found by Annie are slim since she abandoned her."

Rudy closed his eyes in frustration. "We know all of that, but sometimes the unexpected does happen. That's what we're hoping for."

Annie was touched by his determination, but she was also aware that Mrs. Cook had barely acknowledged her. It was also beginning to sound like her quest was a losing battle. She leaned forward and looked directly at the thin woman. "So are you saying there's nothing you can do?"

"No, I just want to be up front with the odds. And they're not good." She folded her long fingers together. "Do you still want to proceed?"

Annie hesitated. "What's the fee?"

Mrs. Cook typed on the computer keys and printed out a copy with three separate prices. "We do this so you're not surprised with what we'll offer for each price range and you don't end up with a larger bill than you can afford."

Annie blinked at the first number and bit her lip. She need not even consider the second or third. "Even the basic is more than I brought with me, so it will have to do."

She was aware that Rudy studied her as she spoke, which made her uncomfortable. It was as if they were creating a silent understanding that he would assist financially.

She turned to him and read in his eyes that she'd been correct in her assessment. She finally nodded her consent to accept his help.

"Okay, we'll start right away." Mrs. Cook tapped the papers on the desk to straighten them and put them in a folder. She didn't smile or give Annie any sign of hope.

"One more thing." Annie cleared her throat. "Do I need to be in the area while you're conducting the search?"

Rudy whipped his head her way.

"No. Are you leaving?" The woman tucked the folder into an envelope, sealed it, and laid it on her desk in a pile of others. Her actions spoke louder than words.

"Jah." Annie kept her eyes forward and blinked away the sting at the top of her throat. "As soon as possible."

Rudy didn't say said a word as they walked away from the agency. Annie knew he didn't agree with her decision to leave, but the weeks had flown by with not even so much as a nibble. Her birth mother had left without a trace. Even Mrs. Cook had left her with the feeling that her search was close to hopeless.

"I'd like to make a phone call, Rudy," she said as they got into his car.

He flinched. "You can use my cell phone." He handed it to her. "Are you calling home?"

"Jah. Will there be phone bills?"

Frowning, he took back the phone. "Worry about that later."

Worry? That was just one worry of many. She wanted to go home, but now, especially after all this time, she wasn't sure she would be welcome. Would her family accept her back? Would they understand why she had to do this? She met Rudy's gaze, tried to understand the emotion in his face, his eyes. Taking a deep breath, she wondered most of all if John would understand.

She'd written each month she'd been away, but no response had ever come. She'd rationalized the reasons. Maybe Abraham, who collected the mail for the Amish, hadn't had a chance to send the letters with anyone yet. Or he couldn't get out to her parents' farm. Or maybe the mail took longer than she thought. She'd never used it before, so she didn't know for sure.

Rudy slowed and pulled over. His face was hard. He was hurt or frustrated. Which Annie didn't know, but it made her feel worse than she already did. He'd started out cold and indifferent and had become her search partner.

"I'm ready to go home, Rudy." She could barely say the words, feeling as if she was giving up, had failed, was unwanted.

His demeanor changed, and she saw something else in his face, a warmth behind the hard facade. Something inside her crumbled, and the tears she'd been holding back traced down her cheeks.

He drew her close. She hugged him and sobbed. He didn't say anything; he just let her cry. She'd held it all in each time they were denied access, ran a check with no results, or received a phone call with no answers. She didn't need anymore bad news. The tall, skinny Mrs. Cook, with all her fancy diplomas, had finally made her see the futility of her search. It was as if she didn't exist, which made her cry harder.

Finally she was done with it. But even after the crying stopped, her body shook with each breath. She pulled back, realizing how close she was sitting to Rudy. She blinked and felt her cheeks warm. She was too close. Much too close.

Rudy let her go. "You can't give up now."

"I have to." She couldn't remember feeling helpless, and now she had the added worry of going home without finding what she came for.

As she sat there in the silence of the car, she appreciated that Rudy had fallen quiet, apparently content to let her puzzle through her thoughts.

It was then she recognized something else in her heart—a nudge, or even a push from the Lord. She felt Him guiding her back home, just as she'd felt Him lead her here. But this time she didn't know why.

Rudy rubbed a hand over his stubbly face and let out a long breath, one of surrender. "You must be hungry."

Annie realized she hadn't eaten since breakfast and nodded.

He seemed relieved that he had some way to take care of her and stopped at a Chinese restaurant. "Is this okay?"

"I don't know." She reached for the door handle. He stopped her.

"Of course you wouldn't." He sat back in his seat and looked at the restaurant. "We've expected you to figure out a lot on your own." He gazed out the window and worked his jaw. "I've been so annoyed by having someone around me who represents the very people who turned us away, I hadn't thought enough of how incredibly hard it must be for you here. Bits and pieces, but not the whole picture."

She picked at a Kleenex wadded up in her hand. "It's okay, Rudy."

"No, no, it's not. And I apologize." His gaze was so intense Annie had to look away. She sensed something more than just her feelings was on his mind.

"It's because of me we had to leave."

Annie lifted her eyes to meet his, but he was facing the window. "My education." He turned to her. "Can you believe it? Just because I wanted to go to school past the eighth grade, our whole life changed." He scoffed. "As hard as it's been for Essie here, I'll never get over the guilt of it. I thought at first it'd be worth it, but not with the way it's turned out."

"So that was it? You wanted to go to school, and your parents moved?"

Higher education was forbidden. So was her love for music and her desire to learn to play an instrument. She remembered the time she'd taken Mamm's knitting yarn and made a guitar with sticks and wood from Daed's workshop. When Daed walked through the barn doors and saw her sitting on a milking stool picking at the yarn, he marched right over and pitched the pieces of wood and yarn into the trash barrel. He'd never said a word about it, and neither had she.

"The brethren didn't appreciate my parents' support of my interest in achieving a higher education. There was no reasoning with them."

"Did you expect them to?" She said it out loud, but she shouldn't have.

He shook his head and drove out into the street. "Never mind. You're just like them."

Annie didn't know how to take the jab. Since she moved here, being one of "them" had become a bad thing, quite opposite of how she'd always felt about being Amish. She'd never had to defend herself, but neither could she go idly by and say nothing. "I do agree with following their ways."

Rudy grunted.

"But I also agree with your wanting to learn and get a better education." She meant every word. Annie had always admired John's natural aptitude for knowledge. He seemed to know about everything, and especially the weather. For him it came naturally, but she wondered how far he could go if he had the opportunity to go to college, and she had always wanted to see how well she could do furthering her own education.

Rudy turned to her and studied her face. "You do?"

"Jah, Rudy. I understand why you left. You're going to be an incredible architect some day." She grinned at his wide eyes, full of surprise, and something else she couldn't distinguish.

He scoffed. "I never thought I'd hear an Amish person say that." He stared at her again and then laid a hand on hers.

Annie knew his appreciation for her understanding meant a great deal to him, but the touch, whether it meant anything else or not, didn't feel comfortable. She politely pulled her hand away and tried to picture John's face.

⌒ Chapter Eighteen ⌒

WHEN JOHN WALKED in through the front door of Abraham's store, the unexpected sound of a bell ringing over his head made him flinch.

Abraham and his family ran the store out of the front portion of their home on the tourist strip in town. They made everything they sold, from candles and soap to quilts and dolls. It looked like any other store on the block, except for the hitching post out front and the absence of electrical wires leading to the building. And then there was also the clothesline neatly hung with trousers and capes.

John waited to see which of the nine family members would come out first. Little Ezekiel came toddling out with Abraham in close pursuit and squealed when Abraham picked him up and placed him on his shoulders.

"John." Abraham patted him on the back. "How are you?"

John felt like everyone treated him with special care now, which only made things worse. "I'm fine, Abraham." John tickled Ezekiel's foot and smiled at his giggle. "He's getting big." Ezekiel blew bubbles that popped on his lips when he made a humming noise.

"It's good they're getting older, because I am as well." Abraham pushed his head back into Ezekiel, making him laugh and grab hold of his daed's hair. "This one has more energy than all the others put together."

John smiled at the thought of having seven children at his heels and of the plans he'd made with Annie. Then he wondered whether they had made them together or if they were just his, assumed and unspoken. He had assumed a lot—maybe too much.

"Abraham, I was wondering if you had any letters for me to pick up." It was his last hope in connecting with Annie. Weeks had gone by, and he had to know if she'd tried to communicate with him.

Abraham's face fell. He slowly shook his head and removed Ezekiel from his shoulders. "I'm sorry, John."

John's gut was as tight as a drum, but he didn't let on that he was hurting. There could still be reasons, but at the moment none of them mattered. "Danke, Abraham."

Abraham pointed to the back. "I could check with Mary."

John held up a hand. "No, don't bother her." He pointed to the bell, wanting to change the subject. "When did you get that noisemaker?"

Abraham scoffed. "When one too many of the English decided to make their way into our kitchen."

John gathered his brows. "Don't they know this is your home?"

"Apparently not." Abraham shook his head.

John waved as he walked to the door. "I'll see you Sunday."

Abraham returned the wave and took Ezekiel to the back of the house.

As John walked down the street of the small town he watched the tourists snap pictures of an Amish buggy and horse tethered to a hitching post. Others held bags full of Amish-made goods. Still another held postcards with an Amish girl on the front.

A group of Englishers waited for the next tour through the farmlands of his community. Another tour went to visit the markets where Amish from all around brought their goods to sell.

He'd never thought so much about the English before Annie was living among them. How could she avoid learning of their ways and covet some of them, maybe just to fit into the lifestyle the Glicks lived? He wondered whether she would be different when she returned. If she returned. He had heard talk that Minister Zeke was considering holding a meeting with the elders regarding Annie ignoring strict warnings she'd received not to leave.

"Oh, sorry!" A teenage girl with colored blonde hair bumped into John, pulling him from his thoughts. She fell into step with two other girls, who gazed at him and giggled. "That one would be worth becoming Amish for," she told the others. Not used to such a comment, John felt the heat rise up his neck.

He made a stop at the Horse 'N Tack to negotiate the price on a new harness. "Morning, Tobe." John heard his slow steps but didn't look up. He glanced over the new harnesses, saw the price, and moved to the used ones.

"Almost afternoon. You in the market for a harness for Pete out there?"

John turned to see Tobe's crooked finger point to a buggy tethered out front. It wasn't his, but he didn't want old Tobe to worry about the oversight. He was one of the oldest Amish men John knew. At eighty-nine years of age he still ran his store alone with the help of his wife, Esther.

"Jah, how about this one?" John pointed to one he knew wouldn't work, but it gave Tobe a kick to explain why.

"Nee, with Pete's girth, you need a wider one." He bent over even more than he already was and pulled out a longer and wider harness. "This one should do the trick." He moved his shaky hand over to John, and he readily accepted it, worried Tobe wouldn't be able to hold it much longer.

John held it up admiringly. "Did you make this one?" Because it was used, he asked; all the new gear was made by Tobe's two hands.

"Nee, the Kings brought it in just the other day. Lost old Henry, and the other horses don't need this size."

"The Kings? We had a barn-raising for them not long ago." John thought back to that time. It seemed longer; maybe it was. The days didn't matter so much; their lives revolved around the seasons and where the sun was in the sky, not so much the months and time of day. Another event that had happened without Annie; that's all it amounted to.

"How much do I owe you?"

"I'll put it on Elam's bill. It's about the end of the month, so he'll be coming around to pay it off." Tobe shuffled his way toward the back, where his living quarters were, and gave John a wave. "And don't you be a'worrying about Annie. She'll come around." He walked around the corner, out of sight.

John's head whipped up, not prepared for the comment, and wondered if the old man had read his mind. It wasn't healthy for him to go on this way, wondering, waiting.

He started for home, giving him time to tie up loose ends and make some decisions. When he got to the barn, he unhitched the horse and put him out to pasture, then headed over to talk with Sarah. Maybe she had a letter. If not, it was time to let go.

Chapter Nineteen

THE GOOD-BYE AT the Glicks's was brief. Annie thanked Levi before he left for work. "Will your family understand why you've been gone these last couple months, Annie?"

"I don't know, Levi." Annie knew to be careful, as this had been one of the areas of disagreement between them.

"If you need my help in any way, you let me know."

"Danke, Levi. I will." Annie laid her suitcase and handbag on the couch that would no longer be Rudy's bed. He had been good to let her have his room. The solitude had saved her.

Elizabeth and Essie were making lunch when Annie walked in the kitchen. "How did things go with the agency?" Elizabeth took out the bread to make sandwiches.

"Not as good as I'd hoped." Rudy slumped down into a chair.

Essie and Elizabeth both looked at Rudy and then each other. Annie noticed his claim on the news, as if it was his own more than hers.

Annie took a step closer to Elizabeth. "It's time for me to go home."

Essie was a hard one to surprise, but she seemed more astonished than the others. Her eyes widened, and she furrowed her eyebrows.

"Stay and finish what you've started." Rudy's eyes were steady and unwavering.

Elizabeth then spoke up. "I hate for you to leave before you've found something, Annie."

"Jah, me too, but I think I've done all I can. But I want to thank you—" She turned to Essie. "—all of you, for putting me up. I couldn't have done this without you."

"I hope you hear from your mother someday." Elizabeth wrung her slender hands together.

"My mamm is waiting for me back home. And my birth mother...didn't mean for me to find her."

Elizabeth and Rudy glanced at Essie, wanting her to say something to Annie. Essie rubbed her arms with irritation. "Sorry we didn't get along." Her words came with difficulty, obviously doing something she didn't want to. She turned to the window. "I guess you don't realize how tough it's been to have you here."

Annie wanted to ask them why they felt it was wrong. If they weren't willing to follow the rules, shouldn't they have known they would be asked to leave the community? What she did understand was that she was a constant reminder of a bitter time, one they hadn't gotten over. "Actually, I do."

Essie turned back and rolled her eyes, a gesture to which Annie still hadn't become accustomed. "Do you always have to be so dang nice?"

Annie flinched at her language but tried to focus on what she was saying instead. "I just know it's been difficult for you."

Essie snorted and crossed her arms over her chest. "I can't say I'll miss you, but it would have been cool if you'd found your mom."

Annie nodded, not sure what to say, and was glad Jake came up for her to pet and say good-bye.

The drive to the bus depot was tense; she was consumed with emotions of unfulfilled answers. Rudy squeezed the wheel as he drove slowly down the busy highway. "Are you sure you want to go before the agency contacts us?"

She kept her eyes ahead, not wanting to tangle with him about her decision. "If you hear anything, I'd like if you would let me know. But I don't expect you to."

He turned to her. "You don't want to know when to quit hoping?"

"I already have." She looked away to hide her disappointment.

In the quiet Annie watched the cars clip by, ready for her mode of transportation to slow down to a horse's pace.

"I'm sorry to hear that. The girl who first came here wouldn't have said what you just did," he said with a light tone.

Annie half smiled and gave him a sideways glance. Even though she knew it was hard, she felt at peace with her decision. Gott had brought her there, and now He wanted her home again. Maybe it wasn't even about her birth mother. She looked more directly at Rudy. Maybe it was about something completely different.

"I've learned a lot by coming here."

"Like what?" he asked in jest.

Now that she knew the reason he was callous toward her, she could better handle his cynicism. "That my life back home fits me."

I just hope they still think I fit them. She stopped the thought. She had made every effort to find a way to be accepted by others, to find out why she had not been wanted by her birth mother, when all along the place she came from suited her so completely.

"You seemed to fit in pretty well in Harrisonburg, for an Amish." He grinned. "When will you be coming back?"

"I won't unless there's a reason."

"You mean your mother."

"Jah, my birth mother."

He grinned. "Not to see me." He said it as a statement, not a question, as if he knew the answer.

"You know, Rudy Glick, when we first met, I thought we might never understand one another." Her face was serious.

His head drew back slightly, and he opened his mouth to speak.

"But I think we do." She grinned.

He gave her a weak sort of smile, one that almost made Annie sad.

"Well, then." Rudy's voice broke into her reverie. "We're going to have a night on the town before you go."

She eyed him with apprehension.

He chuckled. "You know me well enough to trust me. It won't be an English night out; it will be a Mennonite one."

Annie still wasn't convinced. These were the things teenagers from their community experienced during their *rumspringa* that Annie had done well to avoid. And being with someone who knew about all of these desires and pleasures would be worse than with the young Amish who didn't know where to go or what to do.

"I know a great place where we can get—"

"No." She paused and let out a breath. "I'm sorry. I'm just not interested."

Rudy pulled over and parked, then hiked up a leg on his car seat. "That hurts, ya know, not believing that I'll make good judgments about where we go and what we do. What kind of a friend do you think I am?"

She couldn't tell whether he was serious but didn't want to take the chance she'd offended him. "I didn't mean to be rude—"

He laughed. "I'm joking; you need to lighten up. I'm sure you have a great sense of humor somewhere in there."

She had been all business since she'd arrived—so into her quest that she'd forgotten how to have fun. But did she dare even dangle her toe in the water? What if she got swept away and went too far, made the wrong choice? "Okay…"

"That's all I needed to hear. Follow me." He opened the car door and stepped out, moving to her side, and opened the door.

He wasn't giving her a choice, and it made her even more uncomfortable.

He squatted next to her and placed one hand on the edge of her seat for balance. "Annie, all you've done since you've been here is work on finding your mother. When I first heard you were coming to stay with us, I balked, like I always do about anything Amish. But after I met you and realized why you'd come, I admired your bravery, and as we went along searching, I realized how smart you were and how determined to do what you came here for."

He took her hand and stood, urging her out of the car. "I know the Amish are committed to their work, but I also remember how they always made time to rest and to have a good time. And that, Annie Beiler, is what we're going to do right now."

He turned around and pointed to a hibachi restaurant. "And this is where we're eating dinner tonight." He practically pulled her out of the car.

"But I'm not wearing my English clothes." She'd left them in Rudy's room with a note thanking him for the gesture but saying she couldn't keep clothes that would never be worn again.

"Don't worry; the attention will all be on the chef." He smirked.

She frowned in confusion, not understanding why they would be watching someone cook. Now her curiosity was piqued, and she willingly stepped in time with Rudy.

As soon as he opened the door, the smell of chicken, fish, and beef wafted through the room. Rudy told an Asian man they were a party of two, and he guided them to a long, square table where eight people were already seated. Annie wondered whether they all knew each other but quickly realized from the way they kept to themselves that they didn't.

The chef walked in to the center area of the square wearing a tall white hat and apron and poured oil on a huge, hot grill. The way he used a spatula to thin the oil and quickly move it around the cooking area fascinated Annie.

"He moves so quickly, I can hardly keep track of the spatula," she told Rudy, her eyes still trying to follow the chef's movements.

"You haven't seen anything yet. Keep watching." He crossed his arms on the table and watched with her. The others around them did the same, and people began to talk with others outside their personal group. This was more familiar to Annie, as she talked with a young couple next to her and another family sitting to the right of them.

There were lots of jokes at the dinner. People at their table had fun getting to know one another as the chef kept them entertained with an assortment of tricks with knives, spatulas, eggs, and vegetables. By the end of their dinner every guest was willing to try catching bits of zucchini squash the chef launched at them. Some were eager to have a second chance. Annie laughed when Rudy snapped his head around like a snake catching everything that was thrown at him.

"You're pretty good at that." She chuckled.

"Depends on how hungry you are." He grinned and watched her feeble attempt to catch a cut-up carrot that bounced off her nose and onto the table in front of her.

She glanced at him but watched carefully in case another bit of food was tossed at her. "I guess I'm not hungry enough yet." They both laughed and watched the chef go around the table to those brave enough to try again.

Small portions of miso soup and salad were served first, and then the chef prepared vegetables, fried rice, and a variety of meats. Rudy ordered steak for himself and chicken for Annie and an extra order of teriyaki sauce, shrimp, and scallops. They watched as the chef cut them up at lightning speed on the tremendously hot cooking surface.

The filet mignon Rudy ordered was prepared to perfection. It was so tender that every bite was a tasty experience. Scallops prepared on the hibachi grill were also excellent—bronzed and crusty on the outside, soft and succulent on the inside.

"I've never had these." Annie stuffed another bite of shrimp into her mouth. "Is it a type of fish?" She savored the delicious blend of butter and lemon mixed with the firm shrimp.

"Actually, they're a shellfish, a bottom-feeder." He grinned after he said it, making her even more curious.

"Bottom of what? The ocean?" The scrumptious bite she was enjoying only a moment ago was becoming questionable as she learned more.

"They eat what others discard." He took a bite of one and watched her as she swallowed hard and decided on the chicken instead.

"Chicken." Rudy teased.

"At least I know what I'm eating and what they eat." She took a bite to get the shrimp taste off her tongue.

"No, I meant you, not wanting to eat something that's good because you can't stomach the fish's diet." He challenged her, all the while eating more shrimp.

Their gazes met and stayed. He'd known she needed this—getting her mind off something that had been turned on for months. It put things in perspective and refreshed her weary mind of all that had driven her so hard for so long.

"Danke." She smiled tentatively, because the word was out of place for the moment.

He snorted. "For what? Dinner?" His eyes didn't waver.

"For making me have fun." She lifted her eyebrows and gave him a grateful smile, waiting for him to accept.

"Thank you for cooperating." He chuckled.

"Jah, I guess I played a part."

"You said yes."

She shook her head slowly so as not to lose eye contact. "No, I never did say the word. You dragged me."

"I suppose we remember things the way we want them to be." His grin broadened.

"Okay then, but we'll need to stick to the same story."

"Which could be anything, since we're creating our own version of what really happened." He turned toward her, enjoying the conversation.

"Jah, as a matter of fact, I think this was all my idea." She nodded and smiled back at him.

"I won't let you have that one."

She furrowed her brows. "Why not?"

"Because it's too far from reality; no one would believe it."

That made her feel better for some stupid reason. There was nothing wrong with what they were doing, at least not yet. The chemistry between them that had been suppressed was now building up, and Annie knew she had to stop it but without ruining their evening. This was a good way to remember this visit, not all about the search.

"Okay then, I get to pick what we do next." Except for the fact that she had no idea where to go or what to do. Rudy could see it in her face and, as always, helped her along.

"What's something you've always wanted to do, eat, drink...entertainment that we do?"

She appreciated that he said what *he* did versus the Englishers. Rudy was true to his Mennonite ways, and she admired him for that. She thought for a few minutes, and then it came to her. "Ice cream."

He stopped short of putting a scallop in his mouth, about which she was now wondering as much as she had the shrimp. "Good answer. I know just the place to go."

Rudy paid the bill, saying he'd be insulted if she tried to use one of her flour dollars to help. She laughed at his name for her mother's money and its spots of white powder.

"So where are we going?" Annie asked as Rudy scooted into his car seat next to her.

"Just enjoy the drive and tell me something I don't know about you." He pulled on to the highway, making Annie wonder even more where they were going, but soon they were so engaged in conversation she stopped noticing.

They hadn't talked about anything other than the very basics and the particulars of her search. Looking back, Annie wished they would have gotten to know each other better a long time ago. It would have made their time researching more enjoyable.

Then she stopped. It may have become too comfortable, and these hidden feelings she felt rising up now and again might have become stronger. She had trusted this entire journey to Gott, and He had protected her from a forbidden relationship as well. Maybe that's why He hadn't had her find her mother as well.

They pulled into a place called the Purple Cow. The place was packed with people, young and old. People drove up to a sign that talked to them. Rudy placed their order, telling Annie to trust his choice for her, and a person answered. Soon a girl on roller skates came out and brought them their order. No churning milk and sugar for hours in a container covered with ice and salt.

Annie felt spoiled as she stared at the perfect ice cream. She looked closer and saw bits of chocolate mixed in with it. "Ach!" She squeaked with delight.

Rudy grinned and dug into his double helping of chocolate ice cream. "Just wait 'til you try it."

When she did, the taste of nuts, chocolate, and the vanilla ice cream made her taste buds tingle. "I've had berries on ice cream but never chocolate and...is it peanuts? She took another bite.

"It's a Snickers bar." Rudy watched her surprise.

"Good choice." They ate in silence for a minute, and then Annie started thinking about ice cream like she never had before. "I've always wondered how the ice cream freezes."

"The salty ice water absorbs heat from the mixture, bringing it below the freezing point of water and turning the mixture into ice cream." Rudy answered as if he were in a college classroom and she were the instructor.

She stopped eating and stared. Sometimes she wished she was as smart as Rudy, that her community let them continue their education if they wanted to. Most didn't, like the average kid, but for those with the talent and desire it would be good for them to expand their minds. It could be beneficial to the community in many ways. But she also understood why their community didn't allow it. The children were needed to help with the family farm, and once they reached a certain age, they were more useful doing farmwork.

"What? You asked." He shrugged and looked away as he polished off his dessert. "What would you say about staying for one more week?"

She started to speak, and he held up a hand.

"You're so close, Annie. I can feel it. Just think about it for a minute before you say no."

Annie immediately thought no, but since he made her stop

and think, she did. She'd come to listen to Rudy's suggestions and ideas and learned two heads were better than one. He'd been right about what agencies to go to and where to find others when they led to a dead end. Maybe he was right again.

Chapter Twenty

HERE'S THE LAST of them." John's sister Mary wobbled toward him with a stack of quilts so high she could barely see where she was going.

He took the tower of sewn-together patches from her and for an instant let his gaze linger on the one on the top. It was much like one Annie had made—one of her first—and wasn't in good shape, but the blended colors of blue made into a star-like pattern looked perfect to him. "I like that one."

"Well, then you can buy it." Mary grinned and turned to go back inside and help her mamm gather the canned goods they would take along.

John liked the Deutschland quilt and thought he might just do that. The mud sale, named for the churned mud caused by the rain and crowds of people, took place each spring. This last spring the land had been doused with so much rain they had to postpone the event.

Now that they were in the midst of the summer harvesting, they didn't have time for such an event, but because the firemen's benefit auction depended on their charity to raise money for the volunteer fire companies, it had to be done. And no matter what else needed doing, today they would gather crafts, food, livestock, equipment, plants, bales of hay, furniture, and quilts and do their part for a community outside their own.

When they had all the goods loaded, John took the reins of one wagon, and his daed took the other wagon, which was already packed and ready to go. They took their time traveling into the small town, which had doubled in size because of the sale. People came from miles away for the mud sale, and even with it being months overdue, people still flocked to partake in the activities.

John helped Mary down from the wagon as the boys scurried away in curiosity. His mamm looked after them with an expression of joy and with a trace of sadness. John took two steps closer to her and leaned in close, trying to guess what was on her mind.

"They're growing up." He kept his eyes forward, watching them shoot blue lines of Styrofoam at one another from cans of Silly String.

His mamm laughed as a bit of string stuck to her dark hair. Her brown eyes glistened, and drops trickled down her cheeks when she smiled. "I'm very blessed to have them." She touched a hand to his face. "And you, Isaac, and Mary."

John didn't believe her. She'd had difficulties with her last pregnancy and not only lost the baby but also her ability to bear any more children, a disappointment that any woman would feel, but for an Amish woman it meant losing your foremost identity under Gott. "Having me makes up for four more, so the numbers all worked out right."

She smiled a real smile and hugged him into her side. "What do you hear from Annie?"

John's parents thought a lot of Annie and had been heartbroken when she left. Just like the others who knew why she was leaving, they'd been surprised she hadn't been born to the Beilers. They weren't to talk about such things and went on with their lives, just as the Beilers had.

"I don't." He hoped that was the end of it. He hadn't told them that he didn't know whether Annie would return, that something in his heart told him she wouldn't as the weeks dragged on. If she did find her birth mother, the Annie he knew and loved wouldn't leave her; she would want to know her and be her family, or part of it, if she had her own. There was also the fact that she mentioned feeling that she was different, not accepted as she once had been in the community. But John knew this impression was coming from her and no one else.

His mamm didn't look up. "Do you know how to reach her?"

"I'm sure Sarah has the information, but I haven't asked for it."

Now Mamm turned to her son. "But why?"

John let out a long breath, wondering the same thing. What was he scared of? Or worried over the most? Losing her was foremost in his mind, and he had to admit he might be a tad envious that she was out in a world with so much to do and see, and his life was going along the same as always. It troubled him that she hadn't tried to reach him. Abraham surely would have let him know if he'd received a letter. And part of it might be just plain jealousy. He vaguely remembered the Glicks. They had two children, one a young man about Annie's age. Another face of jealousy raged within him.

"Lots of reasons." He didn't want his mother to fret about things over which neither of them had control. He didn't even like talking to her about Annie.

Mamm pressed her lips together. "If you haven't heard from her, this could go very badly." He refused to make eye contact. "Are you prepared for that, son?"

He nodded slightly and moved forward, not wanting to continue the conversation. She walked next to him in silence, for which he was grateful. John climbed up into one of the wagons and began handing the goods to Isaac and his mother, who took as much as she could carry and hollered to the boys to come over and help. Once both wagons were unloaded, they walked to the grounds to set up a booth and arranged the goods on and around two tables, with a board behind them to display the quilts.

Mary stayed with Elam and Mamm, while John and Isaac took the boys to look around. John chuckled when she watched them on exercise bikes.

"What's funny?" Isaac scanned the place to see what he was missing.

"I think it's interesting that the Amish are most amused by the things here that are not part of our culture." He pointed to the boys furiously spinning the wheels of the machine but going nowhere. "Strange concept."

Isaac grunted his agreement and found their way to the large building where they auctioned off the livestock. A black-and-white horse in a pen was being bid on. Making it clear he didn't like the spotlight, the stallion ran from one end of the makeshift enclosure to the other. John had seen them this spirited before and wondered whether that flimsy structure would hold him.

"He's a beauty, isn't he?" Isaac asked as he watched the horse fly by, turn, and run back the other direction.

Before John could respond, he noticed Hanna Beiler watching the wild horse. She looked over the crowd, and her eyes stopped on his. He smiled and started to walk over. Just the comfort of being with any of her family filled a hole in his gut. Being with Hanna wasn't the same, but it was something.

"He's got some energy, doesn't he?" John jerked his chin up to where the horse had stopped, its short breaths moving its nostrils.

"I've never seen such a pretty horse." She turned to John at the same moment a loud *bang* of metal shot through the room.

John looked away from her to find the source of the sound. The horse came pounding through the crowd, hooves stomping on the dirt floor, his mane flying through the air and tail straight behind him.

Before John could take in what was happening, the sixteen-hand mass of horse flesh made a sharp turn, leaning to the right to make a dash for the exit. The only thing standing in the animal's way was John and Hanna.

The thundering sound of hooves snapped him to attention. Hanna realized the danger and began to run. John caught her around the waist and pulled her to the side and into the crowd. Hanna swung around him and held on tight.

Feeling her warm body against him, John quickly created distance between them. He looked down at her as he pulled his hand away. "Are you all right?" He searched her face, waiting to hear her speak.

Hanna let out a huge breath, and then a few short breaths followed. "Got the wind...knocked out of me."

"Let me help you." John helped her stand and brushed away some dirt from her cheek. "Are you sure you're okay?" It was then he saw one familiar face and then another, and the circle that had gathered around them, still watching. "She's fine, folks."

"You should know; you got a close enough look," David popped off, but John didn't appreciate the humor. And if John didn't know better, he sensed a bit of jealousy in David's tone and in the way he looked at Hanna.

The crowd was moving too slowly for John, so he created a diversion. "Did they catch that horse?" He looked toward the open gate the horse must have run through and hoped everyone else would too. They mumbled and started to walk slowly in the direction the horse had run.

Isaac rushed over a moment too late, just as John began to ask Hanna if she was feeling better. "That all happened so fast. I didn't know what hit you two."

"What happened to you?" John wished his brother would have been by his side to have someone to vouch for the strange way the whole thing unfolded.

"Got caught up in the crowd, I guess." He shrugged.

John narrowed his eyes. "You mean you ran with them."

"Jah, maybe." He lifted one side of his lips.

Hanna laid a hand on John's arm. "Danke, John. If it weren't for you, I could have been hurt by that wild animal."

"It's what anyone would have done in my place." John turned away, ready to escape those penetrating blue eyes.

Hanna looked toward Isaac. "I don't think so." She turned her attention back to John. "Danke again."

Isaac scratched his head. "Did I miss something?"

John nudged his brother with his elbow as he walked passed him. "Nothing important."

The boys came up to them, ready to go explore. "Mary's

gonna make a doll that looks like Robert." He bent his head way back to look up at John.

"Okay, then let's go back to our booth. Gabriel, are you going to have her make one for you?" John was calculating the time he'd have to roam around by himself while the boys were waiting for the dolls.

"Yep." Gilbert nodded. "I want a mouth on mine."

"You know we don't make faces on them," Isaac threw in. "No graven images. What's the verse?" He looked over to John.

"It's the second commandment. You shall not make for yourself a carved image, or any likeness of anything that is in heaven above, or that is in the earth beneath, or that is in the water under the earth." It was a question so commonly asked among tourists John had it memorized and wondered why Isaac didn't.

"Just the lips?" Gabriel pleaded.

"Why do you want lips more than anything else?" John wondered what his little mind was thinking.

"So he can talk to me." He tilted his head as if John should know the answer.

"You'll just have to use your imagination. And you have a good one, so that shouldn't be hard." John grinned, thinking of the detailed mud castles Gilbert had made at the mud sales.

When they got to the booth, the boys each claimed he wanted his doll first, and John told them the only way to decide was to flip a penny. Gilbert won and asked Mary for a mouth, which she politely refused.

"I don't want one then." Gilbert stuffed his hands in his pockets and pushed the felt hat down on his head.

"I'm gonna go walk around," Isaac said to John, and turned toward the baked goods.

John watched the sulking Gilbert and put his hand on Robert's shoulder. "Looks like your brother needs some time alone. Ask your sister if she'll make one for you while we wait for Gilbert."

"Please, sis," Robert asked, and sat next to her so he could watch and give his input as to what went on his "Robert doll."

Mary used a battery-operated sewing machine to make the body of each doll in two separate pieces. She put the right sides together and pinned the back and front together, and then sewed around them inside out. "Can he wear a red shirt?" Robert stared at her, waiting for her answer.

Mary looked up to John.

"We only wear black, so why wouldn't your doll wear black if it's you?" John hoped it would work. Whenever they came to places where there was diversity, it got their brains churning with ideas. They understood the rules but didn't always understand why yet.

Robert shrugged and looked at John. "When's Annie coming back?"

John and Mary glanced at one another as Robert waited, not knowing the depth his question created. "I'm not sure."

"But she is coming back, right?"

John met Mary's eyes then looked back at his brother. "Jah, she'll come back." It seemed impossible not to think of her. The questions from his family kept her constantly on his mind, and his answers were his own, not based on anything but his own guesses.

Mary gave John a sad smile then went back to her work tracing the patterns of a shirt, pants, suspenders, shoes, and a hat onto the black fabric and cut them out. Then she turned it right side out and put stuffing in through a two-inch hole, sewed up the gap, and stitched the pieces on.

"Are you done yet?" Robert sat on a chair as she worked, swinging his legs, waiting impatiently. Gilbert climbed up with him and watched.

Mary smiled. "I sewed on his shirt, pants, shoes, and hat, but if I don't put on his suspenders, his pants might fall off."

Robert chuckled and watched as the finishing touches were made. "There you go, little brother. What are you going to name him?"

"Gilbert." He blew air into his cheeks, making them puff out.

John and Mary exchanged glances.

Robert took the doll and handed it to his brother.

Gilbert took the gift and stared at his brother. He slapped him on the knee. "Danke." He slid off the chair and gave Mary a bear hug.

"You made him happy, Robert." John commended his little brother with a smile.

"Yeah, it made me happy too." He sat back and waited to watch Mary go through the doll-making process again.

John thought Robert's words described the heart of the Amish culture as well as he'd ever heard it expressed. He wondered how Annie could have ever left it for the outside world.

⌁ Chapter Twenty-One ⌁

RUDY TALKED ANNIE into staying a couple more weeks. "Give the agency a chance, then go," he'd advised. The phone call had come, and now as she sat in the social worker's office, it seemed he was right in asking her to stay.

A woman walked in, pulled a sweater around her thick waist, and held out a pudgy hand. "I'm Mrs. Mason. And you are Annie Beiler?"

Annie nodded. "And this is Rudy Glick." When she gestured to Rudy, he took Mrs. Mason's hand. Annie glanced his way, trying to figure out his demeanor. Something had been said on the phone when he took the call. It couldn't have been much due to confidentiality, but whatever it was, Rudy was in a somber mood.

The short, round woman sat down, scratched her red curls, and pursed her lips. "There has been a response to your registry, Ms. Beiler."

"Annie. Call me Annie." She asked the Lord for strength, not knowing why.

Mrs. Mason looked into her eyes and held on to a piece of paper at the tips with both hands. "Your birth mother has responded. She's has given you permission to see all legal documents involving your birth and all other circumstances involved."

"What other circumstances?" Annie felt a numbing in her fingers that traveled up her arms.

Mrs. Mason handed Annie a file. "This is the police report." She paused when Annie did. "Or I can just tell you."

The woman held her composure, but her gaze dropped, telling Annie it must be best that way. "Your mother gave you up because she had been through a traumatic experience. I want you to understand that. She was not much older than you when you were born."

Annie couldn't imagine giving up a child but tried to hear the explanation with open ears.

"Annie, your mother was raped." Mrs. Mason looked at her intently.

Darkness slid across Annie's mind. Her thoughts paralyzed. Then a thought crept in: *You're tainted.* Then another: *Not worthy.* And the worst—*You're different. You'll never be good enough to go back now.*

Rudy squeezed her hand. "Annie."

She gazed at him, her focus darting from one eye to the other. His gray eyes blinked, bringing her into the moment—a moment she couldn't bear.

"It's hard news, Annie. I know. And I'm sorry." Mrs. Mason's compassionate gaze brought the tears.

Annie stood and walked to the door. She found her feet taking her to a bathroom. Locking the stall door, she slammed her back against the metal divider and slid down, crouching in the corner. She let the sobs come with the tears of humiliation and shame. *How could this be, Lord? Why did You let this happen to me?*

A knock on the stall door made her flinch.

"Annie, come out. Let's go home."

Rudy's voice was stern, filled with concern. With no hesitation, he rapped again. "Annie."

"I'm here." Annie pushed herself up to standing. The snap of the lock made her hesitate. She didn't want to see his face. It was easier before he cared, before he got involved.

The door eased open, and Annie lifted her eyes to his for a second, just to show him she could. His expression surprised her. It was not filled with empathy but determination.

"Wash off your face and let's go."

A woman grabbing for a paper towel stared as Rudy slipped a file under his arm and reached across her to get a towel. He took

Annie by the hand, and they walked down the plain, white hallways and worn, gray tile to his car. It all seemed so surreal.

They drove in silence, and when they reached the Glicks's home, Rudy turned off the car and looked at her. "Annie, talk to me."

She wiped her ruddy cheeks roughly with the back of her hand. "This isn't what I came here for."

Rudy let out a breath. "How could you have ever known?"

"Ach, Rudy. You have no idea," she spouted harshly without intending to.

"No, I don't. But I can imagine what this is doing to you." He reached for her. "And I'm sorry."

The feel of his touch—flesh touching flesh—annoyed her. Her tears of sorrow turned to anger toward her mother, toward the man who raped her, and toward herself for finding out. Why had she ever come to this place? John was right. Everyone was right for telling her not to leave. This was too hard. How could she ever make this right?

"I can't be that person." She looked to her lap in disgust.

"I know it doesn't feel like it fits. You want it to go away. I wish it could." His voice was sincere and trusting. She was so glad he was with her.

Annie reached for the file tucked by his seat. "Maybe it's a mistake. If there's a police record, then they would have come for me. Are there medical records?"

He pulled out the file. "If you want to find out, it's all in here."

"How did you—"

"You signed a consent form. So I could check things out when you left." He leaned back in his seat. "I talked briefly with the social worker on the phone before we came in. I didn't want to give you false hope if it didn't pan out." He stared at her. "It does."

He handed it to her. "Do you want it? Do you want me to tell you?" He shrugged. "Do you want me to burn it?"

"No, no. I don't know yet." She turned away and then back

again, wondering how a small manila folder could be so intimidating. "*This* is what I've been waiting for?" Gazing out the window, she wondered what she would gain by knowing any more.

"She's alive and lives in town."

Annie snapped her head his way. "My mother? Lives here?"

Rudy held up the file again.

"I don't know if I can do this." Her eyes filled again, and she hated the feeling of being so out of control and this ending so horribly. *Lord, You've made me an outcast.*

Annie woke with a jumble of thoughts. She couldn't grasp the concept of seeing her mother while in the midst of pain. But that's why she'd come, even though everything in her being was telling her she couldn't do it. Would she have regrets? She wouldn't have a second chance.

She pulled back the covers and went to Rudy's desk. Staring at the file for the twentieth time, she wrote down the address to the place her mother lived. Rudy had said it was a college area, a boardinghouse, most likely. But could she truly face her mother, a woman who had given her away? Annie didn't care what the circumstances were. She'd left her child out in an open field, and only by the grace of Gott had that child been found.

Annie stopped. *By the grace of Gott, I was found.*

She cradled her head in her hand and let more tears flow. But she didn't want to be comforted by Him right now. *Why did He let this happen? What a horrid way to come into the world.*

She stood and went into the bathroom. Looking at her reflection, Annie noticed the bags under her eyes and her downturned lips, creating creases around her mouth. This whole experience had consumed her. She'd come here to justify the situation to her community, to find a woman who had made a mistake and was so glad to have Annie find her so she could repent and take her back.

A thought came into her head. *Gott didn't have anything to do with you being Amish. Slash your wrists and rid yourself of that rapist's blood.*

She jerked her head up. "Satan, leave me," she seethed through trembling lips, and then broke, slamming her back against the wall with face in hands and letting the cleansing drops fall from her eyes.

A bang on the door woke her for the second time that morning. She lifted herself off the cold tile bathroom floor.

"Annie, open up." Rudy's panicked voice resonated through the door.

She scrambled for the knob and turned. Rudy swung the door open wide and looked down. "Are you okay?" He reached for Annie and pulled her up to him. "What happened?"

"I just need to shower." She took two steps to the faucet and turned the water on. She glanced over her shoulder. "I want to see her."

Rudy moved toward the door. "All right. I'll skip class and take you when you're ready."

She turned quickly. "No, don't skip class."

"It's not a problem." He held up a hand.

"Rudy, it's okay. I want to go alone."

Chapter Twenty-Two

AFTER A TWO-BLOCK walk from the bus drop-off, Annie had plenty of time to talk herself in and out of this meeting. Having such an awful experience happen to a person certainly meant they didn't have a good life, probably before and after it happened. Did she really want to see her birth mother in such a state?

Her shoes hit the pavement with a *click, clack* as she walked down Timberlane Trail Road. Two more houses and she'd have to make a decision. She took in a breath when she got to a white house with green trim. If it'd had black trim, it would almost look like an Amish home, Annie noted with dry humor. The houses next to this one were similar in style but not in upkeep. Fences with chipped paint, neglected lawns, and clutter contrasted sharply. Those were obviously college renters and not owners.

Annie walked up the narrow path leading to the door and knocked once, a hesitant request for an answer. She glanced behind her at a young man hefting a very full backpack.

"Hey!" He opened the door in front of her. "You looking for a room?"

Annie was baffled. "Excuse me?"

"A room to rent. That is why you're here, right?" He took a step in and gestured for her to, as well.

"No, I'm here to see Monica Taylor." Using the name seemed strange. This was her blood, but she couldn't roll the name off her tongue without it sounding foreign.

"Yeah, she owns the place." He'd never stopped walking and went to the first room, which Annie assumed was the kitchen. He came back in and waved her over. "This is Ms. T." He grabbed a handful of chips from a bowl on the table and left again.

A woman stood at the sink skinning carrots. Her brown hair revealed red streaks in the morning sun that shone through a large window in front of her. Her white apron showed stains of many colors, to which she added as she wiped her hands and turned to Annie. "And who might you be?"

Her eyes were Annie's—almond-shaped with brown centers, surrounded with lily white. If this was her mother, she was not the type of person Annie had expected. "I'm looking for Ms. Taylor."

"What can I do for you?" She picked up the end of her apron and wiped a hand, then let it drop.

Annie worried that her being there might bring back her mother's trauma. She hesitated. "I'm not sure."

"You can look around the place if you want to see if it's what you're looking for." Then she smiled, Annie's smile.

"We might be related." Annie fumbled for words. How could she put this in a way that would make it flow any easier? "You see, I'm looking for my mother."

Ms. Taylor's eyes widened. They stood silent for a moment. "What's your name?"

"My name is Annie Beiler." She waited. Was that enough?

Monica put a hand to her chest. "How old are you…Annie?"

"I'm eighteen. I've grown up in an Amish community a couple of hours from here."

The older woman's eyes clouded, and she swallowed hard. "Who are you?"

"I might be your daughter." Annie paused, frozen except for her wavering gaze. "If this file is correct." She held up the folder with a shaking hand.

"I didn't think you'd come." Monica shook her head, as if she didn't need proof. Maybe she could see the resemblance as Annie did.

"You answered the registry."

"But I didn't think this would happen."

Annie thought about how close she had come to leaving. "Me either."

Monica's rosy cheeks went pale as she walked to the table. "Sit, please."

Annie walked over in silence, not knowing what to say next. The sound of the chair scraping across the floor grated in her ears. "I didn't think I'd find you."

"I'm glad you did." She looked down. "I didn't want you to, not for all these long years. But when they gave me word you had registered, I knew it was a sign."

"What kind of sign?"

"God. Telling me to give the information needed for you to come to me, if it was His will. It wasn't for me to decide anymore."

Annie couldn't hold back her surprise. This woman wasn't anything like she'd expected. It showed Annie how judgmental she was of people in the secular world. "I'm sorry."

"For what?"

"How I was conceived."

Monica held her head evenly, as if to steady her thoughts. "Is it in that file?"

Annie nodded. "You gave consent for me to have access to the police information."

"I didn't know if you would still want to come if you knew." Monica twined her fingers together and looked down at them. "The police got involved. There were witnesses." Her face was blank, as if she had to numb herself to talk about it.

"I shouldn't have said anything." Annie didn't know whether she really wanted the facts, to hear such a story. But a part of her wanted to know what her mother had been through to better understand why she would have made the choice she did.

"I was just out of high school, had two jobs to earn money for college. Walking home from work one night two men came out of nowhere." Monica swallowed and averted her eyes. "It was horrible at first."

Annie narrowed her eyes in confusion.

"But when I shut my eyes...squeezed them shut...I felt my lips move. I was praying. As if the Holy Spirit had taken over my tongue." A single tear slipped down her cheek. She quickly wiped it away. "The next thing I remember was one man standing over me and another with his back to me, walking away."

"You think your prayer stopped them?"

"No." The flicker of a sad smile crossed her face. "I just don't remember."

Annie let the quiet sound of her breathing settle her mind. The buzzing in her head had begun the moment she recognized this woman's face as her own. Seeing the sadness in her eyes made Annie wish she'd never come. She felt selfish needing to hear this at the cost of the nightmare coming back to haunt this humble woman. "I shouldn't have brought that anguish back to you."

"It's right that you know." Monica winced as if in physical pain, and then looked up at Annie. "You have my eyes."

Annie smiled. "I noticed that too."

Monica tilted her head, her expression changing. "But you have his features as well."

Annie twisted in her seat, as if she'd been shocked. Those ugly thoughts wasted no time. *You are tainted.*

The tears rolled silently as she sat in that kitchen completely vulnerable. She had the eyes and faith of her mother, but the rest of her resembled a man of hate and vulgarity.

Monica placed a light touch on Annie's knee. "Annie, I've forgiven those men, and look what God has done. He's brought us together."

The words burned into her chest as she heard them. She had been raised in a culture whose foundation was built on forgiveness, but it was Monica who was the one being merciful, not her. She was drowning in self-pity, while Monica had gone through a horrific situation and was pardoning the ones who damaged her.

"How can you absolve this?" Annie meant it as an honest question. Her heart wasn't in the same place as this woman's, and she wasn't the one who'd gone through the trauma Monica had.

Monica smiled slightly, as if she could see the confusion in Annie's heart. "When it's hard and I feel those memories creep in, I think to myself that when I am communing with God while holding those thoughts against others, I need to stop and forgive so that my sins can be forgiven."

Annie puzzled the words together into the verse. "Mark eleven, twenty-five."

Monica nodded then looked down at her hands. "It was difficult at first. Some days I couldn't do it, but now most of the time I can." She touched Annie's arm. "And the freedom has revived me, set me free from the bitterness I once felt."

Annie stared. The depth of her birth mother's faith shocked her. Why, exactly, she wasn't sure. Was it a stereotype she had in her head of what she thought Englishers were like? She had prejudged Monica just as many judge the Amish; Annie never thought she was one of those people.

"I wish I were that far along with all of this." Annie thought aloud, to her own surprise.

Monica leaned back against her chair and narrowed her eyes in thought. "You need a verse, one of your own that will help you remember how to set your mind when you pray."

Annie let out a small grunt, thinking of all her petitions to Gott to wash her clean of all of this, but never had she prayed for her mother or the rapists, only for herself.

"Ephesians four, thirty-two." It came to her from something outside herself, the Holy Spirit touching her mind and soul.

Monica nodded and looked up, obviously trying to place the verse. "Forgive one another just as Christ forgave you?" She questioned her accuracy and looked to Annie for confirmation.

There was more to it, but Annie just smiled. She'd gotten the important part, the part Annie needed to hear. The being kind and compassionate to one another part was something she did well. But doing good works without the forgiveness *hadn't* worked, and it was the piece she needed to heal from this.

"I'm glad I met you, Monica Taylor." Annie felt the heat rise in her cheeks, along with a flood of emotions.

Monica's tender ways were shown to Annie again when she laid a warm hand over hers. "Thank you for finding me, Annie. I didn't have your courage."

The words didn't sound right. In Annie's mind, it was Monica who was brave.

Chapter Twenty-Three

A BASEBALL FLEW PAST him. John leaned to the right, extending his arm to catch it. *Slap!* The pain hit his palm and then spread throughout the rest of his hand.

David chuckled. "Better find a glove, my friend."

The throb flowing throughout his hand angered him, almost enough to call David out, to put it all on the table right then and there. Dancing around this courting game, with him being the third wheel, was more than he could handle.

"Oof!" A glove hit him on the leg at the same time David yelled, "Catch."

John turned to him, narrowing his eyes. "Next time you might let me know before you throw." He took in a deep breath to contain his temper.

The last time he had gotten physical, Isaac had wrestled him to the ground for the last chicken leg. He had innocently laid it on his plate without knowing Isaac had claimed it, not with his mouth but with his stomach. John had teased him by dangling the leg in front of his face. Most everyone had left the table, with the exception of the two of them and Gabriel, who was only five at the time. Isaac had stood to gain a height advantage but tripped on the bench and fell forward, catching himself by placing his hand on the table. This made him even angrier, and he charged him, head down, arms pumping, and nothing between them. Thinking he could block him, John had set his feet and waited for the hit. Unfortunately they hadn't wrestled much lately, and he hadn't expected the bulk Isaac had put on. When Isaac made contact, John had flown backward and hit his bottom on the wood floor. He had raised a handkerchief he'd grabbed off the bench seat to surrender, which had brought Isaac out of his frenzy. Remembering this, John didn't know whether it would end so well if he tangled with David.

John walked over to a basket filled with baseball equipment. He tossed in the glove David had thrown at him and fished around to find another that fit him but stopped upon hearing Hanna's laugh. She walked along with two young women her age, and each had a handle on a smaller basket but couldn't get their stride in sync to carry it.

John instinctively went over to help them, but the closer he got, the less he felt inclined to rectify the situation. Their giggles and smiles showed their amusement, and he didn't want to spoil their fun.

"Mind if I grab a glove out of here?" He bent over to take the one he wanted and moved out of their way.

Hanna placed her hands on her hips. "Well, John, aren't you going to help us with this basket?"

He grinned. "No, I think you're doing just fine." As he walked away, he heard her grunt with disapproval.

He looked out to the field that had been left for pasturing. Having been freshly cut, it made for a good sports ground, Amish style. The short, dry grass made it easy to run and slide, and the size was twice that of any baseball stadium. A large group of men and boys were on the field with a handful of girls. John took his place on a team and chose first base. His brother took the outfield, and David stood in the middle to pitch. Annie's brother Eli claimed third base, and Alma covered second. John smiled, liking that the midwife was on their team.

"We need a catcher," David called out, causing a number of boys to turn and see who would volunteer and brave David's fastball.

Out ran Augustus, heading full speed for his place behind Jacob, who was up to bat. He stood straight, motionless, as David wound up and threw the ball. Augustus's right hand flicked out, and the ball hit *smack* into his glove.

"Ouch!" Augustus shouted, but he shook out his hand and got back into position.

"Strike," Eli called out, playing the role of umpire.

The spectators cheered for whichever team their significant others were on. Little ones made their own little field next to the seating area and ran around in circles until they got dizzy. The women made popcorn with plenty of butter, and others brought drinks to share. They placed the food on a long table until it was filed with cookies, cake, and shoofly pie. The young ones heard that hotdogs were supposed to be part of the menu, so the ladies did their best to make their own. It was a time to relax, enjoy, and have fun. They were hard workers and hard players.

David held the ball in both hands at his waist, waiting for Elam to ready himself for the next throw. David's hand spun out again, and this time Elam's bat contacted the ball. It blasted into the outfield. He made it to first base and stopped when Isaac grabbed the rolling ball.

A good hitter took the plate, so John backed up a bit. The ball shot off like a meteor above the field, flying deep into the grass, trimmed just long enough to make him hunt for it. John made the throw in time to stop him from reaching home, but Elam made it just in time.

As John walked up closer to the base, he looked over to the wagons, barrels, and into the makeshift stadium seating the community had made so they could move it according to which field was with crop. It was just habit to look for Annie's face in the crowd; when she wasn't watching the game, she was in it. He liked it even better when she was out there on the field with him. She'd run for those bases like her shoes were on fire and then try to steal a base when the baseman wasn't looking. Every time she got up to bat, she'd have that huge grin that told him she was enjoying herself. He hadn't seen that face for so long the image had begun to fade. For once in his Amish life he wished he had a picture, one of her doing something natural that would make it feel like she was there with him.

"We need two more outs, Yoder." David's voice brought him back.

So now they were allies, trying to win a game, not a girl. He had to keep up with David, and Hanna too for that matter. Things used to be so clear and simple. He knew what was going to happen each day, each week, each month, and what his future held. And now...

His gaze swept through the stands again and caught Hanna smiling and waving. He waved back, and then saw David make the same gesture. John was behind him, so David didn't see that they'd both thought she was waving at them. He shook his head.

This was an awkward situation, one he didn't know what to do about, a vicious circle that left him confused and uncomfortable. Did David really care for her, or did he just not want John to be in the picture? He had seen David with Emma as well. As far as that went, John wondered what exactly *he* felt for Hanna. Was she a replacement for Annie? He knew for sure it was a reason for him to be with her family. And why wasn't Hanna clear about her feelings toward them? Was it honest confusion on her part as to whom she really cared for, or was it just to fill Annie's shoes, as she seemed to be working so hard to do? John's world had gone upside down, and if Annie didn't return home soon, he couldn't ever see it turning right side up again.

Chapter Twenty-Four

WHEN ANNIE HEARD the news, the only thing she could think about was how desperately she needed to talk to John. For the first time since she'd been at the Glicks's home, she stood and stared at the television. Reports of five Amish girls being killed at gunpoint by a frequent visitor sent shock waves through her.

Although the location was faraway, up north, she couldn't help but feel that she was grieving along with that Amish community. Her sisters in Christ had lost their lives. It was so difficult to understand how violence could take place among such peaceful people.

The news droned on about the particulars, which Annie didn't want to hear; she just needed to know that their needs were being taken care of and the community was holding strong.

"It's hard to believe." Rudy's sudden appearance made Annie start and turn slowly to face him.

She hadn't realized how absorbed she was in the story until she heard his voice. "Doesn't seem real." Her voice strained under the stress and came out more like a whisper.

"Why?" was the only word that would squeak out, but as soon as she said it, she realized there couldn't be any reason that would make a difference.

"He went to the school; let the boys go, but kept the girls. Within the hour all ten were shot, along with the gunman."

"I know what happened. *Why* would this happen—to them?" She stared at the screen, watching the women with white prayer kapps and capes with black dresses as they cried into their handkerchiefs. The men gathered around with worn faces, embracing the women and holding their children. It all looked too familiar, too close to home, and she was so far from *her* home.

Annie felt Rudy's arm wrap around her, and she tightened. Engulfed in the story, she ignored his touch and took a step closer to the television, then randomly pushed some buttons until the volume went up.

"You could have used this." Rudy offered her the remote, but she brushed it away, not knowing how to use it any better than she did the buttons on the TV.

Different Amish people were asked about the incident. Many responded with a polite, "No, thank you." Others spoke a few words, but those small numbers were profound and shocked the secular world. An anchorman held a microphone toward a daed of one of the boys who were in the school. "We are struggling but urging forgiveness of the killer and quietly accepting what comes our way as Gott's will." He nodded slightly and walked away before the man with the microphone had a chance to ask him anything further.

Rudy grunted. "In most other communities there would be an outcry for tighter gun laws, better security, and threats to the gunman's family."

Annie turned slowly to him. She never would have guessed that those thoughts would come about after something like this. But Rudy, after being on the other side for all this time, would instantly think of those responses.

A mother of one of the victims spoke next when the reporter asked how she felt about the killer. "Judgment is in Gott's hands. 'Judge not, that ye be not judged.'" The woman's voice cracked as she quoted the scripture. "We are looking inward, relying on our faith; we know our children are in heaven and that we will be with them again."

The pride she'd always felt for her people shone through as she heard these words of faith from a group of people she admired. Jah, she had needed to do this, to come and find the person who gave her life, and in doing so, she now knew more than ever where she belonged.

Shame struck her as she realized how sad it was that such a horrible event was what finally made her realize where her heart was.

Rudy shook his head. "It would be hard to do."

She came out of her thoughts and turned to him. "What do you mean?"

"It's a lot harder for me than it seems to be for them." He looked at her with a mix of anger and disappointment in his eyes. "I understand, but not at that level."

Annie felt as if she were saying those words right along with those Amish people and without a war going on in her soul as Rudy was experiencing. He understood and appreciated their ways just as much as she did, but he didn't live in the community anymore, and that's what Annie was instantly thankful for. The freedoms, conveniences, and luxuries she'd discovered in Harrisonburg were nothing in comparison to the depth of faith she'd just witnessed.

The newscaster continued in a stunned voice. "Not only do these people say they forgive this man, but they want his family to stay in the community."

The phone rang and the front door opened at the same time. Rudy answered the phone as Elizabeth walked in. "I've just heard." Tears formed at the edges of her eyes. "Of all people...," she mumbled, and sat in a chair by the television. "The effect of this is great. In looking for anything good to come from this, my hope is that others see this way of thinking, that they might turn the other cheek if they ever experience loss like this."

"It's hard to find the positive, but I think you may have found it." Annie smiled meekly, and Elizabeth wiped her eyes.

When Levi walked in the door, Elizabeth went to him, and they talked quietly before entering the kitchen. "I heard about the shootings on the radio on the way home. How old were these girls?"

"Six to thirteen. Five are in the hospital." Rudy seemed to find the need to place the facts in order to process what was happening, the logical, engineer side of him kicking in to cover his emotions.

Levi shook his head but didn't respond; he just kept watching the repeating scenes on the TV. Annie couldn't and didn't talk about it anymore. She quietly prayed long prayers that filled her up and gave her peace, not the kind of peace that soothes you to the bottom of your soul but a peace that Gott was in this and in control. And then Essie walked in.

Essie slowed as she took in the mood of the room. "What's going on?" She pushed back her springy blonde curls and focused on the blaring television. She was silent for a long time while Annie and Elizabeth started dinner, not that anyone was hungry—it was just something for them to do, a soothing ritual. Rudy and Levi helped, just for a distraction. Everyone was silent except for questions concerning the meal.

Annie kept a constant praying vigil as she worked, asking for strength for the families, community, and the message they were giving.

Essie suddenly stood and stepped closer to the television. "That reporter is totally right. No one should be forgiven unless they show remorse for what they've done."

"Essie," Elizabeth said with disappointment.

"Oh, Mom. It's true. It's like you're not admitting evil exists. And this just goes to show that it's everywhere." She pointed a finger at the TV, ready for battle. She had to have known that everyone in the room disagreed with her, but then again she was probably saying it to push buttons that were so vulnerable at this moment—especially Annie's.

Essie looked around the room, just waiting for someone to say something against her. Elizabeth continued cutting carrots, Levi sighed and then turned away, and Annie ignored her. Rudy, however, stepped in.

"This isn't the time to let out your frustrations. Not now, Essie."

He looked at her like he understood but didn't agree. Maybe he'd been where she was and had come out of it. There seemed to be some silent communication going on that she didn't understand.

Essie looked to Annie and stammered, "You're *not* perfect." She crossed her arms over her chest and walked away.

Rudy came to Annie's side as if to protect her and placed a hand on her shoulder. Any feelings she'd formed with Rudy during her time here suddenly seemed wrong. No matter how innocent she had claimed them to be, right then she was ashamed. And the doubts she held regarding John vanished. He had always been the one, and her own selfish pride had kept her from thinking any differently. She'd had her time away to discover who she was and what she wanted to be, and now all she wanted was to leave.

Annie lay in bed that night in internal agony. She hadn't said a word to Rudy and had asked that she not be disturbed. Although dinner had been brought up, it sat by the door in the hall, untouched.

The news of the shootings seemed unreal, too horrible to comprehend. Her mind replayed the mourning families who looked so similar to the people she knew and loved. *What if something happens to one of them while I'm gone?* The thought stung her heart as tears flooded her eyes.

Sleep would be the only way to have any peace. She willed herself to close her eyes, shutting out the words of the conversation she'd had with Monica, but she would not pray.

How could it have been any worse? Annie wished she'd never met her, never come to Harrisonburg. The self-pity exhausted her enough to finally find rest.

The voices in Annie's head began as a murmur then grew into a lingering whisper. She woke in a startle, sat up in Rudy's bed, and scanned the room. *No more of these thoughts.* But she became aware these were of a different kind. These woke her up at night and spoke with strength. *Go home, my child.*

The comforting voice put her into a drowsy state, and it was in that moment she realized how much she missed John. Annie's dreams took her to him.

John carried the metal holder full of bottles of milk for the calves as he and Annie made their way through the thick mud. The giant baby bottles held a powder mixed with water made for the newborns. The older calves were in a bigger corral but still close to one another, and they were covered with mud from the previous night's rain. John set the holder of four bottles away from the group and handed one to Annie. He hadn't hit his growth spurt yet, so Annie almost looked him in the eye.

"I want Cowlick." The skinny calf had wiry swirls all over his black and white coat.

"What if I want him?" John tightened his lips into a surly grin.

Annie ignored him and walked over to the coveted calf. "Beatcha to him."

"Bet he'd like mine better." John teased the calf with another full bottle sloshing around in front of him.

"Don't, John. You're getting him all fired up." The calf sucked so hard they could hear huge gulps going down his throat. Cowlick pulled on the rope that held him to the hut.

John laughed and shook the bottle, urging spurts of milk to spray out onto Annie and the calf.

"John Yoder!" The minute she yelled his name, the calf broke free and scrambled over her to get to the second bottle in John's hands. Cowlick's back hooves kicked Annie forward into a heap of mud mixed with other stuff Annie didn't want to think about.

John laughed at the scene until he heard Annie's cry.

She sat up and looked at her clothes covered with brown, dripping sludge. She thought of how her mamm would react when she came home, and that's when she huffed out a cry.

John came over and crouched down next to her. "Are you hurt?" His brown eyes glistened in the sunlight.

"No, just in trouble when Mamm sees this." She gestured with her

hands to her clothes.

"Come on, I'll take care of you," he said with a confident grin, and she knew he would. He always did.

He helped her up and brushed the big chunks of mud off her dress. "Take off your apron."

She did and handed it to him.

"Follow me." He took her by the hand. She had thought about how he always did that too.

They walked through the princess lace and flying insects to the pond. "Feel like a swim?" John took off his shoes, rolled up his pants to the knee, and stepped into the brisk water. It was a seasonable spring day, but the pond hadn't been touched by the sun enough to have warmed up for a comfortable swim. Annie studied the water. Tall grasses edged its perimeter, where dragonflies chased each other. She took a deep breath and walked in until she was up to her waist.

John washed out her apron and shook it out for her. "Good as new," he told her as he held it out for her to see. A few brown stains remained, and it was wrinkled and wet, but Annie would look much more presentable when she walked up to the kitchen door for lunch.

"It's soaking wet, and so am I." She brushed off most of the mud and stepped onto the bank of the pond. John helped her squeeze out the excess water bulging at the hem of her dress and took her hand again. He tugged on her to get her to run in the warm breeze until they reached the top of a nearby hill.

"Here's a good spot." He lay down in the swaying Kentucky bluegrass with tall weeds intermittently sprouting around. He patted next to him where he wanted her, and stuck a blade of grass in his mouth. "Better?"

She felt the moisture in her clothes start to warm in the midmorning sun and breathed in the fresh spring air. "Better. We should go fetch Cowlick."

"We will." He took her hand and laid it on his chest and then put his other hand behind his head. She copied him and turned to face him. He returned the stare with a smile, the blade of grass sticking out from one side of his lips.

Annie thought right then and there that no one had ever looked at her like that before, and she doubted anyone else ever would.

She found sleep and woke when the sun came up. Annie didn't let her mind wander as she packed and readied herself to leave. Whatever reason the Lord had for her to come here, He also had a reason for her to go home. She owed it to Rudy to have some closure of her time here, but even more, she needed to make amends with her family, and foremost John, after being gone for three long months. It would be an awkward time to return with all the couples being announced, but the nudge she'd felt the night before couldn't be ignored.

The Glicks gave her another farewell, this time more somber. Knowing their response, Annie decided no one would know the truth about her mother in the community. She didn't need pity along with being chastised. The sympathy she felt for her sister community gave Annie another reason to go.

Rudy checked her bag and paid for her ticket. She didn't have a choice, so she accepted his charity once again. "Danke, Rudy, for everything. If it weren't for you, I wouldn't have ever finished what I started to do here." Even though her feelings were mixed about the entire experience, she couldn't be anything but grateful to him for his time and support.

He held up a hand, avoiding eye contact. "It wasn't what you'd hoped for, Annie. I'm sorry for that." He looked up at her now. "I'm sorry about that part of it, but I'm not sorry I met you, Annie Beiler."

His intense gaze made Annie uncomfortable. She felt as if he wanted something more that she couldn't give. She stood as the bus rolled in, appreciating the lack of intimidation this time regarding the huge machine. "I'm glad I met you too, Rudy."

He took a step forward to embrace her. She gave him a quick hug and turned to go. Annie felt his gaze as she walked away but didn't turn around. She was ready to go home.

⌒ Chapter Twenty-Five ⌒

THE STEEL CLOMP of the horse's shoes against the hard ground created a familiar, settling rhythm in Annie's head as Abraham drove her home.

"I had more visitors asking for your letters than customers while you were gone. And I'll be if it wasn't right before you left that I installed that bell above that door."

Annie smiled at Abraham's ability to always lighten the mood. She couldn't keep still in the bench seat, and when she unfolded her hands, they were damp from nervous sweat. "They don't know I'm coming."

"No one? Even your daed and mamm?" Abraham's eyes widened, but he kept them on the road. He gave the reins some slack and waved the leather so it made a slap against the horse's hide. The animal picked up the pace as they turned to go up the long dirt path to her home. "So you don't know."

Annie studied his face and knew it was something bad. Had they already had a judge, jury, and trial before she even arrived home? Maybe she wasn't even allowed to be here. "What is it, Abraham?"

"I don't know how to tell you." His eyes darted from her to the path. "Your daed's daed passed away, Annie." He pursed his lips. "I hate to be the one to tell you. I figured that's why you came home."

Annie's heart dropped. She cupped her hand over her mouth as tears blurred the dirt path before her.

How could they keep this from me?

He hadn't been sick. Dawdi was never sick.

"What happened?" she asked in a whisper.

"Just didn't wake up one morning." He pulled the buggy to a stop and tied the reins. Then he surrounded her with his burly arms. She accepted his warmth and took a moment to prepare herself for how this might turn out. She didn't want to be more of a burden, along with what was already happening. She would need to put her needs aside and take care of her mammi and her daed. Ach, her daed would be so hardened.

Abraham pulled away. "Are you ready?" His soft eyes and gentle way didn't match his stocky build.

She nodded and adjusted herself in her seat. As they got closer to her house, she noted the number of buggies at her home. "Is this the wake?"

Abraham nodded. "If it's all right with you, I'd like to pay my respects." He reached back and pulled out a black jacket.

"Jah...jah, you should." Annie watched a couple walk out of her home and another get out of their buggy to go in. The entire day was spent this way. Once the death was announced to the church and the obituary appeared in the local paper, the numbers for the viewing grew large.

Abraham jumped down and got Annie's suitcase. She stepped onto the hard dirt path, feeling the pebbles scratch against the soles of her shoes, the same way the grief for her dawdi made her bruised heart raw. The anticipation was greater than she'd ever imagined, with the grief added to her return. More death. She knew her community was grieving with the Nickel Mines community as well.

The door seemed almost as if it was coming to her instead of each footstep drawing her closer. A silhouette flashed by the front window, and then another.

How many are in there?

Her homecoming was meant to be for her family only, not the entire community—not yet.

She inhaled, taking in the fresh air, and let the wind seep out through her lips. Annie looked out over the hills, now brown and naked against the gray sky. Then she turned to the valley. The river moved peacefully through the fields and meadows. She had missed the fall colors, and inside Annie knew she'd missed a lot more.

The chatter stopped as they entered. In her mind's eye everyone seemed to surge up to her then back away, with less and less sound. So this was it, the moment when all would show their true selves. She held her head up and caught the eyes of her mammi.

Before Annie had a moment to speak, Amos came through the maze of people filling the small home. His shoes clomped on the wood floor in quick rhythm as he strove to reach Annie before anyone else did. He squared his shoulders and stood more erect with each step.

He stopped in front of Annie and rested both hands on her shoulders. His touch was light and gentle, as if needing to feel her to believe she was really there. Annie had never really noticed Daed's eyes; he was always head-down in his work. But at this moment she noticed how dark brown they were, almost black, just like her dawdi's. Ach, if only the others would respond to her the way her daed was right now. But this alone was a complete surprise, for her daed to come to her without her pleading for forgiveness. Her mamm, jah, but never Daed.

Annie waited for the words to come, not able to imagine what the first ones would be. A hint of a smile crossed his lined, tired face. "Annie."

His one simple word, her name, gave Annie the courage to speak. "I'm sorry I wasn't here when Dawdi passed."

"I knew you'd come. I've been waiting for you to return." His eyes watered but held strong to hers.

Just the sound of her name on Daed's tongue caused tears to prick at her eyes. She could only nod, and she glanced around the blurry room. Annie felt a hand grab her arm, strong but gentle. She turned to see the worn face of her mammi. Annie's bottom lip trembled, and then she noticed Mammi's hand shook too as she stroked Annie's cheek. She nodded and walked away. The gesture, so quick and sweet, touched a part of Annie she'd pushed away. She hadn't expected support from her mammi since this whole thing began.

Omar, the bishop, sat in a chair with a cup of tea in his lap. He held a spoon in his hand and appeared frozen with the shock of her arrival. Minister Zeke had both hands placed across his large stomach. He stared at her as if she were a ghost.

Eli came to Annie and sighed before reaching out and embracing her. Augustus and the boys were close behind, saying things that meshed together in her mind.

"We're glad you're home."

"Missed you."

"It's good to see you."

Other family friends came over to her then and offered their condolences, but few welcomed her home, as if they didn't know whether her return was condoned. Many watched Omar or Zeke to see whether they were watching and whether their comments were acceptable. A very few close friends did say they were glad she was there without worry of consequences, but they were the minority.

Omar stood and cleared his throat, and then tapped his cup to get everyone's attention. "We do not speak of the dead, out of respect, but I thought it should be known that five of our sisters in the Nickel Mines community were laid to rest yesterday. Gott rest their souls."

He looked around the room at the many faces. "I can only hope that we, in our own community, would respond in the same manner. Forgiveness does not prevent a tragedy or pardon the wrong but rather constitutes a first step toward a future that is hopeful." Omar looked straight at Annie and then addressed the room again. "Keep their families in your prayers this day most specially."

She made her way through the room with Mammi by her side. "Did the bishop look at me when he spoke, or was it my imagination?"

Mammi stopped and looked at Annie. "There have been as many conflicting opinions about your leaving as there have been about the Amish forgiving that man in Pennsylvania." She cupped her palm against Annie's cheek. "In my mind they can't be compared. I think Omar was just trying to make a point, and I hope he did."

"I see." So everyone had formed their opinion about her in her absence. Could she expect any less? Of course there had been talk, but with the enormity of the shootings at hand, couldn't her small infraction be put aside? "I'm going to get a drink, Mammi." There were refreshments in the receiving room, but Annie needed more than the water to cool her.

As Annie stepped into the kitchen, John and Hanna walked in through the back door. She paused as the sight of him. Although all people were to be thought of the same in their appearance, Annie wondered how everyone could ignore certain attractiveness some held. John was one of those.

Her eyes stopped on Hanna's arm touching his. He had his hands nonchalantly in his pockets, but it caught her attention, all the same. When John noticed her, he stared so hard it hurt. Annie saw the wound, raw and overflowing, in his dark brown eyes. And she looked away.

She set the image in her mind of the two of them. Arms touching, their stunned faces, both at her presence and of being found out this way. This couldn't be—her closest confidants together. But after looking into his eyes, she knew it could be true.

Annie lifted her head and tried to hide the shock and betrayal she felt. They were still, waiting for something that none of them seemed to know. John cleared his throat and moved away from Hanna. "I didn't know you were coming back."

"I didn't have much in the way of communicating." Annie's voice wavered. At the brink of tears, it was all she could do to get out a single word, let alone have a conversation.

"How are you?" She was asking John. Annie realized she was hurt by John but angry with Hanna. The separation wasn't clear to her, but those were the emotions that spilled out, on her sleeve and every other part of her.

Hanna answered, which irritated her even more. "We're all fine, Annie. The question is, How are you?" She took a step closer, next to John.

So are they a united front? Against my coming back, or leaving? Are they together? Questions flew through her mind like a swarm of bees. She knew Hanna had asked a question but couldn't think of an answer. Her mind reeled, and then all went black.

When she woke she couldn't differentiate whether she was in a dream, having the flashback she'd had at the Glicks's, or whether this was happening in the present. It was all the same, but vivid, as if everything was now in vibrant color. The braided rag rug seemed to completely cover the floor. A quilt Mammi had made hung folded over a chair full of various hues, and the smell of her mamm's cooking made her taste buds swell.

Thomas sat in a chair beside the bed with his teddy. His eyes widened when hers opened. "Mamm!" He quickly jumped off the chair and ran to the door. A minute later her mamm was there with a bowl of soup in hand.

Mamm didn't say a word, just fluffed a pillow behind Annie's head and leaned over to feed her the soup.

"Mamm."

"Take a bite." Her eyes never met Annie's. She took a few bites but couldn't stand the silence.

"It's good to see you, Mamm." Annie reached up and wiped a drop of soup from her chin. Sarah's face was still as stone. Her blonde-gray hair was neatly pinned under her kapp, and her dress looked newly pressed.

Mamm handed Annie a napkin.

"What time is it?" Annie waited for a response that never came. "You're not speaking to me?" Annie felt the tears come but was too weak to cry. She was under the bann. What other answer could there be for her mamm's silence?

Do I deserve this treatment? Does Mamm feel shunned due to my relationship with my birth mother?

"Why did the others speak to me?"

Mamm leaned back and set the bowl of soup down on the chair and stomped out, her low-heeled shoes banging on the floor, even on the braided rug in the center of the room. She grabbed the door as she left. Just as it was about to slam, she stuck out her hand to catch it and eased it shut.

Annie couldn't put the pieces together. No one acted as she'd predicted. She had prepared herself for certain things, people to act specific ways, but nothing she planned for was happening the way she thought it would. Now she had no defense, no plan at all. She felt helpless not knowing who to trust and who to confide in, or talk to, for that matter. Nothing made sense.

⌒ Chapter Twenty-Six ⌒

THE NEXT MORNING Minister Zeke came to prepare for the funeral. Annie helped in the kitchen to make refreshments for those who stayed after the ceremony. Thoroughly confused regarding who would speak to her, she remained silent for most of the morning.

The furniture had been stored in the barn to make more room for people. The house couldn't hold everyone, so many stood outside. More would come to the gravesite to grieve at the burial. Annie thought of the funeral for the five girls in Pennsylvania and was humbled. The miracle was that the other five had lived.

Zeke stood near the coffin and addressed the congregation. No eulogies were given or talk of the deceased. He spoke from Genesis. "From dust we are created, and to dust we shall return."

He kept one hand on his protruding belly and held his Bible with the other. He turned slowly back and forth from one side of the room to another.

Annie felt the weight of many eyes on her. This seemed so wrong in her heart. This day was about saying good-bye to her dawdi, not scrutinizing the one who left and came back.

Zeke went on. "The New Testament says if Christ be preached that he rose from the dead, how say some among you that there is no resurrection of the dead? But if there be no resurrection of the dead, then is Christ not risen. And if Christ is not risen, then is our preaching vain, and your faith is also vain."

Annie stared into the coffin. Dressed in white pants, vest, and shirt, Dawdi looked like an angel. The Amish undertaker used no cosmetics, so her dawdi was more than pale. The lines in his face were pronounced, as was the white of his hair, much like

Mammi's. Annie looked to Mammi, now standing next to her. She held her head high, although her ruddy coloring revealed her emotions. Mamm held a white hanky that soaked up the tears that continually ran down her cheeks. Annie noticed her glancing in her direction more than at Zeke.

Annie knew John was in the room. She had seen him briefly when he first came in. Hanna had walked over to him, and they spoke quietly.

How could they be so blatant?

Annie tried to avoid any contact with them by staying in the kitchen. She didn't know what hurt more—the death of her dawdi, or the relationships she left behind. But this was her dawdi's day, and she would keep her mind on him.

Eli gestured for her to come into the kitchen as soon as the minister finished. He led her to the barn, where Daed was hitching up the team.

"Why are we here? We should be with the other mourners." Annie was annoyed at Eli's silence and mystery as to why he had asked her to leave.

"I thought you might want to see Otto," Eli responded without emotion, as if he were completing a chore.

Annie stopped. "You want me to see a horse instead of pay my respects?"

Eli turned to her. "With the mess you've made, I suggest you just do as you're told and hope you come out of this without too many restrictions."

The shock sunk in deep. Eli had not been one to discourage her leaving, but in her absence he had obviously changed his mind. As Annie looked into his eyes, she decided not to have any expectations or predictions. She didn't know anyone the way she had before and shouldn't expect to.

"Your choice has affected all of us, ya know." He headed for the barn and opened the big, heavy door.

John followed Annie out to the barn. His eyes flowed over her, taking in every detail. He knew how she walked, the way she swung her arms as if she were in a hurry but never was. With the exhilaration of a shooting star, her patience with children, and the love she had for her people, she always created an emotional eruption in him.

When he realized Amos was in the barn, he lagged behind, not wanting to hamper their first conversation. But John's heart swelled at the effort Amos made toward her. He hadn't expected it, and by the look on Annie's face, neither had she.

He propped himself against the doorjamb and watched Annie slow her walk when she saw Amos. "Did you need me, Daed?" Her voice sounded small but steady. Amos didn't tolerate weakness, which was why it was so strange he'd been the first to greet her.

Amos pointed to Otto. He didn't appreciate the practice of treating work animals as pets, but it was past that point with Annie and Otto. She hugged on the horse's big head and spoke to him. Annie watched Amos begin to hitch Otto, but he stopped long enough to gesture for Annie to help. The silence between them stung. Even as an observer, John could feel their sadness, the misunderstanding, loss of time, and inability to talk it through. Annie's wide eyes darted from Amos to the horse. That's when John stepped forward to help harness Perry, the other horse.

Annie startled at his presence. She gave him a smile and looked down at his boots. Unsure of what to say, he didn't say anything until Amos noticed him. "John, can you finish up here?"

When John agreed, Amos left without a word.

John watched the buckle on the harness Amos had been working on dangle below the horse's belly and knew he wanted them to be alone. Amos would never leave a chore undone.

"It seems like such a long time..." Her eyes seemed to plead for the time that had passed between them.

"It *has* been a long time." John felt a spark ignite in his chest, making his heart beat rapidly. "Did you find what you needed?" He waited for her to answer.

"No, but I learned so many things I hadn't expected that the answer is also yes."

Her leaving had cut him deeply, even before she left, but he'd had no idea until now how badly. "It was worth the bann, or whatever else Zeke decides?"

She took a moment to answer. "You can't know unless you listen to what I have to say."

"You're right. I don't know why you left and hurt everyone you loved to go chasing around after some stranger." He raked his hands through his hair, upset with himself for talking out of anger, and let out a breath.

"The discovery of not knowing my birth mother stripped me of who I was. I thought finding her would fill in that loss. But it didn't. Only coming home did."

"Then why did you leave at all? What *did* you find?"

Annie leaned against Otto's big, brown side. "I learned why it bothered me so much that I wasn't a natural-born child of my parents. Because it made me different."

John bunched his brows. "But you were raised in the way of the Amish. Your situation was different, not of your choosing."

"But still set apart." She folded her arms across her chest and looked up to the hayloft, holding back the tears. "You know, one of the Glicks told me I was more Amish than any he'd ever known." Annie forced a sad smile. She pushed off of Otto and stared into John's eyes. "That was the nicest thing any of them said to me."

John hadn't realized until that moment what it was really all about. It wasn't so much about finding her biological mother as it was knowing she was still accepted here, still Amish through and through. Some in their community sought things to make them different, but Annie lived the Amish life with joy and pride.

"Did you ever stop to think about how hard it was for me not to know how you were?"

"I had the same thoughts." She took a step closer to him.

"Then why didn't you write to me?" John's spark spread into a flame with the frustration of losing her.

"Write to you? I did. Why didn't you?"

John stood back and stopped. Annie had the same look on her face that John was sure he did. "I did."

Her voice softened. "I didn't get any letters."

"I never sent it. I never got a letter from you and didn't want to ask anyone for your address. I figured you didn't want to communicate with me."

"I wrote to you, Hanna, and Mamm." She paused for a moment. "Mainly you."

When she turned toward Otto, John noticed her eyes close, and she took in a breath. "I didn't send them all. It was more a journal for me, to keep in touch with all of you. It just made you seem closer."

As much as he wanted to believe in her again, he couldn't—not yet. But with her here, he felt whole again. "I wish I would have known that." He reached for the buckle still unattended. They both worked together in silence to ready the horses.

John rubbed his chin in thought, wondering what he'd gotten himself into. His anger toward Annie had caused him to make a commitment he knew now he shouldn't have. His impulsive words of retaliation would hurt the Beilers, no matter what he decided.

Chapter Twenty-Seven

JOHN PULLED HIS buggy in behind one belonging to Amos. The long caravan snaked along the dirt roads that led to the cemetery. Each buggy had a number written on it with chalk and a matching number assigned to them at the graveyard. They pulled up to their number in front of the white fence surrounding the burial ground.

Annie was struck by how similar they all were. Even having been away just a short time, the formality of their black dress today was even more pronounced. Each woman wore a black dress and hat. Not even the unwed wore white aprons as they usually did, and married women wore black kapps today instead of the white. The men's black felt hats varied in brim size, disclosing the wearer's age and marital status. The number of shoulder straps and whether they crossed designated different church groups. One was of the New Order, which was less restrictive. Annie's family was associated with the Old Orders, which followed the original ways upon which the community had been founded.

She glanced over the uniform gravestones. Simple, white, rounded stone with basic information, they showed no status or wealth. The older stones were written in German, but newer stones were engraved in English.

Minister Zeke found his place by the grave and opened his Bible. "Marvel not at this: for the hour is coming, in the which all that are in the graves shall hear his voice, and shall come forth, they that have done good, unto the resurrection of life; and they that have done evil, unto the resurrection of damnation." Zeke stopped to push up his wire-rimmed glasses.

When he began again, Annie whispered the last verse with him. "By myself I can do nothing. I judge only as I hear, and my judgment is just, for I seek not to please myself but him who sent me."

Those close around Annie set their eyes on her. "Him who sent me," she repeated. Others turned to listen, knowing what she was referencing. Zeke's face reddened, and he forced air through his nose as the pine coffin was lowered into the black earth. He cleared his throat and read a hymn as the pallbearers filled the grave.

Everyone said the Lord's Prayer together and then prayed silently. Mammi's sobbing ceased as Zeke approached her, offering his condolences. Then he grabbed Annie's arm and walked down yards of white fences to the gate.

He led her to a large oak tree and shoved his face into hers. "I would appreciate your silence during my homily, Annie."

Annie watched his nostrils flare and the lump of skin darken around his collar. "I'm sorry. I thought the verse held relevance to my situation, as well as my dawdi's."

"We will talk of your situation after there has been proper time to grieve."

"I believe Gott intends everything to happen for a reason, Minister Zeke. My dawdi's death happening at the same time I returned home holds great significance to me."

He took a moment then retorted, "A time of judgment for you both."

Annie couldn't help but flinch. Zeke had always been a strict man in the way he conducted his ministry and handled situations that would arise in the community. His treatment of her had always been favorable. Did this one venture change his whole opinion of her?

"I'd like to think that my dawdi now understands my need to leave and accepts me back without judgment now that I've returned." She stopped and took in a breath.

His fists were balled and breathing labored. Zeke being a

heavy man, Annie worried for his health as well as his condem-
nation. It wouldn't bode well if the minister passed out during
their first conversation since her return.

"Gott is the final judge." He opened his hands and tightened
them again.

Annie tilted her head. "I hope that is true in my case, if I'm
brought before the elders."

Zeke raised a hand in frustration. "You have brought this
upon yourself, Annie."

"Is it a sin to want to know the person who birthed me?" Annie
knew she was being disrespectful but didn't feel she had much to
lose. She had embarrassed him due to his puffed-up ego, something she'd not witnessed personally until now.

"This is not the Annie I once knew. Surely this attitude comes
from the influences of the world you came from. We will speak
more about this at the appropriate time. Until then, I advise you
to remain silent about—" He was about to go on when John
walked by and stopped beside them.

"Sorry to interrupt, but Annie's family needs her." He offered
his arm, which she gladly took.

Annie walked away without a second glance. She'd never felt
more rescued. Although she'd held a firm front, inside she was
melting. The change in the way Zeke treated her tore at her heart.
She'd never seen this side of him, but then she'd never broken the
rules before, either. Now she understood how it felt and what was
to come.

John looked over his shoulder to see the bishop approach the
minister. They walked together in deep discussion. The look on
Annie's face told John of the hurt and confusion she felt. As angry
as he was at her for so many things, he couldn't stand by and
watch her be mistreated.

"Are you okay?" He pulled her arm in closer to him.

He seemed to draw her from her thoughts as Annie's eyes flashed up to his then back to the cold ground.

"Danke, John." Annie kept her head down, watching each step she took.

"Annie, there are a lot of things I don't understand..."

"Then ask me." She stopped and pulled away.

John looked over at the bishop and Zeke. He didn't want to see Annie's sad brown eyes. "I can't right now."

"Why? Because of the bann?" She scoffed and crossed her arms over her chest. He'd rarely seen Annie sarcastic and knew she was at her wits end to act in such a way.

"No one has said I can't talk with you."

"But most don't."

When Annie looked away, John took advantage of the opportunity to stare at her pretty face, one he'd dreamt of for many days to keep her image in his head. With no pictures allowed in his community, he had to rely on his memory to keep her face alive in his mind.

"Zeke will eventually talk to the elders, but with your dawdi's passing and the Nickel Mines incident, he's held off with anything formal." John leaned in closer. "But he will, Annie. So just keep quiet, and let's pray for the best."

Annie grunted. "Why? To give me some sort of punishment for finding my family? They won't let me defend myself when I meet with them, so now might be my only chance." She pushed her foot down into the grass, her black shoe tip digging into the hard dirt. "The Glicks were banished from the community because their son wanted to stay in school."

John knew her love for reading and learning. She always had a book in her hand, and when she couldn't be found, he knew he could find her behind a haystack or in the loft reading.

"I remember them. But I never knew why they were asked to leave." He studied her face, hardened and rigid. "You don't agree with the reason why they left?"

"I never really thought about it before. The life we live doesn't require you to have a higher education, but should one be excommunicated for wanting to expand their mind?" She shook her head.

"You admire him because of his intelligence."

"Jah, and because he knew of ways to help me."

"Placing yourself before another creates pride."

Her stunned expression let him know he'd brought her back to Amish thinking and one reason education was to be kept equal.

"But Rudy has so much potential. It would be a shame for someone like him not to go to college, especially since he wanted to so badly."

John's head snapped up before he'd even realized it. "Who's Rudy?"

"The Glicks's son. He goes to the Mennonite University in Harrisonburg."

"They're Mennonites now?" John said it with cynicism. He didn't mean to; he just didn't like the way she'd said Rudy's name.

"Jah, it seems to suit them. Rudy's going to be an engineer. He'll make a good one. I've seen his sketches."

John had never had any real reason to be jealous. He and Annie had always been together, and everyone knew it. But what was flaring up inside his chest at this moment, no doubt, was a flame of jealousy. "Sounds like you spent a lot of time with Rudy."

"He helped me with my research. I don't know what I would have done without him."

"Does he have anything to do with why you were gone so long?" John felt a muscle in his jaw twitch as he tried to hold back from what he really wanted to say. All this time he'd felt guilty about Hanna, and now he was finding out about some guy she'd spent the entire time with.

"He knew how to help me, John."

John nodded and felt he needed to leave, fast, before he said something he shouldn't. "I need to go." He turned and took long, hasty steps away from her.

"If there's any question, it should be about you and Hanna," Annie said with an even tone, knowing she had him.

He stopped and almost turned back but decided to let her wonder about them, just as he had wondered about her for weeks while she was gone.

Chapter Twenty-Eight

ANNIE STOOD LOOKING out the window, rubbing her hands back and forth across her arms. If it was going to get this cold, she wished it would snow. The brown, barren fields needed a white covering to coat their dull plainness until spring. She watched as the midwife's buggy pulled up in front of the house.

She heard the back door slam and her mamm's voice. Alma came into the room with Mamm trailing behind. "She doesn't need to go anywhere." Mamm placed her fists firmly on her hips.

Alma stood as tall as her five-foot frame would allow and challenged Mamm with her eyes. "I need her help. I've already delivered three babies this week, and four more are due. Annie, get ready. Time's a-wasting."

"She doesn't need to be out amongst the community yet." Mamm followed after Alma, who was heading to the back door.

"She'll be with families who are birthing babies, Sarah. They'll have other things on their minds." Alma was quiet until Annie went to get her coat and mittens. "They might even be the very people whom Annie should be around."

Mamm leaned back as if she'd been slapped. "Don't you get in the middle of this, Alma. You don't know what we've been through these last months."

Alma stopped at the door and placed her hands on her wide hips. "I missed her too, Sarah." She turned and stepped down the stairs and was soon out of sight. Mamm stood frozen in the middle of the kitchen floor as Annie passed her.

"Bye, Mamm," Annie said without much thought, just hope, and wishing it was still the normal custom between them.

Mamm grunted and held a hand to her mouth, as if to catch the words. It was then Annie realized Mamm wanted to talk to her as badly as she wanted to speak with her mamm.

"Of course she misses talking to you." Alma handed Annie a bag filled with supplies and took another full of sterile rags and sheets. "She feels she's doing what's right by not speaking to you about anything that happened while you were gone until Zeke does whatever it is he's going to do. Actually, it's for your own protection. If she knows of anything you did that would get you into trouble, she'll have to tell Zeke. She's just a rule-follower." They walked to the door, and Alma knocked once then walked in. "You got it from somewhere, you know."

Annie couldn't deny her mamm following their ways but expected an exception in her situation. "She seems angry."

"Hurt. Maybe angry too. Give it time."

Alma went immediately into the kitchen, where the family was gathered. "Melvin, take yourself and the rest of your brood into the next room."

Annie accepted Alma's curt ways, but some didn't. Melvin raised a skinny finger toward her and wagged the tip back and forth. "Slow down there, Alma. I appreciate you helping out, but if Wilma wants me, I'm staying." He shoved his hands into his pockets. His towering height failed to intimidate Alma as he stood in front of her.

Alma all but ignored him, gathering supplies as Annie brought them in and laid out fresh towels. Clean towels were a constant worry, because they had no electricity. Alma rationed how many she used on busy weeks like this one, especially in the winter when they couldn't count on the sun to dry them. She'd confessed once to Annie that one time she did go into town and use Abraham's dryer when five babies were born in two days. Annie assumed it was battery powered, so she wasn't keeping anything secret.

Alma pulled over a stool and sat at Wilma's feet. "Two inches dilated." Alma stood and brushed past Melvin, who was watching her bop back and forth giving orders and organizing. He stayed nearby until the first shout from Wilma and then disappeared.

Alma took Wilma by the hand and said what she always did before a birth. "Are you ready to see another of Gott's miracles?"

Wilma nodded as red curls bounced onto her perspiring, freckled face. "I don't think I'll do this again, Alma."

Alma lifted Wilma's foot and began massaging the soles of her feet. "That's what they all say."

Wilma's head rolled back and forth on her pillow. "No, I mean it."

"They all say that too."

Annie took the other foot and began the acupressure. Alma found the anxiety dissipated when she performed the method. It helped the birthing process move along more smoothly, as well. Alma moved away when Wilma arched her back and moaned. Wilma reached for Annie's hand. "I'm glad you're here, Annie."

Alma met Annie's eyes. She'd been right to keep Annie busy doing something she had a knack for. It made her feel useful. She enjoyed seeing new life being brought into the world, and after meeting with Monica, it changed her in a way she couldn't quite comprehend.

Annie squeezed Wilma's hand. "Me too." More than she knew. This gave Annie hope that others would accept her too, if given the opportunity.

Two hours later baby Irene was born. The younger girls carried her back and forth from the bassinet to Wilma and brought trays of food. The children knew when the baby was sleeping. There were never the warnings of "shh" or "be quiet," as she'd heard in the city.

Even though Wilma had heard Alma's spiel about children

being a blessing five times before, she told her again and tapped Melvin on the shoulder as they left. "Congratulations, Melvin."

He took the pipe from his teeth but kept his eye on his wife and the bundle she held. "I'll be dropping off a few chickens at your place tomorrow."

"I appreciate that, Melvin." Alma reached for her riding gloves and headed for the door.

"They stopped laying, but they'll make for a few good meals." He clenched the pipe between his teeth and put on his coat.

Alma and Annie packed up the buggy and were just starting down the lane when they saw him again. Melvin reached for a piece of wood and raised his ax. He brought it down with fervor. The sunset barely gave off enough light to see, but as far as Annie could tell, he didn't lift his eyes or a hand in gesture as they rode by.

"If I didn't know better, I'd say he's angry." Annie kept watching as he grabbed another log and split it clean through.

"I think he wanted a boy." Alma adjusted herself on the squeaky bench.

Annie shook her head in disgust. "What is it with men?"

Alma gave a quick response back. "If I knew the answer to that I'd be married."

Annie sat in silent thought. "Why didn't you ever get married?" The role of midwife fit so well with Alma, Annie had never wondered about her being single before. It was just Alma.

"I was a teacher for a while when Benjamin was courting me."

Annie tried to think which Benjamin, as there were a handful to pick from. Then it came to her, but it still didn't quite fit. "Benjamin Quinter?" He was her parents' age, a bit older than Alma, now married, with half a dozen children.

"The very one."

"What happened?"

"I wanted to study medicine. Be an obstetrician. Benjamin said I had to make a choice. So I did." She kept her eyes on the road and spoke as if it were someone else she was referring to.

Annie looked ahead with her, thinking it would take the scrutiny off her. But Alma knew there was none on Annie's part. Annie was becoming more disappointed that her people didn't acknowledge higher education.

"So you never did go to school."

"I took some mail-order classes, but I didn't want to stop being Amish."

"Neither did I when I left. I just wanted to know more about myself."

"And you think you've been ill-received. Just think if I would have left for years to educate myself." Alma's face went taut.

"I guess I expected it on some level, but not from certain people. Then again, the ones I thought sure wouldn't accept me have."

"It's hard to figure. But it will pass. Zeke probably wants to make you an example. Being baptized and all, you can't even trim your nails on the Sabbath or you'll be chastised for it."

"I think it would help if Mamm would find it in her to forgive me. After all, she's the one who gave me names and places so I could go."

"She's got to forgive herself first."

"She's not the one who left."

"It feels like it to her. After all, she is the one who helped you on your way out the door."

Annie had wondered if her Mamm's help had hurt her in any way since she left. Now she knew the answer, and it pained her even more.

Alma gave the horse a quick snap of leather. The sound broke through the night air, which hung thick with humidity.

Annie looked to the dark sky cut with gray and prayed for a cleansing rain.

Chapter Twenty-Nine

ANNIE WRUNG HER hands as the three-hour church service came to an end. She glanced at John, in the front room with the other men, for the eightieth time. She'd caught his eye a few times, but his face was unreadable. This time one side of his mouth tipped, which gave her cause to stare a little longer. She received the same void of emotion from her family as she studied them. Eli and Augustus sat together next to Daed, and the rest sat next to one another with Mamm at the far end, opposite from Annie.

Three preachers and two bishops gave the sermon in German, which many didn't understand, with the exception of her grandparents' generation. They sang hymns from the *Ausbund* between the sermons. The one they sang seemed appropriate for what was to come.

> We alone a little flock,
> the few who still remain,
> are exiles wandering through the land
> in sorrow and in pain.
> We wander in the forests dark,
> with dogs upon our track;
> and like the captive, silent lamb,
> men bring us, prisoners, back.
> They point to us, amid the throng,
> and with their taunts offend,
> and long to let the sharpened ax
> on heretics descend.

All knelt for silent prayer, and then those who were not baptized were dismissed. The men took some of the benches and tables to prepare for the midday meal, and the church spread was laid out. Jams, apple butter, red beets, pickles, cheese, and *snitz* were set out for a light lunch. Mamm made her specialty, peanut butter and marshmallow on bread.

Annie felt lightheaded from so many bodies in the room, and even more so knowing what was to come. "The body of members, please draw together," Zeke called, avoiding Annie's gaze.

She squeezed her shaking hands between her knees and took in a deep breath, watching as the elders sat next to Omar and Zeke in silence. She turned just as John walked in. He glanced back and gave her a gentle smile, but his eyes were sad, turned down at the edges, as if he knew how upset she was.

Zeke waved her forward, but Annie couldn't find the strength to stand. When she finally did, a rush of anxiety filled her. She grasped a chair back and stood for a moment—a moment long enough for Daed to move forward so she could see him. He nodded, and she moved forward to a bench and sat in front of the ones who would decide her fate.

"Ann Beiler," Zeke bellowed, louder than he needed to. "We are here to deal with the issue of your disobedience."

Her thighs felt numb against the hard board she sat on. Her usual intention to make things right and just had left her. She felt unworthy of her cause and wanted to take the punishment due. She only prayed they didn't ask her to tell them specifics, details that would lead to the truth about her, who she was and what she'd really come from. She was not the Annie they knew and one time thought of so highly.

Her face and neck felt as if they were on fire. She bowed her head and listened to them talk to drown out the thoughts in her head. An elder read scripture from Romans. "Now I beseech you, brethren, mark them which cause divisions and offences contrary to the doctrine which ye have learned; and avoid them."

Zeke's narrow eyes found hers as he began. "You have been in the sin of the flesh?"

The verse twisted in her head. Understanding it to mean those who do not believe in Christ, she wasn't a "them." "Jah," she said before she knew she'd formed the word.

Zeke was about to continue, but Omar stopped him with a raised hand. "Is that all you have to say, Annie?"

Annie nodded. But then she thought, she had been *in* the flesh but not *of* it.

"A baptized member living outside our community without the blessing of your family or the council is unorthodox, and for an excessive length of time. There is no defense," Zeke spouted, his ruddy neck pouring over his white collar. His eyes narrowed as he spoke to Annie. "It should be a relief for you to have this opportunity to confess and begin to heal from your sins."

Annie half listened as he talked and thought if she'd only waited to be baptized, this would have all been avoided. But she couldn't regret the decision. She'd felt led and followed the calling.

Omar stroked his white beard, his eyes never leaving Annie's. "That is sufficient."

Zeke paused at the unexpected word from Omar. "Does the congregation agree to place Annie under the bann for the time equal to her time away?"

How many months had she been gone? The time swam in her head. Three, or was it four? How could she live, work, and commune with no one for over three month's time?

Each person placed their vote. A raised hand and verbal consent. *"Ich bin einig,"* Zeke asked if they agreed and waited for others to follow suit. But there was only silence.

"Enough." Amos stood and looked from one elder to another as he began to speak. His tired, watery eyes pleaded with each one of the men who sat before him in their sacred tongue.

"Onze vader die in de hemelen zijt. Our Father who art in heaven." All the elders' heads lifted to Amos. "Our Abba, loving Father. Hallowed be thy name. Thy kingdom come." Amos's voice was

but a whisper. "*His* kingdom, not ours. Thy will be done on earth, as in heaven. Give us this day our daily bread and forgive our trespasses." Amos's voice lifted. "Forgiveness. Jah, Lord, show us how to forgive.

"As we forgive those who trespass against us, and lead us not into temptation," Amos was almost yelling now. "As we have *all* been tempted. But deliver us from evil," Amos lifted a shaking fist. "And we have all stood face-to-face with the devil. For Thine is the kingdom, and the power." He pointed to each of the men. "Help us not to claim *Your* power as our own. *En de heerlijkheid in der eeuwigheid*. And the glory, forever and ever. Amen."

Amos stopped as if he'd come back to his senses and shoved a finger under his nose as if uncomfortable. The room was cold-still, frozen for a second in time, digesting his words of passion.

Annie had never seen him speak more than a sentence at a time. Judging from the reaction of everyone in the room, neither had anyone else. She stood and went to him. Small steps at first turned into a run. The *pat, pat* of her leather shoes hit the cold wood floor. She bent down to where he sat and hugged him. He tilted his head to her shoulder and returned her embrace.

"Order, order here!" Zeke hollered.

Omar went red and jumped to his feet, ready to chastise him. "Silence!"

"But, Omar." Zeke was humbled at Omar's rebuke. His forlorn face resembled that of a wounded animal.

John rose to his full height. "Let him speak."

Mammi stood in the back of the room, then Eli. Mamm remained seated, staring at her hands folded in her lap with Hanna next to her.

Omar motioned with his palms down for all to sit. "I don't need permission to speak as bishop, Brother John." He gave him a stern stare. Then his eyes scanned the congregation and rested on Zeke. "This meeting will now disband." He stepped behind Zeke and down the row of elders to the door. As he passed Annie, he touched her shoulder, and she knew this would be the end of it.

Chapter Thirty

JOHN LEANED AGAINST the barn door watching Annie juggle three glass bottles of milk. Her kapp sat askew, lopsided on the back of her head. She pressed her hand down her wrinkled dress when their eyes met, and she stood tall, the scene so familiar it hurt.

He took two of the bottles without asking. "Haven't seen you since church the other day." They both stared straight ahead. He waited against the thick silence, sure she would speak eventually. When she didn't, he took two steps in front of her and stopped.

"Have you been hiding from me?" He tipped half a smile her way. But to his surprise the face he expected didn't appear. The drawn lips and pinched face was not one he had ever seen. His concerned response was a hand to her cheek. "It's over, Annie."

She pulled away, her eyes misting against the morning sunrise. A small groan caught in her throat. He waited, but nothing.

The feel of her skin swept away so quickly made him take a moment to regroup. John squinted into the rising sun. "It's a new day, Annie." His eyes cast over to her. "It's all new."

"No, it's a continuation of the day before." Her lip trembled. "And the next day, and the next..."

"Annie, what's wrong?" he questioned. "Your daed was incredible."

"He shouldn't have." Annie's head dropped.

Her reaction seemed to be one of disapproval. He guided her to a rock by the barren oak trees and sat by the dried-up brook. The leaves crackled under his boots, filling the silent air.

"The Annie I knew would have wanted nothing more than to

hear those words from Amos." He took her hand. She startled at his touch and met his eyes. "What's happened to you?"

She shook her head and swallowed hard. "So much more than I'd expected."

"Can you tell me what that means?"

She shook her head. "No."

"Okay, you'll tell me when you're ready." He crossed his arms. "But in the meantime, you should be grateful for what your daed has done, and for Omar. Even the elders could have spoken against you, but by the grace of Gott they didn't."

He leaned forward, set his elbows on his knees and looked up at her. "A lot of this was overdone. The timing of the Nickel Mines shootings changed Zeke, all of us, but for Zeke it was different. Not every Amish agreed as wholeheartedly that all should have been forgiven. And you *were* a baptized member that left the community without your family's consent." He stopped, long enough for affect. She needed to hear this, to go to the people who saved her. This was no small thing to them. "But you know all this, and you still don't respond."

There was silence again.

"I missed this place."

John drew his brows together in response to the change in conversation. They stared out to the slopes of the Appalachians' frame and dormant farmland ahead. "What did you miss?"

"I needed the everyday routine of our life here. I lost my stability out there." She gestured, palm flat, toward the hills. "It was the feeling of being disjointed I couldn't bear."

As he studied her, John realized she hadn't even thought to mention him. She was still lost to something. "You found your birth mother. What's missing?"

"My birthright was taken from me." Her lucent eyes stared through him.

The bang of the front door drew their attention to the house. Hanna walked out and looked their way. When she started to approach, John held out his hand. Hanna tilted her head in understanding, but her rigid lower lip let him know she wasn't happy about the rejection.

Annie's expression was unfamiliar, one of malice and envy. "I should go." She stood.

"Are we done talking?" He laid his arms over his knees.

"You shouldn't keep Hanna waiting." She answered with appropriate words but spite in her tone.

He grabbed her by the arm, causing Hanna to stare. She took a long moment before she turned and marched over to the barn. He could fix that later. What he needed to do now was bring Annie back to him. He rubbed a hand over his face. "You used to tell me everything. Is she why you've stopped? Or is it because of what happened in the city?"

Annie rocked back and forth in her boots, similar to a caged animal performing a trick to earn its reward and be left alone. But he could wait. Without communication with her mamm and Hanna, John knew he was the only one she had to confide in, and that Annie knew it too.

Her voice cracked. She stopped and began again. "I can't understand you and her together." She looked toward the door, and Hanna.

"How do you know she wasn't coming out here to talk to you?"

"Because she hasn't talked to me since I came home, except for the night of Dawdi's wake. And I'm not blind, John."

John looked away, not wanting to confess but knowing it was the only way to bring trust again between them. "It was hard."

Annie let a tear fall but quickly brushed it away. "Jah, John, it was."

"I wanted to be with your family, like I always have been. She helped make that happen."

Annie crossed her arms, refusing to meet his gaze. How could she be so selfish to not see what she'd done to him, to them? "And you had Rudy."

Her head slowly turned his way. Unblinking eyes filled with

anger and tears. "I didn't leave you. I went to find myself." Her voice rose with each word.

"She was here for me when you weren't." He turned and walked up to the house. He didn't want to see Hanna. But he would, for all the wrong reasons. With each step he listened for Annie to call to him, waited for those words that didn't come. He grunted. He'd always known what to do with Annie, how to lift her up and when to slow her down. But this Annie he didn't know.

Chapter Thirty-One

YOU CAN TELL me, Augustus. It's been tough on all of us." Hanna's soft voice floated down the hall. Annie stepped slowly and then came to a stop when she heard her brother's response.

"Eli says we shouldn't talk about it."

Annie heard the shuffle of his boots on the wood floor. She didn't dare move, chancing the floor to creek.

"All right, then. I'll tell you how I feel."

Annie leaned to the side past the crack in the door to see Augustus shake his head. "Only if it's good."

It was strange how Hanna had changed to the opposite as before. It couldn't all be about John for her to behave this way. As much as Hanna had hurt her, Annie still couldn't accept that things would stay this way between them.

"Annie's changed since she was *sod*, in the world. It's full of deceitful things out there."

Annie heard the bed springs squeak and pictured Hanna sitting next to Augustus giving him her distorted picture of what Annie had been through. Hanna couldn't know if she'd changed; how could she without breaking her own personal bann that she alone had set between them? Even though she spoke when no one else was around, she apparently was adamant about rules now. Maybe she liked the roles reversed.

"Annie wouldn't do them." Augustus's voice convicted her. He still saw Annie the way she was.

"When you get out there, you do and say things you never thought you would. It corrupts you. Remember that if someone shuns her."

"Bishop didn't say we had to."

"He didn't tell us not to either. Listen to your heart, Gus."

It was so silent, Annie thought she'd been discovered, and her blood went cold. She decided to make herself known. "Hanna, can I speak with you?" she asked, walking to the door.

"Annie." Augustus opened the door wide and walked up to her, giving her a fine hug. "Can we talk to you now?"

Hanna stared at Augustus as if he were now the enemy. "Gus, you go play."

Augustus turned to Hanna. "Are you gonna talk to her?" He looked back to Annie. "She wants to talk to you."

Hanna gave him a shove. "Go on, now."

He stood in front of Annie.

She touched his shoulder. "This is something you don't need to worry about, Augustus. I'll be fine."

Augustus half smiled and ran down the hall. "Walk," Hanna yelled after him.

His boots clomped down the stairs, so loud in Annie's ears it hurt. She waited for Hanna to speak.

"I don't feel comfortable talking with you yet, Annie."

"Then it's personal, not the law."

"In my opinion, Zeke said what should be done. And Omar is still deciding. So jah, I guess it's a personal decision at this point."

"Why were you okay with my leaving before I left?"

Hanna dropped her arms. "A lot has happened since then. It was not acceptable for you to leave without permission. You knew you were breaking the laws when you left. Did you really think all would be forgotten? Why? Just because you're Annie Beiler? When it comes to the law, there is no exception."

"You participated in *rumspringa*." Annie hoped to humble Hanna by remembering that she had experienced things that the outside world does—more so than Annie had in the many weeks she'd been gone.

Hanna had been one to take full advantage of the freedom the order gave the teenagers before baptism, one of which is a party held in one of the teenagers' barns to socialize. But there was always more—alcohol, driving, and couples alone together. Others left the community for a while, and sometimes they didn't come back.

Hanna would come to Annie, who was usually with John, and confess her experiences to her. Most times it was a situation she'd gotten herself into with a boy—any boy—to earn his affection.

"How can you compare the two? Our parents all know and condone *rumspringa*. They don't condone living out of the community."

"This won't get us anywhere, Hanna, and it isn't what I wanted to talk with you about." Even Hanna's eyes were different. Or maybe it was just the way she looked at Annie. "I want to know that when this is over, we can be sisters again."

Hanna grunted. "We're still sisters."

"Not like we were. I want that back again, Hanna."

"Can you accept John and me together and still be close to me?"

A pain went through Annie's chest. Who was this person in front of her? She knew her only choice was to be patient, to wait for her sister to get over the time away from each other. "This isn't about John. It's about us."

Hanna let out a forced laugh. "Everything's about John. And that I have taken on the responsibilities of the oldest child in this house—a duty you deserted."

Annie heaved a sigh. "I didn't leave anyone any duties or relationships." She lifted her palms up. "Why is this about everyone else? Don't you want to know about my birth mother?"

Hanna squinted. "You're so hurtful. Your mamm is downstairs in the kitchen. Not out there." She pointed to the nearest window. "Don't you see what you've done to her…to us?"

Whether her words were true or not, Annie couldn't bear hearing them. As she looked into the eyes of the one with whom she used to share her soul, Annie wanted to scream or cry, wishing that person were still there.

She turned and walked down the stairs, hearing again a conversation she didn't feel comfortable listening to. It was in the way they talked, as if they knew their words were lethal but were compelled to say them anyway.

Annie watched Mamm wash potatoes in the sink as Samuel crunched on a sugar cookie. "Why do people still act funny?" he questioned.

Mamm twisted slightly toward him. "These things take time, Samuel."

As Annie rounded the corner, she joined Samuel sitting at the table with Thomas. He just smiled. Samuel always smiled because he didn't like to talk. He listened and took it all in, sometimes talking with Annie, asking her questions about people's behaviors he didn't understand.

Annie reached over, stealing one of his cookies, making him grin again. Mamm watched and slowly smiled.

"Are you still in trouble, Annie?" A milk mustache lingered on Thomas's upper lip, lifting Annie's spirits. She'd missed this. She glanced at Mamm, who continued to prepare the potatoes as if Annie weren't there. So Annie would act like she wasn't when she answered him.

"I think Bishop has shown mercy on me, Thomas."

"That means he forgives you?" Thomas ran his sleeve across his upper lip.

Annie could feel the swing of his legs under the table, almost kicking her. "It means compassion, kindness."

Mamm lifted her head to look out the window over the sink. "Thomas, Samuel, finish up and do your evening chores." She ran the knife blade over the potato skins, dropping the strips in the sink. Each stroke was harder than the next. "Annie, were those words directed toward me?"

"I didn't mean for them to be." Annie could hardly breathe. She'd longed for her mamm's words even more than Hanna's. Her mamm's understanding was more important than anyone's.

"Your leaving changed everything, Annie." She cut her hand

but continued to peel. "Nothing's as it should be." A trickle of blood trailed down the side of the sink. "Your dawdi is gone. Mammi's alone, wants no visitors. Your daed has become even more silent than before, what with you and his daed gone."

Annie became distracted with the cut, staring at the red line streaming into the drain. "Do you think my leaving would have prevented those things?"

"Maybe, but one thing I know is John wouldn't be with Hanna. She's made a terrible mess of things with David. Now I wonder if my daughters will marry at all. It's not as it should be."

"You can't blame me for all of those things. And does anyone care what I went through?"

Mamm finally turned to see her. "It was your choice to leave. Not ours."

Annie shook her head. "I didn't break the *ordung,* and even if I did, it's our traditions, not a set of rules."

Mamm's eyes glazed. "You found her?"

"Jah."

"Was she who you thought she would be?" Mamm's glassy eyes stared aimlessly into Annie's.

Annie bent her head to look away from her mamm's haunting eyes. "She was nothing like I thought she would be." This being true to her, Annie knew it would be interpreted differently to her Mamm. She chose to let this be, for both their sakes.

Mamm placed a blood-stained potato on the counter and took another. Annie couldn't watch any longer and walked to the sink, taking the knife from her. She stared at her mamm. Mamm dropped her hands as Annie cleaned the vegetables and counter. She held a towel to Mamm's cut in silence. There would be no mercy from Mamm—not yet.

~ Chapter Thirty-Two ~

THE NEXT FEW days were spent tending to the chores. Physical labor was the only thing that helped Annie push the worries away. It was a little better with her family, all but Hanna and Mamm. Others addressed her as usual, but she also heard whispers when she turned her back.

Annie wiped the cow's teats with a newspaper in preparation for milking and then held the suction cups to each. The machine ran on a generator. The hum and slush of the milk being pulled through the cups then letting up created a familiar and comforting rhythm.

The reassuring melody ended at the sight of Hanna. She made her way through the line of Guernsey cattle. She had taken advantage of Annie's eagerness to do the chores that Hanna used to do, claiming she'd done them for Annie during her absence. "When you're finished, why don't you come with me to singing?"

Annie looked into those stunning blue eyes and knew better. "I won't be done in time to get ready." She went back to the front of the line, taking off the equipment she had just attached to the last heifer.

"You look fine."

Annie paused, leery of Hanna's motives, but wondering whether it was wise to refuse the gesture. Hanna was talking to her and making the effort. If she was up to something, it would be her burden to bear.

"Jah, I'll go."

Hanna smiled. Annie thought it was a victory smile but then realized she was mocking her. "I haven't heard you speak much

Deitsch since you've been home. Did they squelch that out of you, too?"

"What do you mean *too*?"

"Your place here is gone, as well."

Annie hadn't wanted to punch anyone ever before. But right there and then her desire to do so was great. *Gott forgive me.*

"I know you don't like to hear the truth, but we are to gently rebuke one another."

"Gently, jah." Annie held her ground, tired of Hanna's ways.

"I'll gather the others. Then I will be ready to go."

As Hanna turned away, Annie realized who she reminded her of. Essie. But now she felt she might appreciate Essie more.

John drove up in his buggy with David next to him. Hanna all but skipped out to the buggy and greeted them, then moved in behind into the jump seat. Annie felt awkward going with the two men Hanna had her eyes on.

Who is with whom?

But the sight of John did make her heart jump, even more so than before. She resented the feeling, not knowing if they had any future together. She chalked the evening up to Hanna's night.

"Hurry up, Annie," Hanna hollered as she placed a blanket on her lap. John whipped his head around to see Annie as she walked through the door, obviously as surprised as she was. The next time Hanna said "others," Annie would know better than to assume she meant their siblings.

David looked like a deer, bewildered as to how he made up the foursome. Annie wondered who was the most confused. "So it's the four of us tonight?"

"The more the merrier, as they say." Hanna spoke with such enthusiasm John could only stare.

The minute they rode up to the Bucholtzers's home, the stares began. Hanna walked up to the door, leading the way for the rest of them. The house was cleared of larger furniture. An intricately carved hutch holding an assortment of china was even pushed to the side, making room for benches.

Songs were sung from the *Ausbund*. No harmonizing or accompaniment was added. Some were folk songs, other chants of the times past. No musical notation was needed, as they were passed down through each generation.

Hanna made a point to stand next to John, so Annie did as well. She felt sorry for David and gestured for him to stand with them. He shook his head, adamantly refusing.

Good for him.

"I'll be finding my own ride home as well," he told Annie.

She nodded with a smile. "Let me know if there's room for another."

He lifted his brows and turned down the sides of his lips. "Are you giving up the fight?"

Annie thought quickly. "I was never in it."

He nodded approvingly and then made his way to the back of the room. Hanna turned and watched with a small pout.

Other couples stood together, a tactful way to let others know who was together and possible announcement of the nuptials within the next month. Annie figured she would keep everyone guessing by standing beside John with Hanna.

David stood with a group of young men who were not courting anyone. But unlike them, David and Hanna had been considered a couple before Annie left. No commitments had been made, but everyone felt sure there would be in time.

John leaned over to her after the first hymn. "I'm sorry. I didn't know."

Annie shrugged, trying hard not to notice the way his breath felt against her skin.

"Are you as confused as I am?" The next song began, drowning out the last of his words.

Annie nodded with tears in both eyes. It was too loud to talk, and they shouldn't anyway.

When the last song was sung, Annie set her mind to get home as fast as possible. Each group she passed looked her way and talked in low whispers until she reached David and his group of friends.

"Still need that ride?" David's voice was welcomed.

"Sure. Let me tell John."

"Nah, they'll figure it out." He took her hand and led her out to a buggy for just the two of them.

"Adding fuel to the fire?" Annie smiled.

"What do we have to lose?" He held Annie's hand to help her in while she was thinking that couldn't be truer.

They passed the dirt road to Annie's house. "Why aren't we turning?" Not that Annie cared. She was curious.

"I'm not ready to go home yet. Are you?"

She'd never noticed his green eyes. He had a nice smile too, crooked on one side, different. She liked that. "Where are we going?"

He pointed to the largest, flattest part of the community's farmland, tucked in under the mountains. "Did you know the Indians used this valley as a hunting ground?"

"I'd never heard that. I mean I assumed, sort of." She sighed. "Actually, I had never given it much thought."

"Well, you should."

She grinned at his passion.

"Did you also know the pioneers moved in on this land, right here where we're riding?"

"Nee, didn't know that either."

"Well, you had to know about the Civil War battles that were fought." His hopeful face almost made Annie laugh.

"I did hear about that."

"You did?" His eyes flashed.

"My daed told me not to talk of it, us being against violence and all." She almost hated to disappoint him.

"We didn't fight in it. It's history." He clucked to the horses. They picked up their feet, their hooves eating up the dirt beneath them. "I have to say if there was ever a good cause to go to war, I'd like to fight."

Annie sucked in air. "I've never heard anyone say that before."

David chuckled. "Does that offend you?"

"Nee, I just keep noticing how so many Amish want to do something they shouldn't." She took note of his drawn eyebrows. "I'm not judging, just making observations."

"That's refreshing." He smirked and took in a breath. "Love this country air."

"You don't know any different." Annie giggled, actually giggled. She couldn't remember the last time she'd done that.

"Nee, I do. When we go into town, I swear the air gets thick."

Annie laughed harder. "You're not supposed to swear."

"I didn't." He snapped his head over and saw her holding her side in laughter. "What's so funny?"

"You."

"You seem like you need a good laugh. But the air really is polluted."

Her laughter turned to tears.

"Annie, what's wrong?" He pulled back the reins. He hesitated to hold her, but when she didn't stop. he took a quick glance around then embraced her.

"Sorry. I'm just tired."

"Jah, tired of all the grief you get for trying to do what you thought you needed to." He squeezed her tighter.

She suddenly felt awkward and pulled away. Not in his arms, but to be seen together. Annie looked into his eyes and realized how good it felt. She'd never thought she'd fit into another's arms other than John. "I can't believe it."

"Sorry, I shouldn't have said anything. It just steams me." His hands drifted to hers, warming the chill in them.

"No, that's not what I meant. That you understand."

"Oh, that. Well, jah. If I were in your position, I'd have done it in a second. Now, everyone might not want to find out about their real mamm, but if you do, by gum you should."

"Unbelievable."

"Jah, I can't believe the way people act—"

"No." She squeezed his hands. "That you appreciate what I did and why."

"There are more people than you know. As a matter of fact, if Hanna had kept her mouth shut, I don't think it would have gotten so bad."

Annie sighed. "What happened to her while I was gone?"

"I guess I wasn't moving fast enough. But she's younger than me."

"Hanna's always been in a hurry." Annie shook her head.

"What?" His eyebrows drew together in question.

"You remind me of someone."

"Who's that?"

"A young man I met in Harrisonburg."

"Is that good or bad?"

"It's good. Very *gut*." Annie smiled, remembering Rudy and everything he'd done for her. And now she understood his bitterness, more than she'd ever wanted to.

"How could she?" Hanna cried to Frieda, who had just become old enough to attend the singings. She stomped to the window, waiting for Annie and David to come home.

Annie appeared in the doorway. "Frieda, it's time for bed."

Frieda walked quickly past Annie down the hall.

Hanna took a step forward. "So where did you two go?"

"I never knew, Hanna."

She drew her eyebrows together. "Never knew what?"

"How much you thought of John."

Hanna grunted and shoved her hands onto her hips.

"Why didn't you ever tell me?"

"Why would I?"

"We used to tell each other everything, remember?" Annie sat on Hanna's bed.

"It didn't matter when you were here, Annie."

"Do you really care about him, Hanna?"

Hanna's lips twisted as she held back her emotion. "I noticed I got more of David's attention when I gave mine to John. But I'm not stupid; I know how John feels about you."

Annie's heart jumped and then fell in one swoop. How could she take joy in John's feelings for her but know Hanna's heart was breaking? And why did she care?

"It's hard to walk in your shadow. Everyone noticed me when you were gone. Daed asked me what you said before you left. The siblings all listened to me like they did you." Her eyes filled. "But it was all false. As soon as you came back, it all changed. Not instantly, but slowly it's going back to the way it was." She threw her hands to her sides. "Even John."

"Did he make a promise to you?"

"It was more like I made one to him and he didn't disagree, but now that you're back...did he to you?"

Annie paused, and Hanna's lips tightened.

"Nee, he didn't." Annie tried feverishly to sort out the facts and feelings that were flying through her mind. She almost felt sad for her sister, so desperate to earn a man's attention. And to hear John was really part of their relationship made Annie realize the connection between John and Hanna was lost. "I guess we'll leave this in John's hands."

Hanna held a hand to her forehead. "It has been in his hands for weeks now, Annie. You gave him plenty of time to realize where he stood with you."

"None of that changed."

"Maybe not for you, but it did for all of us. Do you think time just stood still while you were gone?"

Annie hadn't thought of it that way. Everything had moved forward, significantly. "When I left, David was courting you. What happened?"

"Humph. He was so unpredictable. Asking me to singing then sitting by Emma Smithson."

"Like you did tonight?"

Hanna dragged her toe along the braided rug's edge. "I suppose. I just got tired of waiting."

"You're younger than I am, Hanna. You don't need to rush into anything with David, or anyone."

"Why? Don't you like David?"

"As a matter of fact, I haven't had such fun since before I left for Harrisonburg."

"Really?" She pushed out her bottom lip in thought. "Why?"

"He made me laugh."

Hanna smiled. "He does have a sense of humor."

"Jah, he does, and he made me feel normal."

"What do you mean?"

"He told me things he felt passionate about and wanted to do."

"You mean things he shouldn't do."

"Some jah, some nee." Annie looked into Hanna's eyes. "Like we all do."

Hanna turned away, telling Annie she wasn't ready for reconciliation yet. "I wonder if I'll ever win David's affection." Her lopsided smirk told Annie she was enjoying the thoughts running through her mind. Then her eyes narrowed. "You're in the same situation. John has a lot to work through before he can truly forgive you."

Annie felt the dagger hit her heart. "And how do you know this?"

"Because he told me." Hanna's expression held no apology for the stinging words. She shrugged. "I don't know why you look so hurt. What did you expect?"

Annie didn't know the answer, only that her world had turned upside down, and she didn't know how to make it right again.

John watched David pull up to the Bucholtzers's house. The hum of the generator lights rang in his head. He'd gone out of his mind waiting for Annie to return.

Doesn't Annie realize the position she continues to put me in each time she makes a rash decision?

David tethered his horse and walked up the steps to the wooden porch. He whistled a familiar tune as he skipped up a couple of stairs.

"You're in a fine mood." John leaned against a wooden beam that ran from the porch to the roof.

David stopped fast then took a final step up. "I am. Very observant of you."

"You weren't earlier."

"No, neither were you. I don't like to be used. I assume you don't either."

John tightened his lips. "Where's Annie?"

"Home."

"She lives ten minutes away. You've been gone over an hour."

"We took the long way."

"What way is that?"

"Down by the Indian hunting grounds."

John shook his head and stuck his hands into his back pockets so he wouldn't hit him. "Do you think that was wise? Annie's had enough talk go around about her."

"Just like living in a small town, isn't it? Only we don't have beauty parlors or gossip magazines."

He felt the burn in his chest and spoke before he should. "You don't care anything about Annie. You just want to play games with Hanna."

David rocked on his heels and looked away.

John took two long strides and stood tall, making his height advantage noticeable. "I want to know what you're up to."

"Whoa, whoa!" David held up his hands. "Calm down."

John didn't budge.

"Okay. All right. I'm tired of Hanna chasing after you. It's embarrassing."

He took a step back. "Maybe you should have thought about that when she was pursuing you. You gave other girls the same attention."

"Jah, well, I'm not ready for what she wants."

"Then tell her." John snapped his suspenders, pleased he'd put David in his place.

"You mean like you're doing?"

"You don't know what you're talking about."

"Why are you with Hanna now that Annie's back?"

John didn't like the question and got in his face again. "Annie has a lot to work out before she can think about us."

"She needs you. And you're with Hanna."

That shot a jolt through him. "She needs time. And Hanna's with me, not the other way around." John stepped past David, the convicting words building.

"Are you sure about that?" David snapped *his* suspenders and walked inside.

Chapter Thirty-Three

"ACH, ANNIE..." ALMA'S normally loud voice was tender, causing Annie to move closer. She held a blanket out for Alma to lay the tiny baby on. As she did, Annie saw why Alma's eyes misted, eyes that always remained dry.

Small, twisted legs lay limp in the warm blanket that had been heated by the fire. His cry made them smile as they met eyes. "He's a gift," Annie whispered.

The exhausted mamm watched them silently. "What is it?"

Alma went to her and clasped her hand. "Your child is special, Ellie."

Ellie put a hand to her lips as Annie placed the tiny bundle on her chest. "Ach." She touched his arms and chest and then his tangled legs. She caressed the small limbs as if to bring life back into them that had been lost.

The family gathered around her and the little one. Ervin lifted the blanket to see where Ellie's focus was. The children gazed at the withered legs and made cooing noises, ahhs, and soft prayers. Some laid hands on the babe. Others stroked him.

This was why Annie loved these people, this community. Unlike the outside world, they looked upon this as a blessing, an opportunity to minister to one of Gott's meek children. No hospitals or doctors could replace the insurance of brotherly love between them. It was the same with the elderly or sick—a chance to give, as all are called to do.

Alma and Annie busied themselves by cleaning up so they could to leave the family to bond with the child. Little Ana watched them intently and made her way over to Alma.

215

"I remember them, Alma." Ana always spoke slowly and quietly, and now even more so.

Alma clapped her hands and gave Ana her full attention. Child-rearing rules were part of Alma's work. She encouraged the children to know what was expected of them so they would make their parents proud.

Ana grinned. "Do you want to hear them?"

Alma nodded and spoke to little Ana as if she were her own daughter. "Attitudes are caught..."

Ana's shy voice could barley be heard. "Not taught."

"Always tell the..." Alma bent over so she could hear the small child.

"Truth." Ana gave her a smile, gaining confidence with each correct answer.

"Never question those in..."

"Author-ty." Ana rocked back on her heels.

"Be sure the cup is half full."

"Be cheerful." Ana smiled.

"Always help..."

"Those less fortun..." Ana's dark brown hair slid back and forth across her back as she moved her head.

"...nate. *Fortunate.* Good, that's a hard word." Alma smiled a mamm's smile. "And the last one...Don't..."

"Gossip." Ana shut her eyes and beamed a smile.

"Well done, Ana." Annie patted Ana's head and watched her walk away with pride in her step. She turned to Alma. "You forgot one."

"'Don't remove the twinkle in their eye'—should be for adults, in my opinion."

And Alma always did have an opinion. Annie nodded in agreement. "I never thought of it that way."

They left the house with the satisfaction they'd helped twins enter into the world. The first had come slowly, but the second was almost right upon the first—two boys, to their daed's delight.

"After five girls, that's a nice sight to see," he had told Annie.

"You could do this alone, Annie." Alma's rosy face took on a serious expression as she marched to her buggy. "You delivered that second one so quick I didn't see it happen."

"You were busy with the first." Annie knew better than to get sucked in to what Alma was referring to. No one could do what Alma did the way she did it. "And I've learned from the best."

Alma lifted one side of her mouth in response and shoved her medical bag into the back of the buggy. It creaked with the weight of the old leather handbag, full of everything, much more than Alma needed.

They pulled up to the chicken coop, where the proud daed stood with twice the eggs he'd promised. "Considering they were twins," he explained as he handed one basket to Annie and the other to Alma. They carried their compensation to the buggy and wedged the baskets in next to the bag to keep them from shifting. There would be more eggs in the coming days. Alma needed the payments more than Annie because she was busier with her work, but Mamm always appreciated any extra food for the family.

Once Alma got situated, she fell silent for a moment before speaking her mind. "What are you going to do, Annie?"

Annie stepped into the buggy and paused before she sat down. She knew what Alma was asking and didn't like the answer. She thought constantly of her birth mother, trying to decide whether it was right for her to pursue a relationship with her or whether it was impossible. Yet a small voice inside her yearned to know more about this woman who had braved so much and received her so openly, unlike the reception she had received upon her return home. "It seems I don't have the luxury to decide."

Alma picked up the reins and stared at Annie. "Of course you do."

Annie sighed in frustration. "Then when will the stares stop?"

Alma grunted. "When you quit looking."

Something Alma could do and Annie should learn to. Annie wrinkled her forehead. "Do you think it would work?"

"Without a response, there isn't much encouragement to continue."

"I never thought people would react this way. They didn't before. Why now?"

"It was there, although I have to say your generation has made it worse."

"Why is that?"

"They experience more of the world than we did. And the world has more to experience."

Annie looked over at Alma. "Why is it everything you say makes sense?"

"I don't know that it does. I just keep things simple."

"Maybe I should do more of that." Annie thought about how her secret continued to haunt her. She could not accept the thought of being a rapist's daughter, and if she couldn't accept it, how could others? She had kept the circumstances of her conception a secret, but her parents had kept her identity a secret as well. How could one be right and not the other? There was nothing simple about it.

"What's on your mind?" Alma slapped the horse's hide, increasing the *click, click* of the horse's steel shoes.

"Everything. What I've done, if it was worth it, how to get on with life, how to change it."

"What's done is done. You move on by making a choice and setting it into motion. Then things change on their own." She looked at Annie out of the corner of her eye. "What about John?"

Annie felt a shot of loneliness at the sound of his name. "I haven't seen him since singing on Sunday."

"Probably 'cause of those stories David's been telling."

Annie looked over at Alma. "What stories?"

"Nothing I believe, but those kids who go to those *rumspringas* sure do love to tell a tale. Something about a ride in his buggy the other night."

Annie believed Alma. She made her way around the

community delivering babies, gaining more information than she cared to hear. "I did take a ride with David."

Alma turned toward her. "So it's true?"

"Hanna was pulling one of her tricks, so David and I decided to find our own way home."

Alma pursed her lips and leaned her head slightly. "Sounds like John believes it. Maybe he should hear from you."

Annie looked out over the brown earth and barren trees, much like she felt since she'd come home, dark and hollow inside. "I don't know if he still wants me...us."

"He just doesn't know what to do with you. You up and leave him, then come back silent as a mouse." She steered the horses around a bend in the dirt road. They both leaned left with the turn. "I say it's about time you told somebody something about what happened to you while you were gone."

Annie sat stiff on the wooden bench, which gave no comfort to the ache in her back. "If it was good, I would have shared what I learned."

Alma was abnormally quiet for a couple of minutes. "Even more of a reason to tell someone you trust."

Chapter Thirty-Four

AT DAYBREAK JOHN headed for the eastern edge of the valley. His black horse, Rob, kicked up dirt as John urged him into a lope. The morning was new and crisp, perfect for a ride before more chores needed to be done.

John slowed his horse at the sound of another set of hooves pounding behind him. As soon as Otto's hooves hit the first field, John knew Annie was there. He pulled back the reins and let Rob settle down while he waited for her.

A dark blue coat, far too large, was gathered onto the horse's bare back in front of her, covering her dress. Her kapp was held loosely with a few pins that barely held it in place. John guessed it was Eli's boots she'd rushed off with, because they came up to her knees.

"Morning."

"Good morning." Her tight smile told him she was up to something.

"Are you following me?"

She squinted into the early morning sun creeping up over the hills. "Jah, I am."

He couldn't contain the swell of emotion her presence created in him and smiled broadly. "Don't you want to know where I'm going?"

Annie scanned the direction he was headed and made a confident guess. "The caves?"

He grinned and turned his horse. She followed and stayed close by his side. This slowed his pace, but he enjoyed her presence much more than a quick run on a horse to blow off steam. He wanted to glance at her again. It wasn't often he had seen her hair so tousled, and he liked it flowing down. She was close to defiling herself by wearing her kapp so carelessly. This was abandoning one of their sacred rules, exposing her hair to a man who was not her husband.

When the wind picked up, he had to turn to her. Her smile was as fresh and clean as the morning, bringing back memories of their many rides in the summer, before the sun became too hot to ride.

The silence between them didn't bother him, and the look of contentment on Annie's face told him she was comfortable with it as well. This was so familiar; he felt for a moment that nothing had changed between them.

"Delivered twins yesterday." Her voice was thoughtful, sentimental in fact.

"I heard. Two boys. I bet Ervin was bursting with pride."

"Jah, we were happy for him." She gazed at him. "One's handicapped."

John nodded. "Blessed are the meek."

"The girls were all over him. Patting him, caressing his withered limbs."

"What is the babe's toil?"

"He has no strength in his legs."

John thought of an uncle who had lived in a wheelchair for as long as John could remember. The chair had grown dust over the years since his passing, but it seemed that it would be used again soon.

"They're fortunate to have him." Annie smiled thoughtfully. "Ervin's mamm said it had taken her sixty-fourth grandchild to show her true humility."

They rode the rest of the way to the cave in silence. The entrance had been carved out into a larger opening due to the increasing popularity of tourists who came to visit. Limestone stalactites hung down, the crystals shimmering in the bright sun. Light bounced off the tiny pools full of rimstone.

John made his way over to a group of level rocks to sit on.

"I'll never get used to these lights." Once the caverns had been acquired, the owner had installed electrical lights and paved pathways through the tunnels.

"Hide-and-go-seek just won't be the same." Annie scanned the place.

"You haven't been here for a while."

"Not since Frieda made us a picnic."

"Bread and crackers don't make for much of a meal."

Annie scowled at him. "No one ever found you when we hid. Where were you?"

He pointed to a dark cubby just past the first tunnel.

She smiled and then folded her hands in her lap as if garnishing her courage to say something important. He thought he'd help her along with a little history.

"Did you know the first Deitsch immigrants settled just north of here in seventeen fifty-five?"

She gave him a skeptical look. "How do you know this?"

"I hid in that same cubby during a tour."

"You listened to a tour guide?"

"Jah. Did you also know the slaves sought refuge here during the Civil War?"

She wrinkled her brow, trying to look interested, but her mind was obviously elsewhere.

"Deserters from both sides of the conflict hid out here."

"Really?"

"Can you imagine the conversations that went on?"

"Is that all?"

He almost stopped so he could admire her beauty, but he didn't want to be distracted. "Actually, no. The Native Americans stored their food here. The twelve-degree-Celsius temperature in these caves enabled them to store buffalo meat here year-round."

"Why are you telling me this?" She wrapped her arms around her legs.

He hesitated long enough to get her full attention. "To remind you that there are larger problems, harder times, and bigger lies than anything you've been through."

Annie hugged her knees and closed her eyes. "I found out why she gave me away."

"You found her." John moved closer. "Where?"

"In Harrisonburg."

John was momentarily disappointed that Annie's concern was more for justifying why she was unwanted than the fact she'd found her mother. "Go on."

"She runs a boardinghouse near the college. She's round and short." Annie half smiled. "She wore a blue dress and a white apron. She almost looked Amish."

"Is this the Mennonite College?"

"Yes, but most of them dress like Englishers."

John rubbed his forehead, taking in the information.

"She had my eyes too."

John's heart warmed to the light in her eyes as she said it. "You mean *you* have *her* eyes. How did you find her?"

"She'd gone to a hospital, so there was a record. I was then able to fill out a form at the registry to give her information if she wanted to contact me. A few weeks later we got a phone call from the registrar telling us she'd responded. I'd almost given up, but the Glicks encouraged me to stay on a bit longer. At first I was glad I did…until I went to see her and found out."

John suddenly felt guilty accusing Annie for staying longer with Rudy, now realizing it had been to wait for a response from her mother. "That's why you were gone so long?"

She nodded. "She was assaulted."

John felt a pang in his heart, not expecting those words. "She was hurt?"

"She was raped."

A rush of emotion flooded his mind, knowing why this had been so hard for Annie to share. "I'm sorry, Annie." He drew her to him, trying to know how this must have felt for Annie when she first heard it. "So that's why you've come back accusing your-self, expecting the shunning."

"I feel so tainted."

"Like the rest of us?" John grabbed her by the shoulders. "A sin is a sin to Gott. We are the ones who categorize them, not Him."

"That's not the reception I've been given. People I thought would accept me didn't, and the ones I thought sure would accuse me haven't." She looked at him with red-rimmed eyes. "I'm so confused. I don't know how to redeem myself."

"Gott's already done that."

She nodded and squeezed her eyes shut.

"The others might not have gone so far if it weren't for Zeke."

Annie whipped around to look at him. "But he's one I thought sure would understand me."

John scoffed. "Zeke's a hypocrite." He heard Annie suck in air at his accusation. "He lives by legalism and the laws."

"I'd never seen him that way."

"That was before the shootings. For most, it strengthened them, but Zeke went a different way with it." John laughed sarcastically. "And you were one of his chosen." John smiled. "You would have been one selected to know the Torah if you'd been a boy back in the days of the Bible."

She shook her head. "Now a rapist's daughter, coming back a prodigal."

"The prodigal son indulged in the worldly things. You didn't do that. And even if you had, the Father would have forgiven you." John hugged her to him. "He's glad you're home."

Annie's body shook with sobs of cleansing tears as John caressed her back and spoke softly to her. "Think of what is true and noble, what's right and pure. Whatever is lovely and admirable, excel-lent or praiseworthy." He repeated this verse over to her until she was still, exhausted of the self-hate and loss of identity.

When she looked into his eyes, he knew he had his Annie back.

Chapter Thirty-Five

MAMM'S ATTEMPT TO bring Annie and Hanna together hadn't worked. Sending them into town should be a treat, a special outing, but that had not been the case. They'd gathered the items Mamm requested and started back without even visiting Abraham and his family.

Dusk was a bad time to walk Route 340 home from town. The two-lane highway had seen more Amish fall prey to buggy and pedestrian accidents than any other in the state. The speed limit had been lowered, but the accidents still happened regularly.

"Almost home," Annie said more to herself than to Hanna.

"Jah, 'tis good, since we've been at each other the whole day." Hanna tromped through the tall grass that hadn't been mowed consistently, forcing them onto the road.

Annie felt like doing the eye-roll thing that Essie did and now understood why she did it. "I meant because the traffic is beginning to pick up."

Hanna nudged Annie closer to the ditch alongside the road to avoid traffic. "I think David's asking me to singing on Sunday."

Annie felt what little patience she had left dissolve. "Don't you ever get tired of who's asking who to whatever?"

Hanna stopped and glared at her. "It's because of you that I have to worry about all this." She planted her hands on her hips

"I won't take the blame for *all this* anymore. I went through a lot to put all the pieces together so I could go on knowing the truth."

Hanna waved as if to shoo the words away. "I don't care about that."

"Then you don't care about me."

Hanna drew back as if pushed away. "Your leaving showed us the same."

"What I did had nothing to do with you. That's become your problem, Hanna. You only think of yourself." Annie heard herself shouting.

The roar of an upcoming car caused Hanna to wait to answer, not wanting to compete with the noise. Annie turned to see an approaching vehicle. It was close, too close to the edge of the road. Annie heard Hanna scream. She reached out to shield her from the inevitable blow.

The car swerved in attempt to avoid them, but the right front bumper nicked Hanna's side and sent her tumbling into the nearby ditch. Immediately Annie felt incredible pain in her arm.

The car whizzed by. The young man driving stared as he passed. That's all Annie remembered before seeing Hanna's body heaped in the ditch.

"Stop!" Annie screamed as the car swerved down the road. Colors flashed by: his blue shirt, the red car, a dark stripe. He wasn't going to stop. She saw the still body of her sister less than a yard from her, heard the engine fade, and saw the dust settle. Then all went black.

Annie woke to the sound of sirens. Her head throbbed as she peeled her forehead from the dry grass. She reached up to adjust herself, but felt a blast of pain shoot up from her wrist. When she lifted her head, she saw Hanna lying next to her toward the edge of the ditch.

Annie fought the pain and moved her head slightly, just enough for her to see Hanna crumpled into a ball. Her arm twisted strangely over her still body. Her blonde curls held bits of pink and red—dried blood. A deep shade of red flooded the dry dirt around her and dripped from the colorless grass. Annie pushed herself up and sat next to Hanna.

"Hanna. You okay?" Annie's voice echoed in her own ears. She looked down the road to flashing lights. The blue-and-red lines grew longer and thinner until completely obscured by the rise in the road. Then the ambulance was on them with a shriek of sirens.

Annie looked over at the next bed, where Hanna lay. A tear slipped down Annie's cheek at the sound of the voice in her head—John's. Now he was in the room walking over and embracing her.

His eyes met Annie's as he pulled away. "Where are you hurt?" He began to look for injuries and then saw the cast on her right hand. "Is this it?"

"That and a bump on my head. Otherwise, I'm fine." Tears flooded her eyes. Since she'd come home, she could show weakness with him, and only with him.

He reached for her hand. "You finally break now. Not when you were running into dead ends finding your mother or taking grief from me and the others."

"Well," she sniffed, "this hurt." She grinned, trying to make light of the horrible experience.

He smiled. "I really do wish you wouldn't have gone into town without me."

She took in a tattered breath, remembering how glad she had been when she arrived home from Harrisonburg, thinking she wouldn't have to worry about cars anymore.

"I have a lot of questions." John turned as the nurse came in to see about discharging Annie and to check Hanna's condition. "But I'll wait."

Mamm and Amos talked with the nurse concerning Hanna. She had lost some blood due to a puncture wound to her side but was stable. A couple of nights for observation, and she should be ready to leave the following day.

Then the nurse came over and checked Annie's vitals. "You're ready to be discharged, Miss Beiler."

"I'll take you home." John took her hand with such care she felt instant comfort. As she set both feet on the floor, he watched her intently.

"You okay?"

After a brief dizzy spell Annie answered, "I'm fine." But she wasn't. With everything that had happened in just the last month's time, and now this, Annie was losing her will. The once-positive attitude and trust in Gott was waning.

Let something good happen, Lord.

"I'm staying here with Hanna. I'll see you both tomorrow." Mamm's soft voice reminded Annie of her mamm's gentle touch when any of them were ill. When she had awoken in the hospital, it had been her mamm she saw first by her bedside, comforting her as if all were forgotten.

"I'll see you at home, Hanna." Annie forced her best smile, and Hanna did the same. She almost felt Hanna's apology.

She went into the bathroom to dress, then let John help her to the wheelchair and out of the hospital, all the while feeling something was different. It was probably just pity, or maybe guilt, but his demeanor had changed. She tried not to be affected by it. Annie had decided not let herself be concerned with what anyone here thought of her anymore. With John's gentleness, she almost felt as though she could follow through with that pledge.

They made their way to the front of the hospital, and John waved at Abraham, who pulled up in his buggy. Annie's eyes watered again at the sight of him. Only around Amish land would a buggy be a common mode of transportation at a hospital. "Danke for leaving the store to take us home."

"Ah, now, don't get all mushy on me, Annie." He helped her in, and John moved in beside her. "How's Hanna?"

"She's okay." John put his arm behind Annie. "We'll all be okay."

She knew he was trying to keep her spirits up, but it wouldn't work for her tonight. Nothing would.

John let out a long breath. "I've been so angry with Hanna. I felt terrible when this happened to her."

Annie felt the same way. Hanna's bad choices had made the entire family suffer; this was just one more. "Can we not talk about this right now?"

"Fine. May I ask another question?" Abraham held tight on the reins.

"Jah, I suppose so." Annie had been ready for silence but knew Abraham to be a sensitive man and couldn't say no to those big, blue eyes.

"Have you made any contact with the woman you met in Harrisonburg?" Abraham glanced her way.

"Nee, not since I've returned." It stung Annie to say the words. She thought about her birth mother all the time and wondered whether Monica Taylor ever thought of her.

It was silent too long before Abraham spoke again. "Why?"

Annie was considering her response when John interjected, "Out of respect."

Abraham nodded. "I see." His face fell as if he felt disappointed for Annie, and Annie suddenly felt very sorry for herself, unable to finish the search for a relationship.

Abraham dropped them off and went back into town. They would need him to bring the others home in the morning.

Annie took a deep breath and said a silent prayer. She worried for her sister. The concern she felt for Hanna was intense, bittered by guilt and anger.

As she walked into the house, she told herself to let the anger go, to forget these feelings of Hanna being responsible for any injuries she had, inside or out.

Chapter Thirty-Six

THE COUNTY POLICE showed up at the Beilers' late the next morning. The tall blond standing next to his muscle-bound counterpart seemed to enjoy the call.

"Coffee, gentlemen?" Mamm already had the pot in her hand ready to serve.

"Thank you, ma'am." The short one sat at the table with Amos. "You Amish always make the best coffee."

Annie decided that was a compliment and sat down with them. The *clomp, clomp* of John's stride was heard coming up the back stairs. Annie's heart jolted, but not as it had when she'd first came back, worrying and wondering what his response would be. Now she knew.

His eyes met Annie's first and then wandered around the room. "Hallo, I'm John Yoder." He shook both of the officers' hands and sat next to Annie.

The tall policeman brought out a pad and pen, while the short one asked the questions. "As you know, Mr. Beiler, we spoke to your daughter Hanna and your wife at the hospital last night after you left. We'd like to ask you and Annie a few more questions."

"Do you know who did this?" Amos's voice was calm but firm.

"From what we can conclude from talking with your daughter, the vehicle was a pickup truck." He turned to Annie. "Do you have any more to add?"

Annie nodded. "It was red with a black stripe down the side. It looked like an older model. Did she tell you what he looked like?"

"No, she said she didn't see him."

"He was a young man with a blue shirt on."

"Is there anything else you can remember?"

Annie studied the table. The whole scene played out again in her mind. "He didn't stop."

"Yes, we've concluded that. It's being considered a hit-and-run."

"A red truck should stand out a bit." John offered.

"You'd be surprised how many red pickup trucks there are out there. The black stripe helps a little." He looked back to Annie. "We're on this, Ms. Beiler. We want you to know that."

"Do you have any idea if you'll find him?" Amos spoke.

The tall cop chimed in. "We'll do everything we can. And please keep us updated on your daughter."

The short officer stood to go. "We'll be checking in. Feel free to call." He handed Amos a card and talked more about a few particulars Amos was concerned about. Just Amos talking that much showed Annie how concerned he was.

John and Annie went out to the milk barn. The Guernseys had waited long enough, and the milking had to be done. "I don't know why Amos doesn't buy Holsteins. You get more milk out of them."

"Jah, but the Guernseys' cream is richer." Annie walked past the stalls. The name of each heifer was written on a blackboard above her stall. The blackboards had been adopted because every once in a while they had to move one when she decided she didn't like her neighbor. For the most part the cows knew which stall to go to without much direction.

While waiting for the milking, Annie began to churn. It was a daunting task that went on for hours. "I'll see you later?" Annie asked John as he rushed out of the barn.

He began to walk backward toward his house. "I'll be back for some of that butter to put on my sandwich for lunch." He pointed at the churn and then turned around. She watched him until he was out of sight.

Three breaks, breakfast, and a few hours later John was back, ready for his lunch with fresh butter on Mamm's homemade bread. He peered into the churn and turned up his nose. "Why does it do that?"

Annie chuckled. "It always turns to liquid right before it's done. The curdling turns to water."

"And white in the winter."

Annie nodded. "You like yellow better?"

"Definitely." John sat in a chair across from her.

"It tastes the same."

John leaned into her. "Sometimes I feel like going into town and getting me some yellow butter that I can eat in five minutes, not five hours."

"John!" She smiled. "You wouldn't appreciate it nearly as much as you will this."

"You're right about that." He leaned back in the chair. "Sort of the cycle of things, I suppose."

"How's that?" Annie felt the curds set and knew she was finally done. Warmth and satisfaction filled her.

"Things usually seem the hardest when you've *almost* achieved the goal."

"Like running a race," Annie added.

"Jah, like Paul talks about. To run a good race to reach the prize." John placed his elbows on his knees. "Have we forgiven each other for everything that's happened?"

"I don't know. Have we?" Within a matter of minutes of her coming home he had taken her over rolling hills of emotions. She let out a breath in hope they could reconcile.

His brown hair slipped down over his forehead. "I felt like we were there, ready to make a life together. Then after you left, I wondered if it was only me who was ready, that you never were."

Annie laced her fingers through his hair, pushing it back to see his serious eyes. "I assumed too much, that everything would go as it should without action from me. Everything had always gone the right way." She sifted through his brown wisps, thinking how much she had taken him for granted. "Then I came home and found no one the same, most importantly you. I always thought we'd be together. That's why it was so hard for me to see you with Hanna."

John lowered his head.

"It surprised me more than anything." She caressed his cheek with the back of her hand, loving the feel of him again.

John scoffed. "Me too."

Frieda came rushing out and stopped in front of Annie. "Mamm says we're going to the hospital."

"Why?" Annie was surprised to hear that they would all go.

"We're going to make quilts."

"A quilting bee at the hospital?"

John grinned. "Leave it to your mamm to organize something like that."

"Guess the butter will have to wait." Annie stood and took off her apron. "Help me with my patches?"

"Ach, there's nothing I'd like better."

She linked his arm in hers. "But you'll get to be with me."

He touched the tip of her nose. "Then that's enough."

Chapter Thirty-Seven

WOMEN FROM THE Amish community flocked around Hanna's bed. She looked much better today and was ready to leave, but not until after the quilting bee.

Two circles of women sat closely together in the room, all chatting like clucking hens. Annie sat with Mamm, her mammi, Frieda, and John's mamm. Hanna hadn't spoken much to anyone since the accident. Most figured it was angst over the car incident, but Annie knew it was something more.

Annie took spools of orange, yellow, and dark threads to make a sunshine-and-shadow quilt true to how she felt, expressing dark and light, spirit and form. The challenge was bringing the two together as one in the center of the quilt.

Mamm sat next to her, tension still between them. "Why did you choose the sunshine and shadow?"

Annie started at her question, no longer used to being addressed by her mamm. "It's complicated."

Mamm's eyes darted to Annie and then back to the wedding pattern she was patching together. Annie wondered who she intended it for but dared not ask.

"Tell me." Mamm's lips tightened, etching lines around the corners.

Annie was wary at first, then decided to let it out, not knowing if her thoughts would be accepted. "It's my journey."

"And...?" Mamm glanced at Annie then back to her work.

"The meaning of this quilt is contradictions coming together, conformity and freedom, discipline versus imagination, acceptance or doubt."

Mamm stopped sewing and set the patches on her lap.

"It's about balance—something I learned when I came back home and realized I didn't have to choose one part of me over another."

Mammi stopped her sewing as well, along with Ida and Frieda. "What were your two opposites?" Mammi questioned.

"Humility or self. I felt I'd done something wrong by leaving, and maybe in a way I did. But I needed to find myself, and in doing so, I've found a balance."

Alma, not one to sew, laid a pile of patches she'd sorted on the table. "I'd say all that thinking is more than most do when they repent." She looked to Mamm. "You have a very thoughtful daughter, Sarah."

Her words hung in the room. Silence like thunder filled the air waiting for Mamm's response. She picked up her sewing and began to stitch. "Jah, I guess I do."

Another hour of pleasant conversation passed until Omar appeared in the doorway. "My, we can't keep you women from sewing, even in a hospital." His gray beard jiggled with his laugh.

He greeted everyone and then went to Hanna. They talked briefly before Omar asked Annie to come with him into the hallway. "Come sit." He patted the chair next to him.

Annie sat down, not knowing what this would be about and nervous to find out. "Is there something wrong?"

"Why do people assume that when I ask to talk to them?" He placed his palms on his knees. "I just want to see how you're doing." He stared at her. "Look into my eyes."

She did, and saw the merriment there, a regular Amish Santa Claus, even more so when he stroked his white beard. "I've heard word you and your birth mother found your way back to one another."

She'd always liked the way he phrased things, so gentle and unassuming. "Jah, we have. The decisions I made to see her were difficult for my family to understand, and for others."

"Jah, well, they'll get over themselves too." He pulled on his beard and stretched out his legs.

"Themselves?"

"There are just certain people who are quick to judge without putting themselves in someone else's shoes." He shook his head. "I hope we've all come back to what our faith is grounded upon after what happened up in Nickel Mines."

"Forgiveness. I thought I knew the meaning of the word until I met my birth mother. Then it became hard because it was real, not just a word that was easy to say."

"If you're sincere, it's not easy to say, and it's even harder to do." He leaned toward her. "I gather you've learned a lot while you were gone and after you returned."

His words encouraged Annie. "Then why don't we allow others to go on their journey as I did and learn these things too?"

"We can't be just like everyone else. Our separateness is what makes us different."

"Then how do we find contentment?"

"Accepting and achievement together make a person content. They stop questioning who they are and where they belong. This brings the freedom you found—by accepting who you are."

"Why aren't we taught these things?"

"You can't teach this; you live it." He lifted the ends of his skinny red lips. "Was your faith tested?"

She nodded without thought. "It became personal to me."

"In what way?" He scooted up in his chair, interested.

"That religion should be a felt experience, not from the vanities."

"People get caught up in the works and not in the relationship."

Annie nodded again, loving this man. She only wished he spent more time in their community, but she knew he had others to tend to, as they were only one in his flock of communities. "When will you come see me again?"

"At your wedding." He grinned with those rose-colored lips again.

She grinned, enjoying his playfulness. "Do you know something I don't?"

"If I didn't, I wouldn't be much of a bishop, now would I?" He stood and squeezed her hand. "Good day, Annie Beiler."

She watched his penguin-walk all the way to the elevators and waved to him as he turned around in the elevator before the doors shut.

Annie went back into Hanna's room. She glanced at Hanna, who was giving her a blank stare. Maybe it was time to find out what was truly bothering her.

Annie studied the room to find everyone preoccupied with their quilts, ironically leaving Hanna to herself in the bed. "Do you feel up to sitting with us?"

"I'm not a very good patient."

"Jah, I know." Annie smiled. Hanna didn't.

"Are you upset?"

"Of course I'm upset."

"This will pass, and hopefully the driver will be found soon."

"This is just my life." She rolled her head against the pillow and stared at the ceiling.

"I'm sorry you feel that way, Hanna. It could have been a lot worse."

She grunted. "It's just not fair."

"What?"

"No matter what you do, it turns into your favor."

"I hardly—"

"I was upset when you left, sad and lonely. That's what brought John and me together." She hit her head against the pillow. "I pushed things too far, and now I look a fool."

Annie remembered how much Hanna used to think of others before herself. It saddened her that through all of this her sister had become indifferent and callous. "I don't know what to say."

Hanna turned to her. "You always know what to say."

"You've changed, Hanna."

"I wanted to change, to be better than I was."

"You change when you stop trying to change, Hanna. You can't force it. It just comes when it all fits."

"I knew you'd figure out what to say."

"I didn't know if you wanted to hear it."

"I don't. I just wanted to see if it felt like it used to."

Annie couldn't imagine it did but hoped all the same.

"But it doesn't." Hanna rolled to her side, holding the bandage over her wound, and closed her eyes.

⌁ Chapter Thirty-Eight ⌁

IT WAS SOON after fall communion that the couples who provided the proper credentials were published. This being known, many of the young adults fidgeted in their seats during the two-hour sermon.

Zeke listed the beliefs of the Amish. "We believe the Bible is the inspired Word of Gott, we believe in the Trinity, and we believe Christ died to save us from sin."

So far Annie wholly agreed with everything he said. She'd learned not to automatically accept everything he stated, as she used to, but she felt all the wiser for it.

"As Romans twelve tells us, 'Be not conformed to this world: but be ye transformed by the renewing of your mind, that ye may prove what is that good, and acceptable, and perfect, will of Gott.'"

He didn't look at Annie as he used to, but during that verse she thought she saw his eyes meet hers for a second.

After Sunday service Zeke boomed out the names as if he were Gott Himself. "Kenny and Lydia, Eli and Miriam, David and Emma..." The names went on.

Hanna snapped up her head up at the sound of David's name. Annie was sure if he had been there, Hanna would have given him a mouthful. But all the couples were at the homes of the first bride-to-be having a private meal together, so David would have a reprieve until tomorrow.

"Did you know?" Annie asked as carefully as she could.

Hanna shook her head.

Frieda pushed her way in between them. "Ach, Hanna."

Hanna stuck out her bottom lip, pressing her top lip against it. "It's okay," she replied more to herself than to answer Frieda.

As everyone left, murmurs were heard of congratulations to family members and talk of what good matches they were. Mamm took Hanna by the arm. "You're too young, Hanna. That's all. You're too young." And they marched out ahead of the crowd.

The next couple of weeks were filled with weddings, at least one a day, so they could then place their focus on the Thanksgiving holiday. After the ceremony the reception took place at the bride's home. There was never a day away from chores, so the timing of the events varied greatly.

As Annie entered Emma's home, she scanned the room. All the furniture was pushed to other rooms or against walls. There was a wooden bookshelf and tables of food from those who gathered to talk with the couple.

The bride and groom made a list of the couples who were dating and would be seated together during the meal. They sat with the bride and groom at the corners of two tables called the *eck*. Those married sat at the far side of the table. Emma called off the young ladies' names and placed a hand at the chair they were to sit in.

When she had called out a fair number, Annie's question was answered. At one time she and John would have been the first couple called. Now they might not be called at all.

"...and Annie Beiler."

At the sound of her name, Annie's senses were awakened. She glanced at John, who stood with his hands in his pockets, grinning, staring at the floor. Annie went to Emma and sat in the assigned seat. Then her eyes went to David, who was ready to call the young men to their places, and she knew it was he who suggested putting her and John together.

Leafy celery stalks in jars were set at the table for decoration. The meal itself was a feast, with Mamm's roast beef, Miriam's chicken, Alma's best mashed potatoes, Mammi's slaw, applesauce, and creamed celery made by the bride's and groom's mamms, and then came the dessert. When the meal was over, the party would continue on for hours, well into the night.

Annie finally had a moment alone with the hostess. "Emma, you look beautiful in that dress." All the dresses were blue but newly made and different styles. Emma's black hair and eyes stood out against the deep blue.

"Annie." She grasped her hand. "I'm so glad to see you." She pulled Annie to a quiet place by the bookshelf. "Hanna's upset, I know." She wrung her hands. "I wish I could say I'm sorry, but I can't. As soon as David and I started spending time together, I knew he was the one."

"And you're marrying age. Hanna understands that." Annie wanted to save face for Hanna. Not that she deserved Annie's help, but with the way things had gone for her lately, Annie couldn't stand to let this go too. "Congratulations, Emma." Annie kissed her on the cheek and went to find David. He was in the kitchen with a group of young men his age, most of whom were recently married or going to be soon.

"Any words of advice, David?" Jacob asked with candor.

David grinned. "I'm still looking for some myself." They all chuckled in low baritone growls. He pointed around the room. "Who's the first married guy here?"

Gerry held up his hand. "I'm the one first this year. So if you need to know anything, just come to me." He stuck out his chin and bobbed his head with teasing bravado.

"Hey, Ruth." David jokingly called Gerry's wife's name, looking beyond Gerry.

Gerry started and looked behind him to an empty space. They all laughed, enjoying the joke. David's laughter ceased when he saw Annie, and he moved toward her.

"Congratulations, David." She smiled convincingly.

"Danke, Annie." He drew close to her. "How's everyone at the Beiler house?"

"We're on the mend. Healing, moving on with life." When she looked into his eyes, she saw sincere joy and knew he was happy.

"Is Hanna doing well?"

"She'll be fine. A lot has happened."

"Jah, it has." He leaned in closer. "Do you understand why…?"

"I don't need to, but jah, I do."

He nodded his appreciation. "So, you and John?" He shrugged.

"Maybe next year." Annie's heart pounded at the thought. It all seemed so real with many celebrations that had gone on recently.

David looked over her head, behind her, and nodded. Annie turned to see John a few steps behind her. Her eyes trailed up from his boots to his legs and then further up to his chest. Annie had never been intimate with him in any way, but still she knew every part of him—his physical features and, even more, who he was. At that moment, standing with him, she knew who she was too.

She took long, slow steps to him, smiling all the way over. "When did you come into the room?"

"Just now." He turned and looked at her out of the corner of his eye. "What are you thinking about?"

"All of this." She raised her hands to the celebrating of new lives together. "And about this being us someday."

"Someday?"

"Someday soon."

His answer was a smile.

She grinned to herself, hoping he was seeing things her way a little more than he thought he would. They knew they needed time, but they also both knew this would have been them if the events of the past months hadn't come between them.

David and Emma walked through the room hand in hand, ready to start the hymn-singing. Annie watched Hanna's lifeless face as she stared at them. There would be more to come for her to endure—a weekend honeymoon was customary, then overnight visits with relatives who presented them with gifts. Annie mouthed the word *time* to Hanna, but she was saying it as much to herself as she was to Hanna.

Chapter Thirty-Nine

JOHN WAS READY to have a word with Amos and Sarah. He thought back to how long he'd waited for the right time before Annie left. This helped him find new courage in asking for her now.

Not finding Amos at home, he went to Mammi's to find him. John tapped on the door and glanced at Becca's withering garden. The cold fall nights had finally turned the colors to browns there, as in the hills and pastures. John thought of how long ago he helped Annie weed that garden right before she left. It now seemed like a long time ago. He was glad it was over but also realized now how important it was that she'd gone.

When Zeke answered the door, John felt like making a retreat, then thought maybe this was an opportunity to clear the air with him as well. "Minister Zeke." He took a step inside, and Zeke closed the door behind him.

"I'm glad you're here, John. Sarah is in here with us as well." Zeke walked through the house as if he owned it and joined the ladies.

Mammi smiled pleasantly when she saw John. He took her hand. "How are you today?"

"I'm well, now that you're here." She glared at Zeke and began her knitting again.

He nodded to Sarah. "Morning."

"Good morning, John. What brings you here?"

"I was looking for Amos."

"He'll be along soon."

"How's Hanna healing?"

"She's well. Annie's broken bone and Hanna's wound seemed minor compared to what could have been done."

Mammi piped in, "Hanna's bumped and bruised too." She scrunched her nose. "All black and blue. Poor girl. Wish they'd find that fella."

Zeke laid a hand on her knee. "Now, Becca, the Lord is our avenger."

"Yeah, that's in due time. I'd like to see some now." She yanked on the ball of yarn at her feet.

John couldn't help but smile inside. So much for forgiveness today with the mood Mammi was in.

Zeke let out a long sigh and turned to John. "What did you need to speak to Amos about?"

John took caution; he didn't want to show disrespect but preferred confidentiality with this matter. "I'd rather wait until he gets here."

At that moment the front door opened and shut, and in walked Amos. His stature always made an impression impossible to ignore when he appeared in the room.

"Morning, all." Amos sat next to Sarah on the couch and nodded to John. "Zeke, what's this about?"

"I'll get right to the matter." Zeke sat up at the end of his chair. "I'd like to confirm with Annie that our set of practices are to provide a context for morality in her choices from here on out."

"Could you explain that in English or Deitsch? Maybe Deitsch would work better," Mammi requested brashly.

Zeke said it again in Deitsch.

"Still doesn't make sense." She looked over at the rest. "Does it make sense to you?"

Sarah was the first to answer. "I think what the minister is trying to say is that we want to be assured that Annie understands what she did was wrong and to make sure she doesn't do anything unlawful again."

Amos grunted. "I think we've done that."

Zeke's pensive eyes stuck on Amos for a moment and then slid to Sarah. "That is my concern."

John couldn't hold back. "Do you really think Annie will do anything to upset the *rules* again? She didn't mean to do anything wrong the first time. She just wanted to meet her birth mother."

Zeke held out a hand, palm down, to quiet him. "I only want to restate the oath that we are admonished to live a life that is separate from the world."

"I think you made that clear in the service on Sunday." Amos stood. "Are you going to leave now, or am I?"

Zeke's look of surprise was priceless as he looked up at Amos with his beady eyes and small spectacles. "Amos, denial of this situation will only cause more grief—"

"This situation is over. My Annie's been through enough." Amos paused. "I guess it's me that's leaving." He made his way to the door before Zeke could put two words together.

"Well, I suppose I'll give him a minute before I leave. Ladies, John, I hope you all support me in—"

"I agree with Amos. This is done." Mammi clicked her needles louder and faster, staring up at Zeke until his neck turned a blotchy red.

"I will bring this matter to the church board, *gmayna*, to see that the matter is closed." He excused himself and stood.

It was silent until he left. Then Mammi started in. "I never liked him."

"Mammi, don't say things you'll regret." Sarah touched her arm.

"Ach, I won't regret them, the *welsh* of a man." She let out a breath and slowed the *clickety clickety* of the knitting needles.

Sarah looked to John. "I suppose Amos is in the barn if you need to talk with him."

John nodded. "I reckon so."

"Are you asking for Annie's hand?" Mammi didn't look up; she just kept clicking.

"Mammi," Sarah hushed her.

"Well, look at him. He's enamored, *ferhoodled*."

Sarah shook her head and stood to get more tea. "Would you like something to drink, John?"

"Nee, thank you. I'll be on my way." He put a hand to Mammi's shoulder. "I want to see that scarf when you're finished. I like that color of blue."

"I'll save it for your wedding present."

Sarah grunted with approval, then she turned to go into the kitchen.

John whispered, "I'll look forward to it."

Mammi smiled and tugged at the ball of yarn, satisfied.

John took in the country air as he walked to the barn. Hard chunks of dirt kicked up under his boots and crunched with each step. Amos wasn't an easy man to talk to, but John knew Amos favored him, and that would be his advantage.

The double-sized wooden barn door slowly creaked open. John shut out the winter cold now approaching and searched for Amos, following his ears to the sound of tinkering in the work-shop. Amos's hobby was his tools. He adjusted, cleaned, and even invented ways to make them perform even better than the orig-inal tool maker.

"Hallo, John. You were right about this cold front moving in," Amos greeted John before he was in the room.

John nodded. "What are you working on?"

Amos held a stripped-down sanding blade used for smoothing wood to make furniture. On the worktable before him was the knob that screwed into the cylinder. John couldn't figure why he'd taken out the knob, which was the handle to move the sander back and forth across the wood.

Amos held up a clip. "This here will allow the knob to rotate laterally to adjust across the surface of the wood to improve the control." Amos placed the clip and then the knob in the sander. "Here. Give it a try."

John laid a scrap of pine on the workbench table. He moved the sander knob in between his thumb and first finger. The slight movement the clip created was forgiving in not keeping the tool in direct line with the previous stroke.

"Smooth as butter." John continued until the entire piece of wood was sleek and smooth.

The edges of Amos's lips lifted slightly—the most he ever smiled.

"The new and improved sander, by Amos Beiler," John announced.

"Ahh, it's just a little something." Amos took the sander and tried it out himself. "Hmm," was his noise of approval. He had never learned how to whistle, so he hummed instead.

It might be hard to get his attention off the sander and onto his eldest child. John leaned back on the worktable and waited for a minute to see if he'd tire of testing out the tool. "You could get a patent for that design, you know."

Amos waved the thought away. "Nee, wouldn't want to do anything else to upset Zeke." He stopped and felt the underside of the sander.

"Amish do it all the time. We create the tools that the Englishers use for hobbies. They spend a fine penny on those pastimes."

Amos pursed his lips in thought, but only for a second. "You here about the sander?"

John crossed his arms over his chest for warmth. "I'm here about Annie."

"Figured so." Amos eyed jars of different nails and screws, which were glued to a shelf by the lids. He unscrewed one and fished out a tiny screw. "You two finally got things straight?"

"I think so. What do you think?"

"I'm just waiting." He stopped his task and looked directly at John, a rare gesture. "You know I approve of the two of you together."

"There's no hurry. I just don't want anything to interfere again."

Amos paused a second time. "Hurry or wait. It doesn't matter; there's always going to be something that comes up."

John slapped Amos on the shoulder. "We'll make it through the next obstacle just like we did this one."

"I know you will." Amos screwed the jar back into the lid and began to work on his sander again. Their conversation was over.

Chapter Forty

WHEN THE BEILERS returned from church, they found a police car parked in front of the house. The same two officers were in the kitchen with Hanna. She'd missed church, saying she felt sick, *grenklich*. Annie thought it was more her spirit than any physical illness.

Amos hurried in with Mamm and the others close behind. Annie brought up the rear, catching the end of the conversation.

"We brought the driver in last night. He was pulled over for a DUI."

"Hmm?" Mammi shook her head.

"Drinking and driving, ma'am," the tall officer yelled to her.

"I'm not deaf. Just didn't know what that stood for."

"Sorry, ma'am." He looked back over to Amos. "We'll let you know when the trial is. We'll need both young ladies to be witnesses."

Amos grunted. "It's not our way."

"I understand, sir," the short, dark-haired cop answered. "But if we're going to have any justice involving this incident, we'll need to hear their accounts."

"You'll have to take it to our minister." Amos left it at that and walked out of the room.

"Thank you for coming, officers." Mamm seemed ready to be rid of them as well. To their way of thinking, the situation was best forgotten, especially with everything else that had gone on recently.

"We'll be in touch." The tall cop led the way to the door.

"Would you like to join us for noon meal?" Mammi asked, as was the way of the Amish, but it wasn't heartfelt.

"No, thank you, ma'am. We need to get back to work." The shorter officer tipped his hat and followed his partner out the door.

"Danke." Annie smiled at him as they left but was uncomfortable about the possibility she might need to appear in court. The police seemed to think they were a bother due to the Amish disinterest in the legal system, and she most definitely didn't want to see the young man they'd identified. She tried to distract herself preparing the meal.

With the excitement over, the men and boys went out to do chores, and the women and girls started the noon meal. Chicken and dumplings would be served with potatoes and gravy, one of Annie's favorites.

As Annie filled a large pot with water and began to cut the chicken into bite-size pieces to make a broth to boil the dumplings, she began to think about how the legal process worked. The young man was caught doing an illegal activity, and now he would go to court to see what his punishment would be, much as she'd gone through when she had returned here. But it sounded like this man could walk away with no punishment if she didn't tell of his crime. Annie compared her situation to his, and although she understood one better than the other, it seemed strange to her that this young man could get caught in the act and avoid repercussions by simply not telling the truth. It was all a matter of others proving his guilt.

She mixed the flour, eggs, and water together as further thoughts came to her. Since her visit to the outside world, she contemplated these situations more; she'd never had any reason to think about them before. The more she thought about it, the more she appreciated where she was and the lifestyle the Amish lived. She rolled out the dough and let the noodles dry and thought of the young man and all the material possessions he had. That seemed to give him more control of the situation in that he could get his way because of the money.

When the noodles were dried out enough, she put them in the

boiling broth and went over to help Mamm with the side dishes. A vegetable, bread, and sometimes a fruit were usually served with every meal.

"What are you thinking about?" Mamm's voice broke her concentration.

"Ach, I was just wondering about that young man and how this all works." Annie went on, explaining to her mamm all she'd thought through. But Mamm remained silent. "What do you make of it?"

"It's not our worry. And it's not our way. I'm praying, and that's all that can be done at the moment." Mamm pulled out two steaming loaves of bread from the stove and set them on the counter to cool a bit before cutting slices.

Although Annie didn't respond, she understood completely and took her mamm's words to heart. Once Zeke got involved, it would be taken care of, so she needn't spend any more time trying to figure out something that was over as far as they were concerned.

As she placed the food on the table, Annie looked around the kitchen. The room glowed. It went beyond clean; it was simplicity too. The large table, black metal stove, and linoleum floors were nothing special in color or fashion, but the air vibrated. There was no place she'd rather be.

As everyone began to gather around the table, Annie felt the light atmosphere, as it had been before all of the changes happened. When they finished, the young ones poked one another and bantered back and forth. The adults talked about the weather and how thankful they were for the bountiful crop they'd brought in to get them through the upcoming winter. There were no harsh words or tension; only kindred spirits reunited. But through it all the nagging thought of the upcoming trial drew her away from the calm. Annie prayed she wouldn't have to set eyes on that young man ever again.

Chapter Forty-One

ANNIE WALKED OUT of the chicken coop twirling a basket of fresh eggs around, bumping her leg as she walked slowly to the house. She stopped to admire the sunrise. The yellow sun wore a skirt of red just above the mountain range, and the chilly air bit at her lungs as she breathed in deeply.

Looking across at the nearby farms, Annie thought of each of the families individually and how they had dealt with her adventure. She'd realized most of the speculation was when she was at church with Zeke nearby. She hadn't thought of Zeke's power negatively until John had told her his true feelings on the matter. She wondered how many others shared his thoughts.

Time had healed the wounds inflicted when she first returned. It took some longer than others, but overall most understood, and some even supported her decision to make the trip to the English. Still, there were some wounds that might never mend. Hanna, for one, was so different when she came back, Annie didn't know whether their relationship would ever be the same again.

"It's awful cold to be standing outdoors without any work at hand."

Annie welcomed John's brisk voice. He had been hurt and reacting out of pain when she returned. She understood that completely now.

She pulled her light jacket around her. "I should have listened to you about the cold weather." She took in his mud-splattered pants and soiled shirt. "Have you been wrestling with one of the hogs?"

He looked down at his clothes and brushed off some of the

dried dirt. "Robert spooked the milk cows this morning while I was in the pen trying to herd 'em in to the milk barn."

Robert was John's youngest and orneriest brother. "I can't imagine he did it on purpose," Annie teased.

"Ach, I'm sure." The ends of John's lips turned down with a small shake of his head. They walked in silence for a moment. "Why don't you talk about your birth mother?"

Annie turned to him. "I think about her all the time. I feel awkward talking about her. That's what all the fuss was about." She glanced at the house. "And I don't want to hurt anyone's feelings."

"Everything's quieted down, but you shouldn't limit your relationship with her. I think people might understand that now."

"Maybe. I just hate to stir things up since peace has settled in again."

He squinted into the bright sun. "It is nice out here."

"Nice and quiet." Annie kissed him on the cheek and then looked around to see if anyone might have seen.

John chuckled. "I'll see you later."

She nodded and took the eggs into the house. Then she went to her room and sat at her desk. She fiddled with a tablet of paper for a while and took out a pen.

She peered out the window for a moment to take in the rolling hills and never-ending pastures before beginning to write.

Monica,

I hope this letter finds you well. I think about you often, about your haus that reminded me so much of the one I live in. I thought since I've seen your world that you might want to know about mine.

We have fifty acres to the south and another hundred north of our haus. We grow crops and raise livestock, mainly corn, tobacco, and Guernsey cows that make us a good profit selling their milk and cream. It's prettiest in the summer here when the leafy tobacco is a shade of yellow and the corn is plump. Honeysuckle wraps around the fence lines and in Mamm's garden, creating a sweet scent as you pass by. You can pick a bloom off the vine and suck on the end. It tastes like honey, which is why the bees swarm around those flowers more than any others.

I spend my day milking, gathering eggs, churning, canning, and cooking. In the off time we quilt, make candles and dolls. I'll send you one of my quilts if you like. I just finished one called "sunset and shadow." It means a lot to me. Maybe it would for you too. It's about finding the balance in life. You might understand if you could see it.

Annie looked at her bed with the orange, yellow, and black quilt folded over the steel footboard. Would she think it was silly to send the quilt to her?

I should go help with the noon meal. Write to me if you want to. If not, I understand.

She hesitated on how she should sign the letter. They weren't living the lives of mother and daughter, but Annie felt a connection with this woman who had struggled so from Annie's conception to meeting with her eighteen years later.

Yours truly, Annie

She scrunched up her nose, feeling funny about the word *truly* but unable to think of another to replace it. She folded the letter and stuffed it into an envelope, addressed it, and went downstairs. After lunch she would find an excuse to go into town.

The small town of Staunton bustled with tourists. The approaching holidays brought them in by the droves. Annie pushed her way through the hordes of people huddled together listening to the guide talk of the first Deitsch settlers.

John held her by the arm, not wanting to lose her to the mass of people. "How did you talk me into this?"

"It was your idea, remember?"

"Contacting your mother, jah. Coming into town, nee." He looked for cars, found an opening, and pulled her along quickly to reach the other side. A pickup flew past them, causing Annie to scream out in protest.

She turned just in time to see the truck fly down Main Street. She pointed. "That's the pickup."

John glanced down the street to the oncoming traffic. "I didn't see it. Are you sure?"

"Jah, it was red with the dark stripe on the side." Annie bent over to catch her breath.

"Are you okay?"

"It's all coming back to me. Like it's happening all over again." The cars seemed to move quicker, the lights flashed brighter. More and more people came into view. The feel of John's grip on her arm brought her back.

"Annie. Annie." His stern face drew her attention to him.

"What?" she squeaked out.

"Come with me, out of the street." He guided her to a bench where three tourists sat staring. "Can we have this seat, please?" They quickly moved away but continued to stare and did nothing to help.

Annie sat and held her face in her hands. "I thought he was gone, in jail or somewhere."

John sat next to her. "Me too. Something must have happened."

"Like what?"

"Like Zeke."

"What do you mean?" Annie remembered her contemplations after the police left the other day, thinking everything would be taken care of without their involvement. This made her wonder whether it was necessary for them to do something to make sure he wouldn't be able to drive. It seemed a natural consequence.

"If Zeke told those officers you and Hanna wouldn't help

identify him, he might not have gotten any punishment." John's serious expression made Annie wonder what he was planning. He wasn't one to intercede unless absolutely necessary, but she had a feeling this would be one of those times.

"Do you feel well enough to walk to the buggy?" He took her by the arm and helped her up without waiting for an answer.

She nodded as she stood. "What are you going to do?"

He narrowed his eyes and tightened his lips. "Something I should have done from the beginning."

Chapter Forty-Two

T HEY HURRIED HOME in John's buggy with cars whizzing past by the dozens. "I hope this dies down after the holidays." Annie sat back in her seat holding onto the door handle with white knuckles.

"It usually does. Once they get their Amish doll for their niece and quilt for Aunt Betsy." John didn't mean to be sharp, but he'd had it with Englishers. From the time Annie left to the car accident to tourists, it was enough.

"What are we going to do?" Annie still seemed a bit out-of-sorts. The hit-and-run must have upset her more than she'd let on. This gave him another reason to figure out a way to stay away from town for a good while.

"Talk to Zeke and wait for the police to contact us."

"Maybe we should have just gone to the station while we were in town."

He'd thought about it but wanted to get Annie home, and then there was the matter of Zeke. "Let's see what Zeke has to say for himself first."

"What do you think he did?"

"What he always does. The Amish way, no matter what the cost."

"Aren't we supposed to?" Annie seemed confused at John's disobedient remark.

"Sometimes our lives cross, and we have to work together. This Englisher who has caused harm to us and is still on the roads, able to hurt others, is something we need to help stop in whatever way we can, even if it means bending our rules." They pulled into John's, and he began to unhitch the horse. "Let me finish here, and I'll walk you home."

Annie fidgeted as she waited. "Nee, I want Daed to contact Zeke so we can figure out what to do."

"Are you sure you're okay to walk home?" He didn't feel comfortable with her being alone. The sight of that pickup again had upset her more than he'd expected.

"Jah, come over when you're done." She walked over to him with quick steps.

He rubbed her cheek with his rough fingers, wanting to get a good look at her before she left. Her heavy eyes and tight lips didn't give him any comfort. He'd just hurry things along.

He watched her go and went to work on cooling down Rob and putting away the harness and bridle. He'd just moved the buggy into the shed when he heard a commotion coming from Annie's. A scream had him in a full run down the hill and across the dried-up creek, through the trees, and up another hill to her home.

The front door was wide open, and it was silent. John took a step forward, his head spinning with a mix of fear and the need to protect. Just as he was about to step inside the house a flash of red whizzed by. He turned to see the red pickup truck hit the dirt road. Its tail slid back and forth across the loose gravel. Dust lifted as the truck drove out of sight.

There was no way to catch him. John just watched helplessly until he heard sobs come from inside.

Annie.

He couldn't move fast enough. Soon he was by her side, but it wasn't Annie in tears. It was Hanna. Her body shook with anxiety and fear. "What happened?" John rested his hand on Hanna's shoulder.

Annie tried to explain. "I only saw him leave through the back door and drive off. Hanna's so upset I can't get her to talk."

"He must have followed us here." John lifted her face to his with two fingers under her chin. "Hanna, tell us what he did."

She sucked in air, trying to calm herself. "He didn't do anything."

"Then what happened?" John couldn't stand not knowing. He wanted to belt the guy, but he knew he could have no quarrel with another soul.

She hiccupped and tried again to explain. "He told me not to show up."

"He threatened you?" Annie shook with anger as well, or maybe fright.

"Jah, and I won't." She shook her head back and forth several times.

"Won't what, Hanna?" Annie rubbed Hanna's back.

"Say he's guilty." She trembled.

John hated that the Englisher had the freedom to do this. It was wrong in Amish culture and should be in Englishers' culture. "If you don't, he'll be free to come torment you again."

Annie looked at John. "Why is he able to be out around us?"

John didn't understand the system but figured he'd worked himself out of jail somehow. "Maybe he posted bail."

"What kind of justice is that?" Hanna cried out.

"English justice," John sneered. "I'm going to talk to Zeke."

"Now, at this hour?" Annie asked, as if she didn't want him to leave her.

John didn't care what time it was. He walked through the door and to the barn, grabbed a bridle, and tacked up Perry. He raced down the hill past Amos and the others, who were on their way back from hymn singing. He didn't stop. They'd find out soon enough.

As John approached Zeke's modest home, he prayed for patience and self-control, neither of which he had at the moment. The small clapboard house was only big enough for Zeke and his wife. Louisa was barren, a tragic and unbearable way for an Amish woman to live out her life, as John knew through his mother. Although others were kind and said it was Gott's will, their lives were made up of family and children, making it uncomfortable at times for the childless.

Louisa opened the door before he reached the first step. "John, what brings you here at this hour?" Her flannel, floor-length nightgown flowed against her as the night breeze blew in.

Zeke stepped in front of her, blocking John's view. "What is it?"

"The man..." John leaned over to catch his breath, "...who hit Hanna and Annie came to their home."

Zeke's eyes widened with surprise. "That's crazy, *narrisch*."

"Why isn't he locked up, Zeke?" John stood to his full height.

Louisa peered around Zeke, irritated. The fire in John's belly went upward into his throat and came out in his words. "What do we need to do? Hanna was harassed by the same man who hit her. Annie's just as distraught watching him drive down Main Street and then finding him in her home." John took a step forward. His eyes narrowed at Zeke. "You and I need to talk." John walked past him and stood in the living room.

Louisa's eyes darted from John to Zeke. With no response from Zeke, she frowned and started for her bedroom. "Well, I never."

"Hanna had a difficult experience. I understand. We'll contact the police." Zeke crossed his arms over his round belly.

"Why is he on the street, Zeke?"

"Humph. We'll go to into town tomorrow and sort this all out."

John took a step closer to him. Zeke backed away. "You'll tell me now."

Zeke heaved a sigh and went for his glasses as an excuse to dodge John. "If you insist, I'll tell you what I know, and we'll leave the rest for the officers to answer." He sat in a large chair.

John remained standing, hovering over him. "What did you tell the police when Amos sent them to you?"

"Amos sent them to me to decide the best course of action to resolve the issue." He wiped his sweaty brow with his hand.

"That should be decided in court."

"The Beiler girls would have to take the stand in order for that to happen."

John leaned over, his face directly in front of Zeke's. "Then let them."

"It's crossing a line, John. Has Annie's influence caused you to fall away as well?" No sooner had the words left his mouth than Zeke recoiled, as if knowing he'd pushed too far.

"Then cross it." John turned and walked out. He needed to cool his temper. He felt Zeke's mouse-like eyes on him as he collected his horse and road down the trail from their house. By demanding that Zeke cross a line of Amish law, he'd crossed the minister of his community. There would be a penance to pay.

They went to the local police station early the next morning. The red brick building with cracks in the mortar looked its age. A sign with chipping paint claimed the place as the police department and gave the precinct number.

As they walked to the witness room, Hanna reached for Annie's hand. They had come to identify the man who came to the Beilers's home and to see whether it was indeed the same man who had hit them. Annie was reminded of walking through the sterile hallways at the adoption agency.

The thick glass between them and the six men standing on the other side called for caution. One man's gaze seemed as if he was looking right into Annie's eyes. "Can they see us?"

An older officer answered and guided them closer to the glass wall. "No, ma'am. We wouldn't have very many willing witnesses if that were the case, now would we?"

His sarcasm made Annie feel even more uncomfortable than she already had. She knew Hanna felt the same, or she wouldn't have made the gesture to take her hand.

Zeke walked in, making Annie's heart heavy, knowing he would only make matters worse. "Minister," Annie greeted him.

"Annie, Hanna."

Hanna didn't respond. She just stared at the men opposite the glass from them.

Zeke looked at the camera up high on the wall. "I've only come to offer moral support." He shouted, directing his words toward the camera. "I'll go back out to the waiting area." He nodded to Annie and then to the officer and left.

Annie breathed a sigh of relief and decided to get this over with. "Can we start?" she asked the compliant but disinterested officer.

"Yes, ma'am." He moved forward. "Do any of these men look like the man who came to your home, Ms. Beiler?" He stared at Hanna, making her squirm.

Each of the six men were so much alike in appearance it would be difficult to narrow them down. They were all in their early twenties with blond hair, but they didn't all have the same color of eyes; but then, they were never close enough to see what color he had, anyway.

Her forehead began to perspire as she looked at each man. "The one on the end."

"Which end?" he huffed out with annoyance.

"To the right," she sputtered.

"You." He pointed to Annie. "Is he the one?"

"I didn't see him that night. Only the hit-and-run, and it happened so fast I'm not sure. I only know what the truck looks like."

"So, we have one identification?"

Hanna and Annie looked at one another. "Jah, I guess so."

He filled out a form on his clipboard and then led them to the door.

"Is that all?" Annie questioned.

"Thanks for coming, ladies." He closed the door behind them.

As they walked down the hall, they saw Zeke and John talking. Their serious expressions told Annie not to interfere. "Let's wait here." Annie tugged on Hanna's arm.

Hanna looked to where Annie was staring and sat with her on some metal chairs. "What are they talking about?"

"I'm not sure. But by the looks of it I'd say John's in a bad way."

It was a cold winter day when Zeke called the elders together to discuss John's disobedience. John took it well. His goal had been to have justice done, and it had been, so the berating was well worth his efforts.

"Wait for me?" he asked Annie after church and council were held.

"I'll go in." She took his hand, and they walked in together. The council sat in a row at a long table with Zeke and Omar in the middle. They stopped their chatter when John approached.

Since Zeke was in charge, he brought the meeting to order as usual. "John Yoder, do you confess your insubordination?"

John replied with a simple nod.

Omar smiled at John with his thin, ruby lips. "What do you feel is a fair atonement, Brother John?"

John watched Zeke look sideways at Omar. He was learning to put his power aside when Omar expected it, and it seemed to humble him.

"I'd like to help Zeke plant his back field, come spring."

Zeke's eyes lifted. "That pasture hasn't grown a good crop for years."

"I hear a season of growing soybeans will liven up the soil enough to grow a healthy crop the following year." John was obviously prepared with his offer.

"It sounds as if you've put some thought into this, John." Omar sounded pleased.

Things were so automatic and fluid, Annie began to wonder whether the two of them had talked earlier.

Zeke raised his finger and opened his mouth, but John carried on. "Jah, I have."

Omar turned to Zeke as if on cue. "Do you accept these conditions, Minister Zeke?"

"Well, jah...I—"

"Good, then." He clasped his hands together. "Is there anything further?"

The elders grumbled their nees, and Zeke watched the meeting deflate before him. "Once this commitment has been completed, we will consider the matter closed," Omar said, and stood.

John winked at Annie, who sat with her mouth open. "What just happened?"

He grinned. "I bet Zeke's asking himself the same exact question."

Chapter Forty-Three

BEAMS OF LIGHT filtered through the clouds, creating rays of illumination that looked as if Gott was reaching through the sky to connect with the earth.

Annie appreciated the picture in the sky and the calm of the day. The days of quiet seemed far away, but it had only been the last few months that life had turned upside down.

"The heavens are beautiful this morning, aren't they?" John walked up the hill behind her from the path to his home.

She could feel him standing behind her like they had so many mornings before this one, but today felt different. The struggles they'd been through had eventually brought them closer than they had been before. They had grown up assuming what was to be between them, but now it was defined.

"I have news."

"I hope its good news." Annie turned to him.

He grinned and held out a letter. She grabbed for it, and he pulled it away. "Changed my mind. I want to tell you about Jeffrey Walker first."

"Who's Jeffrey Walker?"

"The guy Hanna identified at the station. It seems he has a rich daddy, a rancher who raises race horses. He's bailed his son out of worse situations than this one."

"So what's going to happen?"

"His father paid off his crime again. He'll do some community service and be under house arrest for a couple of months."

"Is that the way it's always done?"

"The policeman I talked with seemed to be more bothered with us than the criminal. So I'm thinking it is."

John nodded and then pulled out the letter again. Annie crossed her arms over her chest, not willing to play the game again. He smiled and handed it to her.

She read the return address. Harrisonburg. Her stomach jumped. It could be from her mother or from the Glicks. She looked at the street address, Timberlane Trail Road. "It's from her."

"I know."

"You couldn't have known her address."

"It looked like a woman's handwriting. I might not have given it to you if it had been from Rudy." He grinned.

She pushed up on her tiptoes and laid her forehead against his chest. "I'm going to the house to read it."

She leaned back, and he cupped her cheek in his hand. "I'm happy for you, Annie. And I'm sorry I didn't understand before."

Her eyes filled. "But you do now." She took a deep breath to keep the tears at bay.

"I'm anxious to hear about it." He pointed to the letter and began to walk back home.

Annie waved and hurried to the house. It would be too much to ask not to run into a family member on the way to her room. She wanted to keep this to herself. Abraham would only give the letters to her or John, and for now that's the way she felt it had to be.

She squeezed the letter into the front pocket of her dress as she eased the back door shut and made her way through the kitchen with only her brother to pass by.

"Where are you going, Annie?" Eli asked as he placed the milk back into the cooler.

"Upstairs, just for a minute."

"Are you sick?"

It was a fair question to ask. Everyone was always doing chores. "I'm fine. I just need a minute."

He shrugged and headed for the door. "Mamm needs some beans from the cellar," he informed her as he walked out the door.

Annie fought off the anxiousness that zinged through her. She opened the creaky cellar door and took two steps at a time down the stairs. She knew exactly where the beans should be and went straight for them. As she grabbed the glass jar, she turned to her left, staring at the black space that had always frightened her. Her vivid imagination as a child had fabricated all kinds of creepy things in the dark hole.

She took a step toward the darkness, and then another, until she was in as far as she could go without ducking. Annie made herself close her eyes. They popped open, and she forced them shut again. She took in some air through her nose, smelling the musty aroma. She didn't let the unknown scare her; just let the quiet calm her and listened to her breathing.

When she opened her eyes, the black had lifted. She could see the slant in the earthen wall at the end of the small tunnel. The intimidation that had filled her was gone. The ghosts her mother claimed she ran from deflated. Annie turned her back, and without turning around, she walked slowly up the stairs.

But when she turned the corner to the flight up to her room, Annie's feet felt like bags of feed as she climbed the stairs. She couldn't get to her room fast enough. When she opened the door, both Frieda and Hanna were in their room. "What are you both doing in here at this time of day?" Then she realized how ironic it was to ask.

"Why are you?" Frieda pinned her kapp and then helped Hanna with hers, who was milking the healing wound to her side as much as she could.

"I'm going to write a letter." This much was true. Who she was writing to would be her own secret.

"Daed wants us all to help in the corn crib. The winter mold's gotten to it, and we need to sort through to see what's left to keep." Hanna's gaze dropped for a second to where Annie's hand held the letter in her pocket.

"I'll be there shortly." She sat at the desk and took out a piece of paper and pen.

As they left, Annie let out a long breath. Finally alone, she opened the letter. The first words warmed her heart.

> Annie,
>> I can't tell you how happy I was to receive your letter.

After weeks of waiting for a response and finally getting one she had still felt unsure about how her outreach would be received.

> Some people think peace is something you can learn. So they pretend they have that serenity about them, but inside they're in a fury. I used to be that person, Annie, until I met you. I tried to block out the feelings of self-hate because of what I'd done to you with noise and activity, never sitting still or letting in the quiet.
>
> After you came to visit I felt a kinship with you for trusting me enough to take the chance for us to meet. After you left that day I wanted to contact you but didn't know if you'd want me to. I'd never forgiven myself for my actions, and I never thought you could either.
>
> Then I got your letter, and I felt new mercy. For all of these eighteen years (and yes, I've counted them) I recognized I'd always have a rotted piece in my heart, one that I wouldn't let the Lord cut away. But in bringing you to me He did.
>
> I loved hearing about your world, Annie. Since you came to see mine you know what I do and the people I see. But know there's always a place for you here in my life, if you ever want to take it.
>
> This has probably put you in an awkward situation with your people in the community. I'm sorry for that. But I'm sure you're loved and accepted because of the Amish people's way.

If only she knew. But Annie wouldn't tell her. That would only bring more heartache, and neither of them needed that again in their lives.

Please continue to write, call if you're allowed, and if ever possible, come to see me again. Under the circumstances I know my presence wouldn't be understood, but know that I would come if I could.

I learned that a mother would do anything for her child once you were gone to me. Just as our heavenly Father did for us by giving His Son. I lost you once, Annie. I don't want to lose you again.

Truly yours,
Your Mother

The page wet with tears could not have felt more real in her hands, the words more meaningful, or the emotion so clear. She had done the right thing to seek out her mother. This union was worth the rejection, frustration, and confusion that had come of it. She would have no regrets. In finding her mother, she had found her truth.

⟋ Epilogue ⟍

ANNIE HEARD JOHN'S boots on the porch. Their new home was bare inside. No knickknacks or calendar adorned the house to give it character, but Annie would make it their own. She sat in the rocking chair Amos had made them for a wedding gift, swaying as she worked on John's quilt. He had already given Annie her wedding present—a handmade rug with orange, yellow, and dark threads, a sunshine-and-shadow.

John took off his boots and sat next to Annie in the only chair they owned. He was hard at work to stain a table that was given to them as a gift, but the daily chores came first, and there was a lot to do for a man with no able-bodied children to help him.

"You're so good to take off your shoes, but it will have to be walked on someday." She put the thread she was working with between her lips and bit it in two.

John looked down at the large, colorful rug at the tip of his toes. "It reminds me of your journey and mine, finally realizing everything that happened to us was through Gott's will. If you hadn't left, the change in us would have never happened. He was preparing us to be together."

Annie pulled up the quilt and laid it out for John to see. "It's all Gott's design." Mamm had pieced the quilt together but left it unfinished so Annie could complete it herself.

"Look here." She showed him the few pieces she had stitched together. "Hardships and joyful events, coming of age, our journeys and marriage. But this is what holds it together." She pointed to the thread she was using, three pieces twined together. "A cord of three strands is not quickly broken. It represents the two of us with Christ, throughout the entire quilt, even what's not complete yet."

His eyes softened, and he reached for her. "I thought I knew the meaning of your experience, but I understand even more. You couldn't be as content as you are now without discovering who you were and finding peace in that."

She stood and placed the quilt on the rocker, sat on his lap, and put her arms around his neck. "You were so good to let me go. It helped me see things so much clearer. I wasn't trusting the Lord while I was gone. Only myself and..." She hesitated and glanced at John, unsure whether he was able to be that forgiving yet.

"Rudy. You can say his name. If it wasn't for him, you wouldn't have ever found Monica. You might still be wondering and waiting, and we couldn't be happy together until that happened." He tightened his arms around her waist to look her in the eyes.

She brought his big, rough hand to her cheek and held it there. She didn't deserve this wonderful man, but here he was, had always been there for her. But then, she didn't deserve the for-giveness Gott had given her either.

She glanced around the room that held so little and felt that she had so much. When she turned back to John, she could see a vision of their future, and she admired the view.

Glossary

ach — oh

bann — excommunicated

danke — thank you

dawdi — grandfather

ferhoodled — enamored

gmayna — church board

God — Gott

grumbeere — potatoes

gut — good

hallo — hello

haus — house

Ich bin anschaffe — I am working

jah — yes

kapp — hat

komm esse — come eat

mammi — grandmother

meidung — avoid

narrisch — crazy

nee — no

ordnung — order of Amish ways

puh — ugh

rumspringa — teenagers running around

shunned — disregarded

sod — in the secular world

vorsanger — hymn leader

welschkorn — corn

Welsh — Englishman

COMING FROM BETH SHRIVER IN 2013

GRACE GIVEN

BOOK 2 IN THE TOUCH OF GRACE SERIES

RIPPLES OF PINK clouds covered the blue Texas sky. The sun slowly dipped behind a large oak tree that was almost invisible against the fading darkness. Elsie and Katie walked down a dirt road leading to their family farm after a day at a neighbor's quilting bee.

"I like the orange with the yellow patches." Katie flicked her thick, amber curls away from her blue eyes.

Elsie shook her head. "Not me. I like green with the yellow."

Katie frowned and kicked a rock down the lane ahead of them.

Elsie thought of a compromise, a frequent gesture she made on her part when dealing with her sister. "What if we do all three?"

As they chatted about the patches needed to complete their quilt, an unfamiliar rumbling noise made them pause. Elsie stopped and looked behind her as a car drove up, causing a cloud of dust to fall around them. Her kapp blew off, and the driver whistled.

The three other young men in the car heckled them and laughed. "Hey sweetie, show us more."

"How about some leg, Amish girl," the driver called out to her.

"Hey, ladies, stop and talk to us," another yelled over to them. "No harm in being friendly."

Each word made Elsie feel dirty, as if the men were throwing handfuls of mud at her. The car came to a halt, and the driver got out. She sucked in a breath and took two steps backward. His dirty blond hair was slicked straight up, and his blue eyes hardened as he took her in.

The passenger door opened, and a tall, skinny young man walked around the front of the car. He looked Elsie up and down and moved toward her. She took another step backward, whirled, and took off running, her heart nearly beating out of her chest. She didn't stop until she got to the gravel road leading to their house. Finally she leaned over, puffing and holding her side. Katie was close behind, catching her breath.

Katie turned around. "They didn't follow us, thank God."

Elsie glanced around. No one had seen them with those men.

"Elsie, Katie. Are you all right?" Their daed's voice boomed from behind them. "I saw you running all the way up the drive." His height and hefty build gave him an intimidating appearance, but his family and community knew him as a gentle man.

"Nee, we're fine." Katie answered before Elsie could think of what to say.

He eyed them with suspicion but nodded. "Okay then." He lumbered away but looked back once.

"Do you think he believed me?" Katie asked with concern in her voice.

"Why didn't you tell him?" Elsie wasn't sure what to do. She only knew that now that they hadn't told him, it became a lie, a secret. Elsie didn't want the burden of either.

"I don't want to upset him or Mamm. Nothing really happened anyway." Katie shrugged.

"It would have if we hadn't gotten away from them. They had something bad on their minds." Elsie frowned at her. "It was embarrassing what those boys said. What if someone thinks we invited the attention?"

"They would know better than that," Katie scoffed. "And they didn't have a chance to do anything with the way you ran off so quickly."

But Elsie wasn't so sure. Katie liked attention—especially when a young man smiled her way.

"Well, I guess it's done." Elsie tried to put it out of her mind, hoping as they walked to the house that they had made the right decision not to tell anyone.

And she prayed it wouldn't happen again.

⌒ Chapter One ⌒

ELSIE BLINKED, OPENED her eyes, and looked out the window. Darkness hung in the morning sky. The storm clouds moved slowly, turning like smoke in the wind. Her heart beat against her chest as she remembered where she was.

They had moved from Virginia a year before, when young men in their large community had needed land of their own. A parcel size sufficient to make a living was becoming harder to come by in the areas up north. Here in Texas her family had more land than they could manage, but as Elsie soon learned, they were not welcomed by some of the locals.

She sat up in bed and looked at the endless rows of golden wheat fields as soft rain hit the windowpane. There would be no outside chores today. Knowing she would have her two siblings in tow made her tired, and then she felt ashamed for the thought. When was the last time she'd felt like herself? She knew but tried to forget. Elsie drew in a breath. The four walls around her seemed to close in, suffocating her thoughts. It was her sister's birthday, but not a day to celebrate. Katie wasn't there.

Forcing herself to get ready for the day was becoming less painful. At first even the simplest tasks had seemed pointless and irritated her. Opening the closet door, she studied her black dress and white apron. They were wrinkled, needing a good pressing. There were only a few of Katie's clothes left in the closet. Elsie thought of packing them up and putting them away in the attic with Katie's other belongings, but she didn't. She left them there to see each morning and night, as if she needed something to hold on to, to feel her sister's presence.

At times she felt Katie was right there with her, even imagined what they might say or do. She wondered what Katie was doing now. Where was she? Elsie also thought of Jake. Her stomach boiled with anger and hurt. She didn't know which of them she resented more. The absence of one was painful enough, but both?

"Elsie, are you awake?" Her mamm came in the room abruptly.

Without looking she knew her mamm's hands rested on her hips, her blue eyes sharp and blonde hair in a tight bun. She didn't want to discuss the significance of the day but turned to face her anyway.

"Sizing up the weather. There is plenty of work to be done indoors as well." Elsie's chipper voice didn't fool even her, and she didn't think it would fool her mamm either.

"I'm sure your daed can find you something to do." Elsie felt her mamm's stare.

Elsie laid her clothes on the bed, smoothed her black dress, and then smiled at her mamm. "I don't want to leave you with the boys."

"I'll manage." Her scrutinizing stare made Elsie turn away. "Today will be hard."

Elsie stiffened her lower lip. She wanted to talk about it, yet didn't. Birthdays were not usually celebrated in any elaborate way in the community. Elsie wondered whether Katie and Jake were celebrating her day together right now as she was thinking of them.

"It'll get better. She'll come home." Mamm shifted forward and rubbed her hand along Elsie's arm. "Soon, it will be your birthday. Twenty—that's a special one."

Her mamm's certainty hadn't waned over the last couple of months since Katie had left. Elsie wasn't as confident of her sister's return, but then she knew more than her mamm did about why Katie left them. Telling anyone now would only add more shame and suspicion to Katie. She hoped it was only a one-time incident and vowed to be careful if she had to leave the house alone. If it weren't for Elsie's friend Rachel, Katie's absence would have been even harder. But Rachel had four brothers and her father to tend to and had little time for conversation or consolation.

The five-year-old twins, Aaron and Abe, flew into the room freshly scrubbed, bringing the clean smell of soap with them. Her fair-haired brothers came to a halt when Mamm stepped in front of them. "Slow down, you two. Save your energy for your chores." She caught them both and gave them a tender hug until they wiggled free from her embrace.

"I'm starving." Aaron scrunched up his freckled nose and held his stomach for affect.

"I'm hungrier." Abe frowned, his heavy cheeks held taut by a scowl.

"You two set the table, please." Mamm patted each of them on the bottom as they headed for the stairs. Abe glanced at Elsie. "Are you coming down?"

"I'm right behind you." Elsie smiled at him before turning to her mamm. "Are you sure about that?"

"What, Elsie?" Mamm's brow furrowed.

"About it getting better." Elsie didn't look her in the eyes. She didn't want to put pressure on her to lie only to make her feel hopeful. She wanted to see them both again, to scold then hug Katie and to ask Jake how he could turn on her so abruptly, so coldly. "And that she will come home."

"I know it will, that she will, and we'll be a family again." Mamm's touch to Elsie's shoulder warmed her. She would try to hold the same good hope that her mamm had and even more so the forgiveness she already gave Katie. "You're a strong young woman. You have so much ahead of you, and Gideon—"

Elsie held up a hand, tired of her parents' references to him. He was perfect—that's why she couldn't be around him. She was tainted with bitterness, unlike Gideon, who never seemed to make a mistake or say a wrong word. Three years her senior, he was more mature and grounded.

"If not him, then at least let someone in." Mamm waited for a reply, but Elsie couldn't tell what she'd been through, not until sister returned and was there with her to share what they knew.

Mamm turned and walked down the squeaky wooden stairs and sighed. "I wish I knew what went on in that head of yours."

Elsie merely smiled and then slipped her shoes on and made her way to the kitchen to help with the morning meal of pancakes, eggs, and toast.

Her daed had been up before dawn tending to the morning milking and was ready to eat. He lumbered in, ducking under the doorway, and rubbed his calloused hands together. "There's a chill in the air." He tapped each of the boys on the head and put his arm around Mamm's waist as he inspected the scrambled eggs. "Smells like it'll taste *gut* to me." His customary comment still made her smile. When he turned to Elsie, he tapped her on the nose and sat next to her. "How's my girl this morning?"

Since Katie's departure she was the only girl in the house, and Elsie had to admit she liked the extra attention. She knew he meant more than his regular greeting due to the importance of the day and was pleased to realize she honestly felt a small sense of peace. "It's going to be a *gut* day." She sounded more like her mamm than herself, but it was a heartfelt answer.

Elsie walked across the spotless white kitchen and took four plates off the shelf, then walked to the matchbox that hung on the wall and lit an oil lantern. She placed the lamp on the large counter in the middle of the room before plucking some of the spices hanging by the window.

After they ate, Mamm went to a shelf by the back door, gathered dirty clothes, and placed them in a laundry basket. Today they would do a week's worth of laundry, come rain or shine. Monday was wash day, even if they had to set up a clothesline in the house. Daed had purchased a wooden washing wringer from Marlin, who lived in their community, which helped the process along.

The boys sat at the spindle table their daed had made and ate quickly so they could see the baby birds. The chicks were new entertainment for them until the next animal was born, which made them very busy come springtime.

Aaron stopped at the door. "Can you help me with my carving today, Daed?"

"Jah, son. I have a whittling knife just your size." He grinned.

Elsie put away the last of the dishes and turned toward her father as he walked to the door. "What do you need me to do today, Daed?"

He stopped with his hand on the door handle. "Axle on the wagon. I need one of the Fisher boys to come fix it for me." As Daed ran a hand over his dark, short hair, he studied Elsie's face. Trying not to stare, he added a smile.

Elsie's heart pounded. Mamm stared at her daed as if he didn't know what he was saying. Elsie asked the question both she and her mamm were wondering about. "You mean go to the Fishers' house?"

Daed opened the door. "Only if you're up to it, Elsie."

Elsie thought of every reason she could say no. The memories of her time there with Jake would be painful. Their families had hardly spoken since Jake and Katie had left. The awkwardness of being with the Fishers would make it difficult to go through the emotions that would arise. She had avoided them, not knowing what to say, and with no forgiveness in her heart for her sister or Jake. But she couldn't stay away forever.

Elsie also didn't feel comfortable walking alone along the countryside. Since she and Katie had a run-in with those young English men, Elsie had made a point of staying put on the farm or having someone with her. She often wished she'd confided in her parents before. As more time passed, the lie seemed to grow, making the telling harder.

Elsie didn't know if she was physically up for the walk. She hadn't felt well all morning, and the temperature had changed abruptly into a warm, muggy day, giving her excuses not to go. Elsie knew her family worried about her adjusting. Maybe this was one way to show them she was. Even more, she needed to see for herself.

"Okay, I'll go." She stood tall but didn't look into their eyes. She was too close to changing her mind.

Mamm stared at Daed as if she didn't approve. Her lips parted, but she remained silent. Daed avoided her gaze, an act of will-power to avoid both of their stares. "*Gut* girl." He nodded and walked out the door. Elsie followed, but her mamm stopped her.

"Elsie, you don't have to go." Mamm took her hand.

"It's okay. They're our neighbors, and I've been to their house since…they left, remember? I'll be all right." Elsie had to believe it herself before she could convince her mamm.

Mamm nodded. "Jah, you did well at their place during the barn raising." Mamm looked at her with hope in her eyes.

She didn't need to know the pain Elsie had felt that day. She'd been fine on the front lawn and preparing the food, but she couldn't go up to the porch where she and Jake had spent so much time together. And seeing the Fishers with their three boys left a big hole where Jake had been. Being the oldest, he assisted his father not only with their blacksmith trade but also with caring for his brother, Calvin, who was developmentally delayed.

She let out a breath. "It'll be *gut* for me and make Daed feel better."

Mamm nodded. "Okay, then." She patted Elsie's cheek and kissed her on the forehead and then caught up to Daed. "Solomon."

"Jah, Meredith." He stopped but didn't look back.

Elsie heard his reluctant reply but turned away when they began to talk in hushed tones. Not wanting to be a burden, she walked on, but with each step her breathing increased and her skin crawled.

Going to the Fishers' was an emotional toil, but seeing the Englishers again gave her nightmares.

FREE NEWSLETTERS
TO HELP EMPOWER YOUR LIFE

Why subscribe today?

- ❏ **DELIVERED DIRECTLY TO YOU.** All you have to do is open your inbox and read.

- ❏ **EXCLUSIVE CONTENT.** We cover the news overlooked by the mainstream press.

- ❏ **STAY CURRENT.** Find the latest court rulings, revivals, and cultural trends.

- ❏ **UPDATE OTHERS.** Easy to forward to friends and family with the click of your mouse.

CHOOSE THE E-NEWSLETTER THAT INTERESTS YOU MOST:

- Christian news
- Daily devotionals
- Spiritual empowerment
- And much, much more

SIGN UP AT: **http://freenewsletters.charismamag.com**

8178